MW00627403

the Keeper

by

JILLIAN LIOTA

Love Is A Verb Books

Book Cover Design and Layout by Jillian Liota

Editing by Jillian Liota

Cover Photo © iStock.com/AleksandarNakic

ISBN 978-0-9982224-2-4
ISBN 978-0-9982224-0-0 (ebook)
ISBN 978-0-9982224-1-7 (kindle)

To my amazing husband:

who has stood by my side through all of my ups and downs
who has been my never-ending support
who has loved me in spite of all of my failures and faults

You are *my* keeper,
and I plan to keep you forever.

<3

Chapter One

"Remind me why I agreed to go to this stupid party again?" I shout to Charlie from the entryway as I shove my feet into a pair of Chuck Taylors. When I look up, I see her prancing down the stairs in what can easily be classified as a shirt and heels. "And please tell me you're gonna put on some pants. What are you wearing?"

"I am *clearly* wearing a costume designed to attract male attention at an event surrounding sports," she responds, twirling in a little circle - without teetering in the slightest - once she's made it to the base of the stairs.

I'm always astounded by Charlie's ability to practically pirouette in a pair of sky-high heels. My ass would be flat on the ground if I ever tried something like that. My body was made fun-sized, and I'm perfectly happy remaining close to the ground at all times. Charlie and I are essentially exact opposites. Where she is long, I am short; where she is dark, I am light. We are living, breathing antonyms.

She saunters past where I stand waiting in the entry, her shoulder-length brunette locks loose and wavy in that 'I just rolled out of bed' look that takes at least an hour to pull off successfully. She's wearing a purple Laker Girls "dress" - I use that term sarcastically - with her favorite pair of heels, accentuating her long, lean legs.

"It isn't a costume party, Charlie," I say as she passes me. Although, internally, I wonder if maybe I missed something when Jeremy invited us. "We're just heading over to watch the game with a few of the guys from the team."

"Of *course* it's a costume party, my sweet, naive RJ. It's October. *All* October parties are costume parties," she calls to me from the kitchen. "And you can't back out because I *need* you there!"

I roll my eyes and follow in her wake.

"You do not need me there," I respond. "You just don't know anything about basketball."

Charlie looks up at me from where she stands digging through her clutch and scowls.

"Exactly!" she responds. Apparently I've made her point for her. "Not only are you my *best* friend, but you're also my *only* female friend who knows sports and can keep me from saying something really stupid." She snaps her clutch closed and rounds the kitchen island with a smirk. "Plus, you have a car. How else am I supposed to get to Jeremy's? Take the bus?"

"You're using me for my car!?" I shout with excessive dramatics, slapping my hand against my heart in feigned distress. "You're making me reconsider our entire friendship."

Charlie rolls her eyes, but I see a smile creeping onto her face.

"You're an idiot." Throwing her arm around my shoulders, she starts walking us towards the door. "But seriously girlie, you need to help me understand what's happening on the field."

"Basketball isn't played on a field, Char. It's played on a court."

"See!" Her smile grows wider. "You're helping already." She winks at me, letting her arm drop from my shoulders, and turns towards the door. "Let's go, bitch! Time's-a-wasting!" And she struts out, heels clicking, ass swaying.

Charlie, Charlie, Charlie.

I exit our apartment, locking the door with as much sass as I can, and begrudgingly follow her out to Trusty Rusty, my light green '66 VW Beetle. *Come to the party with me*, she says. *It will be so much fun,* she promises. I'm already starting to regret acting as her sports translator and we haven't even left the parking lot.

"In all honesty, you don't need *me* there," I say, as we click into our seat belts and I start the ignition. "You just need to find a guy who finds your sports-illiteracy to be charming. Like Jeremy. He won't think you're dumb just because you don't know anything about basketball. If anything, maybe he'll see it as an opportunity to lean in towards you and whisper in your ear." I wiggle my eyebrows and give Charlie a super cheesy smile before pulling away from the curb.

"I don't need Jeremy getting all into my personal space. Thanks, but no thanks." Her reply is quick and sharp. I glance over and catch her eyes before she quickly turns away, her cheeks tinting to a soft pink. She acts like her lust-fueled obsession with my brother is completely off my radar. What am I? Blind?

Her infatuation began freshman year when she returned to our room one night and found him there. Alone. In the buff. Okay, he was in boxer shorts. But still, practically naked. Apparently he was mid-hook up with one of the girls in my building when her boyfriend showed up. Jeremy doesn't 'throw down over chicks', so he didn't put up much of a fight when he was shoved out of the room. Sans clothes.

He showed up at my room at 2am and asked me to go get his clothes, keys, phone and wallet, since he can't really get back to his apartment without his keys, and security would escort him out if he just wandered around the freshman hall in nothing but his boxers. As I was smoothing things over with the girl and her boyfriend and trying to collect his belongings, Charlie returned from a party and nearly had a heart attack when she found 'The Jeremy Jameson' - her words, not mine - sitting on her bed. I'm surprised she didn't drop to her knees and offer to show him *just* how welcome in her bed he actually was.

But Jeremy loved the fangirling, of course, and took his sweet time putting his clothes back on while he oozed his charm and asked Charlie all about herself. *Oh, so you wanna be a nurse, huh? So if I need some CPR I can give you a call?* Gag me. I could literally see the hearts popping out of her eyes as she soaked him in.

It took all of my efforts to get his ass out of my room. And then I had to listen to Charlie go on and on about him until I was nauseated. It wasn't until the following week during our weekly lunch at the quad that I let him know how I really felt.

"You're a 21-year-old senior in college," I growled at him. "What? You've already stuck your dick in everyone your own age and have to move on to the barely legal? You're so gross." He

scoffed, but I jabbed a finger into his chest. "You should be embarrassed that you have to troll for freshmen to get laid."

"Hey, I can't help it if I appeal to everyone," he said with a shrug. I just glared at him and jabbed my fork into my potato. "Besides, Charlie didn't seem to have an issue with me."

My eyes narrowed.

"She is completely off-limits." Jeremy gave me a little smirk that made me think he didn't care. "I'm serious Jer! You've fucked and chucked enough girls this year. Leave. Her. Alone."

"I don't fuck and chuck, Rachel," he replied with what looked like mock sincerity. "That implication about my character is just rude. I'm offended."

"Oh really? So Andi, Rebecca, Jennifer... they were serious girlfriends?" I was, of course, referring to three of my high school soccer teammates that Jeremy slept with over the course of the nine days he was home for spring break during my junior year. They didn't know about each other until Jeremy was back at college and I was left to deal with the rage issues and emotional breakdowns. Needless to say, those girls and I never formed lasting bonds.

"You can't pull out one example of exercising my right to get in some physical exercise," he said, wiggling his eyebrows, "from over a year ago and make it sound like that's how I live my entire life, Rach. What if I really like Charlie? I can do the whole... dating thing," he said with a vague wave of his hand, as if the simple idea of dating was a foreign concept that eluded him.

I sighed, closed my eyes and brought my fingers to the bridge of my nose.

"Jer, you know I have a hard time making friends. Charlie and I get along really well, and I don't want anything to ruin that." Then I looked him dead in the eyes. "Please. I am begging you. Turn your penis off for one minute and do your lonely, friendless sister a solid. Pretend. Charlie. Doesn't. Exist."

Jeremy's face become nearly expressionless as he looked out over my shoulder. After a second, he finally nodded his head, looking back at me.

"You have my word. From here on out, Charlie doesn't exist."

I breathed a sigh of relief and let my head fall back.

"Thankyouthankyouthankyou." The last thing I needed was for my brother's roaming penis to ruin a burgeoning friendship.

Again. I crammed a potato in my mouth and smiled. "So, heard anything from the Galaxy?"

Apparently Charlie never got over her obsession with him, even though she stopped gushing about him to me. But even now, several years later, I see the way she looks at him when we head to his house in LA or when he comes over to our apartment. There's some deep longing there that I don't entirely understand, and their interactions are particularly stilted. But I decided long ago to limit my prodding on this particular topic.

Besides, now Charlie is the 21-year-old senior with a mile-long list of bed partners. If she wants to get it on with everyone and their brother and pretend she doesn't have the hots for mine, that's her own choice.

"So I'm good with being the designated driver if you want to enjoy yourself," Charlie says, bringing me back to the present and making a pathetic attempt to change the subject.

I smile at Charlie's topic choice - essentially her one opportunity to prod into my own issues.

"Nice try."

She sighs and then slaps her thighs with enthusiasm.

"Come on, RJ! You're such a party pooper. You should be able to let loose every so often. It's not like I'm saying you should get shit-faced and fuck some random guy."

"No, that's normally your job," I say with a giggle.

Charlie snorts out an awkward laugh.

"Seriously. But still, have *one* drink. You have been my loyal, devoted chauffeur for months and months. Let me pay you back by letting you get a little giggly tonight." She wiggles her eyebrows up and down.

I sigh loudly. Our constant battle. You'd think Charlie would be thankful that she has a best friend willing to play DD on a regular basis. But she never lets up, even though she knows my many reasons for staying away from alcohol. The primary reason is called Frank Jameson, and he makes the decision easy. Well, he *should* make it easy. My brother and I have different philosophies.

After graduating from college, Jeremy took his soccer skills to the LA Galaxy, the Major League Soccer team in the City of Angels. He was a bed-hopper in high school and college, and it only got worse once he got a taste of the tiny bit of fame and money that professional soccer players get. The guys he spends time with are really intense about staying fit and healthy during the season, but during the off-season, they all live a party lifestyle. Women and booze are abundant. I'm just lucky he can afford to pay for drivers when he and the team go out. The amount of times I've had to drive his drunken ass home or pick him up from some girl's house in the morning was so not cool.

After living a childhood that was essentially swallowed whole by alcoholism, I decided that I would never take the risk that comes along with having a single drink. The smell, the destructive behavior, the poor choices - it just isn't for me. And while it's highly unlikely that Jeremy is an alcoholic since he doesn't really drink very often, he still took the chance when he had that first drink. Like I said, we just have different philosophies.

"I'll be sober. So drink your little heart out, my dear," I respond as I exit the freeway and begin the drive through downtown to get to Jeremy's loft. "Besides, you'd get us lost trying to find your way home," I add with a smirk.

Charlie giggles and lets out an exasperated breath.

"God, I will never get used to LA traffic and freeway mazes. This place is ridiculous," she says, looking out the window in awe, as if she just arrived yesterday. Charlie is originally from a little town just outside of Omaha, Nebraska, but the way she talks about the freeways in Los Angeles makes it sound like she moved here from the Amazon.

"You've lived here for three years, Char. It should be making sense to you by now."

"It would if I had a car. But you crazy-ass California drivers make me squirm." She pauses, seemingly struck by an important thought. "You know what? It's probably best if you stay the DD," she concludes as I pull into the parking lot beneath Jeremy's building.

I laugh.

"Glad to hear we're finally on the same page."

*   *   *   *   *

The minute we walk into Jeremy's loft, it's clear I missed the memo that watching a basketball game on October *third* is actually code for *sports-themed costume party: get out your hoochie mama swag.*

I send Charlie off into the crowd and step into the bathroom. I'm not a big fan of crowds, and I really thought this was going to be a low-key night of watching basketball with Jeremy and a few of his friends from the team. But there were at least fifty people within my immediate line of sight when we entered his apartment.

Yep, missed the memo.

As I'm washing my hands, I take a look in the mirror. My long blonde hair is swept to the side in a loose French braid that falls over my left shoulder, and my makeup-free face still looks clean and fresh, despite the heat. But I'm wearing what I've been wearing all day – a gray and white baseball shirt, tan pants, and red Chuck Taylors. And my glasses.

Maybe I could pull off telling people I came as... well, okay so I definitely don't look sporty in any capacity unless I count the baseball shirt.

I scowl at myself in the mirror. *Whatever.* I've never cared what Jeremy's friends have thought of me before and we've gotten along just fine. Although the crowd in his loft is a bit larger than the small group of friends I'm familiar with, there's no reason to start caring now. Even if I wanted to dress up, I couldn't wear half the shit the girls here are probably wearing. My 5'1" size 8 is okay for cute shorts and tops, but a stick-figure model I am not.

Luckily I prefer to wear jeans and tees.

Choosing not to spend another second looking at myself, I exit the bathroom. Before I can take more than one step, I'm immediately swept into an embrace by someone very tall, and from the feel of him, very strong.

"Hey baby, I've been waiting for you."

For a brief second, I am completely overcome with sensation. I am hyper aware of the muscles wrapped around my frame, of the outdoorsy smell coming from the gray shirt my face is pressed into, of the deep timber in the voice that just called me baby. Every instinct in my body tells me to wrap my arms around this body and snuggle in close.

Until I remember that I do *not* know this man.

The muscular arms wrapped around me, keeping my arms trapped firmly at my sides, suddenly make me feel claustrophobic. Trapped. My whole body tenses and I begin to

13

pull myself free from his arms.

But the hold on me tightens just a fraction, and I hear his low rumble whispering into my ear.

"Please play along," I hear, then feel a soft kiss on my left temple. In a split second decision, I feel my muscles relax, and in turn the arms encasing me loosen just a fraction, the man standing up straight again.

Now that he's dropped the vice grip, I tilt my head back, back, back and get a look at a guy who made my pulse race for several reasons at once. And when my eyes collide with his, my stomach falls out of my body and onto the floor, my lungs collapse, and my heart flies up into my throat, leaving me nauseous, unable to breathe, and mute.

He's handsome.

Like, *really* handsome.

The cover of GQ, campus heartthrob, *Love Actually* silent happy dance, kiss me now kind of handsome.

The first thing I notice is his body, which is so unlike me, but how can it be helped when his arms are still wrapped around me. He's firm and lean with broad shoulders. And he's tall - at least 6'2". He has dark brown hair that's just a little bit too long and curls slightly at the edges beneath his ears. His strong jaw is covered in stubble that makes me think it's been a few days since he's shaved. And his eyes. Damn. Warm, chocolate eyes peer into my soul with a look that is genuine and caring and I can't look away.

As cliché as it sounds, a girl could get lost in those eyes.

"Oh sorry, Mack," I hear from a snippy, feminine voice over my shoulder. "I didn't realize you were with someone tonight."

The guy - Mack, apparently? - releases me as I turn towards the voice. But it seems like he still wants the buffer, as his arm repositions to wrap around my shoulders, tucking me into his side.

A sexy referee is shooting daggers at me from down the hall, her arms crossed, plumping her amazing breasts up to the point that they're nearly spilling out of her top. She's pretty pissed, and the force of that rage is directed straight at me.

Right. Because *I'm* to blame in this situation. It's not like I was randomly grabbed by a stranger or anything.

I'm normally not a troublemaker, but this girl looks exactly like Cassandra Roman, a bitch I went to high school with who slept with my boyfriend junior year.

14

So I take the opportunity to get misplaced justice for the 16-year-old me.

"Oh, it's not just tonight," I reply, leaning my head against Mack and running my hand up and down his chest. His very cut, muscular chest. I mean, come on… I can feel all six of his packs. "Although, he *will* be busy." I'm trying to play sexy and hoping the unpracticed look on my face doesn't come across as if I've recently had a mild stroke.

Apparently it works, because the Cassandra look-alike huffs and stomps off, and I can't help the shit-eating grin that covers my face or the happy dance in my head.

"Well, that went better than expected," Mack's deep voice interrupts my mental high five.

I quickly step out from my happy place nestled against his chest and under his arm, my face flushing warm and red as I realize how ridiculous the past thirty seconds was. I have a hard time looking up at him, but finally manage to drag my eyes away from the ground and give him a small smile.

"Yeah, what was the deal with that?"

Mack shrugs lazily, his eyes roaming my face as he leans nonchalantly against the wall.

"I just met her and she's been following me around like a blood hound for the past hour. I figured I needed a way to get her off my scent."

"So you were just waiting outside of the bathroom for an unsuspecting female to fill your fake girlfriend position?" I ask, my mouth tilting up at the side a little. "What if I had been a guy?"

"Oh trust me, I would have been willing to come out of the closet to get away from *that* girl." His face splits in a half smile so breathtaking I can't help but smile back. "She showed me her nipple ring. Like, literally whipped her tits out for me. And then thought it would be seductive to point out the other guys here she's slept with."

My face quickly scrunches up in disgust.

"Wow that's… like, really disgusting." But then I smile again. "You sure you don't wanna put a ring on it? She sounds like amazing wifey material."

Mack lets out a rich laugh, his smile continuing to grow. "Nah, I'm all set, thanks."

We stand there in silence, just staring at each other, smiling lightly, for about twenty more seconds before I start to feel awkward. But I can't look away.

I've never felt so awestruck by someone before. It's not even just his looks. It's that deep rumble of a laugh that hits me right in the chest, and the easy smile and kind eyes. His eyes are glued to me too, the crinkles in the corners remaining even though his smile has dimmed slightly.

Luckily, someone comes around the corner and claps Mack on the back in greeting, drawing his eyes away from me and offering me a reprieve.

"Well, I'll just head back out, then. Come find me if you need rescuing again." I quickly turn and dart out of the hallway without looking back.

As I enter the main living area of Jeremy's massive loft, I'm pulled out of the little bubble Mack and I created in the past few minutes and thrust right back into a party I don't want to be at. I'm also reminded that I didn't wear a costume.

I head for the kitchen and grab a Jarritos soda out of a cooler, stoked when I find the last Tamarind flavor at the bottom. I pop the top of the bottle with a lighter sitting on the counter and take a long drink before looking out at the room.

My initial assessment of fifty people wasn't even close. There are at least a hundred people here. I didn't know that was even possible in a downtown loft, but Jeremy did get a monstrosity of a bachelor pad.

I'm seeing lots of scantily clad cheerleaders and referees. Dresses so short I can see ass creases, and make-up so thick I wonder if an artist was involved in the process. That shit is painted on.

It's the male costumes that draw my attention and remind me why Halloween season can be so fun. There are a bunch of fun things like old-school baseball uniforms and 70's basketball gear. There are even a few soccer players.

I quickly spot Jeremy on the balcony and can't help the loud bark of laughter that leaves me. He's dressed as 80's tennis star John McEnroe, ridiculous hair, short-shorts and all. My laugh somehow catches his attention, even over the music.

"Rach!" He shouts with a smile, waving me over. He whispers something into the ear of the redhead draped on him and gives her ass a squeeze.

I gag. But only slightly.

She passes me as she walks back inside, gives me an overly bright smile, and trots off to a few friends lurking in the corner of the kitchen.

When I walk through the sliding doors to his large patio, Jeremy greets me with a big toothy smile.

"Favorite brother!" I shout, flinging my arms around his shoulders in a tight squeeze. The hug feels like home, and I realize seeing Jeremy once a week isn't nearly enough to satisfy me.

"Favorite sister!" he shouts back enthusiastically. "I'm so glad you came! I wasn't sure if you would actually come tonight." He pulls away to grab his beer off of the table he walked away from and takes a pull. "I saw Charlie come in alone, so I figured maybe you just dropped her off and bailed."

"I almost did. But then I decided I didn't want to waste all of the time and effort I put into my super creative costume." Jeremy looks me up and down, eyebrows furrowing in confusion. He didn't catch my heavy sarcasm over the music that's making my ears bleed. "I'm a fan," I say in mock enthusiasm. "Go team!" I punch a little fist into the air.

Jeremy lets out a little snort and shakes his head.

"God, you are fucking ridiculous. Okay, the game is currently at half-time, so go grab a drink and get a good seat to watch the second half. I'll be back inside in a minute. I'm a little busy." He smirks and then gives a little finger crook to the redheaded cheerleader he was ass-grabbing when I first spotted him and she slinks her way back onto the patio, giving him a seductive grin.

Rolling my eyes, I step back inside and am immediately accosted by Charlie.

"Where have you been?" she fumes.

"Uhm, the bathroom?"

"Well, while you were in the bathroom, Melody got grabby and latched her fangs into your brother. You'll be lucky if you see him at all for the rest of the night. It's disgusting." Her eyebrows are pulled together in a scowl, and her lips are tight. I notice she said that *I* would be lucky to see him and didn't make any mention of herself.

Part of me wants to say that I saw Jeremy with who I can only assume is Melody the vampire. The other part of me wants to tease her because this is the first time in years that she's admitted Jeremy's slutty ways bother her. But I know neither of those things are a good idea.

"Want me to help get you giggly?" I ask with a smile.

17

"I thought you'd never ask." And she stalks off to the kitchen to, I'm assuming, drown herself in Grey Goose.

*   *   *   *   *

About an hour later, I'm sitting next to Charlie in front of Jeremy's monster TV watching the Lakers and the Clippers. Just to clarify: *I* am actually watching the game. *Charlie* is a little bit drunk and laughing like an idiot at everything the guy to her right is saying. And no, he's not funny. He's actually a total dickwad. I've been clenching my jaw at most of the things he's been saying, trying to focus on the game on the TV, and not on this guy trying to game on Charlie. But I swear if he says one more thing, I'll need to invest in some serious orthodontia.

"And then I told him to fuck off," he says, taking a swig of his beer. "I almost socked that faggot in the mouth."

"Hey!" I bark at him, making both him and Charlie jump a little bit. "If I have to sit here and listen to your pigheaded ass for one more minute, I swear to God that *you* will be the only one getting socked in the mouth." I stand, ignoring his shocked expression that's quickly morphing into a scowl, and pull Charlie up with me. "I need a drink Charlie. Come with me."

With that, I grab Charlie's hand and pull her off the couch and towards the kitchen, away from the idiot. Half way through the mob of people between us and the fridge, I feel Charlie jerk her grasp away from me.

"RJ, stop!" she shouts.

I turn to face her and I'm genuinely surprised at the nasty face she's giving me.

"What?" I ask, because I really don't know what.

"What the hell is your problem?!" she shouts. I'm not sure how to respond, so I just stand there, mute. "I was having fun with that guy, and you get all high and mighty with your bullshit and ruin *everything*!"

I raise my eyebrows.

"You were having fun? Listening to that asswipe throw around the word 'faggot'?" Charlie doesn't respond and just glares at me. "Charlie, your brother is gay. How was that okay with you?" Still she stares, fists clenched, as people talk and dance and move around us.

I take a step towards her, my voice lowering a fraction to give the illusion of privacy.

"Look, I know you're upset about Jeremy, but that doesn't mean you have to listen to that guy's shit just for attention. You can do so much better." I look around quickly. "Come outside and we can talk about this, it's too loud in here."

"You think you know everything, but you know nothing!" she shouts. "Feel free to leave if you don't want to be at this party, RJ. I'll figure out my own way home." She turns around to storm away from me, but wobbles slightly on her heels. And that's when I realize that Charlie is more than giggly. The girl is tanked. Once she regains her balance, she storms away from me, knocking people out of her way as she goes.

I stand frozen for a minute, unsure how the situation escalated that quickly. As Charlie disappears in the crowd, I groan in frustration and turn towards the balcony. Hopefully fresh air will clear my head and provide me with a much needed reprieve.

Thankfully, it's quiet and deserted. I plop down on a lounger, and stare up at the night sky, wishing I could see the stars. The bright lights of downtown and the disgusting bubble of LA smog get in the way, so I just look up into the yellow-tinted haze.

Charlie has always been difficult when it comes to men, especially where Jeremy is concerned, but tonight was different. We've gotten into fights before when she's used guys to make herself feel better, but she practically detonated in there. Normally, I make some crack about the guy and she laughs. I'm not sure exactly what happened to her in the past, but I feel like Charlie lets herself get way too wrapped up in getting male attention. She doesn't stop long enough to remember that she has more to offer a guy than a vagina. And as close as we are, she hates talking about her past, so I know little to nothing about what her life was like growing up.

Well, I guess we are a suitable pair, then, because I never talk about my childhood either.

Frustrated and unsure how to deal with my emotions, I let a growl out into the night sky.

"Feel better?"

I jump a little and look to the corner where the voice came from, shocked that someone else is on the balcony with me. And when I see who it is, I'm sure my face flushes bright red.

Mack.

How did I not notice him when I came out?

"I'm sorry," I say, sitting up in my seat. "I thought I was alone."

"I can tell," he says with a chuckle. "But really, feel any better?"

I give a small smile and nod.

"Actually, yes. Sometimes when I'm really angry, it helps to just scream it out, you know? Get all the pent up frustration together and just hurl it into the sky?"

"So you do this often?"

"Mmmm, not that often. I don't have *that* many rage issues." I smile and he lets out another small laugh. "But normally I head to the field and actually shout or scream. I figured doing that on a balcony in downtown LA might freak a few people out."

He smiles.

"Yeah, I can see how a woman screaming bloody murder might cause a concern." He stands and walks towards me, then grabs my hand to pull me off of the lounger. "However, there is a statute in LA county law dictating that *two* people screaming bloody murder is just a case of young people antics." He leads me over to the railing at the edge of the balcony, then turns to stand next to me as we look out over Los Angeles.

"I'm confused."

"On the count of three, we'll both scream."

I laugh.

"Or, on the count of three, I'll scream, and you'll just stand there letting me look like a complete idiot."

"Oh come on," he says, nudging my shoulder with his arm. "Trust me."

I look into his eyes and for some reason I can't exactly place, I actually believe that I can.

"Okay," I breathe out. "You know, this will be very *Garden State* of us."

He smiles.

"Nice reference. I love that movie" He turns back to look over the balcony, but I see him eyeing me. "Okay ready?" I nod. "One." I smile and look directly at him. "Two." I look back over the railing. "Three."

At the same moment, both of us take deep breaths and fling our voices out into the city. His deep one booming out next to mine makes a smile take over my face. For a brief moment, there is nothing but us and the sky. No frustration or longing or disappointment. No anger or fear of the future. Just two stupid young people, eyes scrunched shut, screaming into nothing. Two ridiculous individuals joined together for a moment of absolute hilarity. We stop after about ten seconds, and I can't help but look at Mack with a huge grin. I literally can't get it off of my face.

"Wow."

"Wow?" I ask. "That's all you have to say?"

"Wow, you scream really loud?" he replies.

"Dummy!" I shout at him playfully. I still have the same goofy smile, and I notice the amusement in his eyes and the gorgeous half-smile that sits on his face in return.

"Well before you called me out, I was going to say, 'Wow, you have a gorgeous smile,' but now I'm not so sure I want to say that. Now I'm more concerned with your increasingly apparent rage issues."

I laugh.

"Rage issues!? So dramatic!" I let my weight fall backwards but grab the railing at the last minute, stretching my arms out. I pull myself forward then drop back and grab it again. "Don't even pretend that wasn't cathartic. I *always* feel better after something like that."

We continue to smile and just stand there looking at each other, like fools. Even though it's kind of awkward, it's also kind of nice.

"What's your name?"

"RJ. Why?"

"Just curious. I'm Mack, by the way."

"Yeah, I know." He looks at me curiously for a moment, his eyebrows scrunching together in confusion. "The referee with the nipple piercing. She said it earlier."

He nods slowly, the furrow on his brow line disappearing. He turns away and looks back out over the city again and I follow suit. After another minute, he pipes up again.

"Hey RJ?"

"Yeah?"

"Can I take you out sometime?"

There are dozens of things that I know happen to people who get nervous in social and relationship situations. Butterflies in the stomach. Sweaty palms. A flushed face. Dry mouth. The inability to string together a coherent sentence. All of the ridiculous things that usually don't happen to me when a guy shows interest. *Usually* being the operative word. And while I haven't turned into a sweaty lobster with a speech impediment, I can feel the flutter in my stomach. Nerves. Who knew it could happen to me?

"Sometime?" I respond, still looking over the railing, actively not looking at him. It's the only thing making this back-and-forth manageable for me. I may be able to throw out a line or two to make him laugh, but I'm feeling very unsure of myself.

"Well, I'd ask to take you out tonight, but I figured you were attending a party or something." I can hear the smile in his voice.

Tonight.

He would have wanted to take me out tonight.

I can't help but smile too.

"Plus, tonight is technically over in about two hours. And I want more time than that. So I'm thinking tomorrow instead."

"Tomorrow?"

"Yeah. You have plans?"

"Just in the morning. But I'll be free after twelve."

"So, I'll pick you up tomorrow at one."

"I never said yes," I respond, still grinning.

"But you didn't say no either."

"Well, there's that."

We're both quiet for a few minutes, listening to the sounds of the city, enjoying the cool fall breeze rushing across us, such a contrast to the typical LA heat.

"So, what do I have to do to get you to agree to let me take you out tomorrow?" he finally says, and I see in my peripheral vision that he's turned to look at me.

I wait, mulling over what I should say, and then ultimately decide on the response I usually give, which borders between honesty and 'lets see how interested you really are.'

I turn my head and boldly look him dead in the eyes.

"To be completely honest, I am incredibly awkward on dates. So... I'll agree if it's a casual day. I'm like a kid, you know? I like it simple. I don't really glamazon. That's not my thing."

"You don't glamazon?" He raises one eyebrow. "What does that even mean?"

I shrug.

"You know. Fake eyelashes and huge boobs and hooker heels."

"Oh, so all of the women inside?"

"Pretty much," I respond with a half laugh, then gesture to myself. "What you see is what you get."

He steps towards me and I feel my heart rate pick up. With complete sincerity, he reaches out and adjusts my glasses, pushing them up my nose a little.

"Well, I can tell you with absolutely certainty that I like what I see," he says softly.

I fight the cheesy grin that wants to bloom on my face and instead just offer him a small smile. Although I am certain my flushed cheeks give away the pleasure I felt at his words.

"So you said one-o-clock?" He nods and breaks out into that breathtaking smile again. My butterflies are going crazy. "One sounds great."

Chapter Two

Mack asks for my number and ends up leaving the party within ten minutes, and then I spend a while lying back on the balcony lounger with a stupid smile. I feel like I'm a 15-year-old going on her first date.

Ridiculous.

I'm not trying to pretend that at 21, I'm some old bird. I'm still very young and have a whole lot of life ahead of me. But there is a huge difference between how 15- and 21-year-olds feel about dating and relationships. When I was 15 and going on my first few dates with Carter Lincoln, it felt like electricity was shooting through my veins any time we would look at each other. Just a single glance from him across the quad could make my traitorous body break out into a deep flush from the middle of my chest, up my neck, onto my cheeks.

Over the years, some of that newness has fallen away. I've dated here and there, but I don't get that squirmy feeling of nervousness anymore. Did I seriously think I felt butterflies when Mack asked me out earlier? Because that's how just those few moments of interaction with Mack made me feel. Like it was all new again.

When I finally decide it's time to stop daydreaming, I wander inside to find Jeremy or Charlie. With no luck, I drive home and crawl into bed at a reasonable hour. But that still doesn't stop me from groaning when my alarm goes off at six the next morning.

Time for practice.

I quickly put on my practice gear before peeking into Charlie's room to see if she made it home the night before. Nope. I cross my fingers, hoping she didn't go home with the idiot.

After shoving a few bites of banana into my mouth, I drive out to the college soccer field wishing that I was still snuggled in bed, thinking about Mack and what our date will look like. Practice on a Saturday morning feels particularly mean. Normally we just practice during the weekdays, but with only one loss this season and a top ten ranking, Glendale College is currently a real hopeful for a spot in the playoffs for the first time in the college's history. So, extra practices it is.

We're stretching when Coach Walker joins us at seven and gets us running the field. After we finish a few laps, she pulls us into a circle.

"Alright ladies, as I've been saying the past few weeks, our focus needs to remain on endurance training. You've all done a great job adjusting to the difficult drills I've thrown at you so far this season, and that shows dedication. But keep up your extra training in your off time to boost that endurance. Regulations dictate I can only have two hours with you this morning, so we're gonna focus on high-intensity drills. We're more than halfway there, but you still have eight games left."

Several of the girls let out groans at Coach Walker's statements.

"I hate high-intensity drills," I hear from my right.

I turn to see Piper Mills, one of our first-year strikers, and I give a small nod of agreement. We goalkeepers have it easier during high-intensity drills, because it mainly focuses on ball maneuvering and quick feet.

But none of us get to lay back and watch. And from the looks of it, Piper wants to curl up in a ball and sleep away that hangover. Her eyes are dull and she still has makeup crusted on her face from whatever she was doing the night before. Someone didn't get enough sleep. Rookie mistake.

Coach Walker grins at the complaints.

"No moaning, ladies. You're in a solid position, but you still have a lot of things to work on. Let's get moving."

With a clap of Coach Walker's hands, everyone sluggishly begins getting into groups and maneuvering the field with cones and soccer balls, and practice begins.

When Coach Walker finally calls it a day, I shout a quick

goodbye to a few of the girls, jog quickly to my car and drive back to the apartment. I can finally put my mind towards what I've been willing myself not to think about all morning.

It's date day.

I'm not normally this person. I don't get excited about dates. I have too much going on in my life at any given moment to get excited about watching someone of the opposite sex chew with their mouth open.

School work, soccer practice, my part-time job, family drama… those take up way too much of my time already. Not to mention my handful of friendships, my social calendar - which, to be honest, isn't completely off-the-charts-packed with fun things, but it should still be a priority - and the endurance and strength training I pack into my free time. Plus sleeping and allowing myself time to relax.

That literally leaves like, six hours of my week available for dating. I've always used those hours for extra study or to eat stupid amounts of food, or more time at the gym. But today, Mack gets those hours. And I'm entirely positive it will be my best use of time in months.

When I open the door to the apartment as I return from practice, I see Charlie's heels and purse tossed haphazardly on the floor in the entryway.

"Char?" I call out.

For a second I hear nothing. Then a small grunt comes from the living room. When I walk in, I find her face down on the sofa, a bottle of water and a package of head meds on the coffee table.

"Rough night?" I ask softly, crouching next to her and pulling her hair out of her face.

She rolls onto her side and looks up at me, remorse written in her eyes. "I'm sorry," she whispers.

I give her a small smile. "Me too." I lean forward and kiss her forehead, then head into the bathroom where I quickly disrobe and crawl under the hot water.

A few minutes pass before I hear a faint knock on the door.

"Come in," I say, knowing that Charlie has come to do our 'post-argument' chat. Any time we have something important to talk about, she waits until I'm in the shower so she can sit outside the curtain and can talk without a face-to-face conversation. I don't really get it, but I guess it's just a thing with her.

I hear Charlie drop the lid on the toilet and sit down. Without even looking I know exactly how she's sitting. She has her feet on the seat, arms wrapped around her legs, chin resting on her knees. We may have done this once or twice.

"So, I have to tell you something," she says in a voice I can barely hear over the rushing water.

My hands drop from where they were scrubbing shampoo into my hair.

"Please, Charlie. Please tell me you didn't sleep with that dick from last night."

"No!" she quickly shouts. "No, no, no. Yeah, that guy was a total dick. You were completely right."

I sigh with relief.

"Thank the Lord," I mumble, and my hands resume scrubbing the shampoo.

"No, this isn't about him. This is..." there's a pause. A long pause. So I know she's trying to summon up the courage to tell me whatever it is. "I had sex with Jeremy."

My hands stop moving in my hair, shampoo forgotten, and I feel all of the color drain from my face. I grab the shower curtain and practically rip it off as I pull it back to see Charlie sitting on the toilet, exactly how I had pictured her.

"You what!?" I shout, completely uncaring about standing buck naked in front of my roommate, with the water still on and now splashing off of my body and onto the floor.

"I'm sorry, RJ," she says quickly, tucking herself further into her body. "I should have told you about it. I told myself over and over that it was wrong for me to keep this secret from you. But I just didn't want you to hate me for sleeping with your brother. Your friendship means too much to me. He said we shouldn't ever tell you because you would be really upset. So I just never said anything."

My face scrunches up in confusion.

"Wait a minute, when did this happen?"

"Freshman year."

"What!?" I shout again. My eyes fall shut. I cross my arms over my breasts, lifting a hand to squeeze at the bridge of my nose. "So, I tell my brother to stay away from you because I don't want to ruin our friendship and he immediately goes and gets you into bed? I am going to *murder* him."

"Oh my god, RJ, pleasepleaseplease you can't tell him I told you!" Charlie's face is contorted in some weird mix of mortified and terrified. "We promised each other we wouldn't ever say anything about it since both of us said it didn't mean anything. It just turns out I might have been lying when I said it, and he wasn't. I'm only telling you now because I feel like you're owed an explanation for why I react the way I do sometimes when I'm around him."

I let out a long breath and swipe the shampoo that is now trickling down my forehead away from my eyes. I'm trying to formulate the words I want to say without sounding like a bitch.

"Charlie, I get it. The way you act is how *most* women feel after he sleeps with them and then breaks things off. I dealt with enough broken hearts asking me why he didn't want to date them when we were freshmen. But I *told* you this about my brother before you even met him. I specifically told you that he was bad news from a relationship standpoint and not to fall for his shit. I mean, after all of the guys you've slept with, why is he the one that has you all up in knots and unable to move on?"

She looks at me a bit confused.

"Maybe you just don't understand because you haven't had sex with anyone before."

I roll my eyes.

"You don't get to pull the virgin card here, okay? Just because I haven't had sex before doesn't mean I don't understand that it can have an emotional impact. I just don't understand what it is about Jeremy that has you hung up on him three years later." And then I quickly add, "And your explanation better have nothing to do with his penis."

Her mouth tips up at the side, and I see her trying to hold in a laugh.

"I'm not saying you don't understand because you're a virgin. I'm saying you don't understand because you don't know the difference between your first time, and every other time. Your first time changes everything."

I pause and look at her.

"You were a virgin when you slept with Jeremy?" She nods. "But I thought... I mean, when we moved in together freshman year you used to talk about the guys from high school that you'd hooked up with."

"Oh, don't assume I was completely innocent. I definitely had my fun in high school," she says, grabbing her hair and pulling it forward across one shoulder. She lets out a sigh as she starts picking at the tips of her hair. "But I was a virgin until

Jeremy."

I sit down on the edge of the tub and stare at the drain, trying to reorganize the past few years to try and better understand. Charlie was a virgin when she slept with Jeremy. Does that mean that her one-night-stand-a-thon for the past three years was *because* of Jeremy? Because she was trying to forget the person she gave her first time to? And all those times she talked about him, but pretended she wasn't interested, she was pretending because she knew I didn't want them together? My jaw tightens as I realize that Jeremy must have slept with her and then used me as an excuse to discard her.

"I'm so sorry, Char. I didn't know."

She shrugs and stands up.

"Well, now you do. So, can you promise me you won't tell your brother?"

I look at her for a moment, unsure whether I can really make that promise. When I finally nod at her, she leans over and kisses my forehead.

"You're a great friend, RJ. Thanks for not kicking my ass for handing my flower to your brother." I shake my head and let out a chuckle. I hate when she calls it a flower. As I stand and begin to close the shower curtain, she adds "And your ass looks amazing, by the way. That extra training is totes paying off."

I glance over and find her grinning at me before she pulls the door closed and I'm left with my thoughts.

*   *   *   *   *

The doorbell rings at 12:45. Having been ready and wandering aimlessly around our apartment for nearly an hour, I come flying down the stairs with such energy that I nearly slip on the tile near the entry.

"You expecting someone?" Charlie asks from the living room.

"Yeah, kind of," I respond, before wiping my hands on my jeans, blowing out a breath and opening the door.

He stands there smiling in Chucks, jeans, and a faded Ramones t-shirt holding a... dead flower?

"Uhm... hi," I say, unsure how to proceed.

"Hey. This is for you," he says handing the shriveled up flower to me.

A choked laugh escapes me as I start to reach out to take it from him.

"I'm not sure what to say. You shouldn't have?"

He laughs and chucks the dead flower into the bushes next to our door.

"It was a joke, RJ. You said you're awkward at dates, so I thought I would start it off awkward to alleviate the stress."

I raise my eyebrows.

"And a dead flower is..."

"Hey, if I can't wow you with some glamorously expensive meal, I at least have to try and make you laugh. Don't tell me I totally ruined everything already." His facial expression is twisted into mock seriousness, and I can't help the smile that blooms on my face. He leans forward, his forearm resting on the doorjamb, his face just inches from me. "There it is."

"What?"

"That smile," he responds, his eyes focusing on my mouth. He's so close to me that I swear we're breathing in each other's air.

I bite my lip to keep from giggling like a mental patient, and glance down at my bare feet before summoning the courage to look him directly in the face again.

"Wanna come in? I still have to put my shoes on."

He nods and follows me into the living room, where Charlie is currently curled up in her pajamas watching reality TV, nursing the remains of her hangover.

She flicks her eyes to me for only a second when we walk into the room, but then double-takes when she realizes I'm not alone.

"Charlie this is Mack. Mack, my roommate, Charlie."

"Nice to meet you," Mack says, nodding at her.

Charlie gives Mack her megawatt smile.

"You too. So, where are you two going?" she asks, flipping onto her knees and facing us from over the back of the sofa.

"Not sure," I reply as I tuck my feet into socks and slip on one of my Chucks. "Somewhere casual, right Mack?" I look up at him for confirmation as I lace my shoes.

He nods.

"Yup. Casual."

After finishing with my shoes, I stand and say bye to Charlie. With Mack's back turned towards us as he walks to the door, Charlie's eyes grow wide and she gives me a quick thumbs up before mouthing *Oh. My. God.* I giggle and wave at her before walking out the front door.

When we get out to the curb, I see a truck with two bikes in the bed. Without a word, he drops the bed of the truck and begins to unload.

"We're riding bikes?" I ask.

"Well, if I remember correctly, your exact words were 'I'm like a kid. I like it simple.' So, we're going old-school, pre-drivers license days." He pushes a Schwinn towards me, complete with basket and bell.

"Wow, Mack. Pulling out all the stops," I throw my leg over the bike and get comfortable on the seat. "What would you have done if I was wearing a dress and heels?"

He looks at me with a smirk.

"After your glamazon comment last night, I figured you in jeans was a safe bet."

"I have to be honest. I've never been on a bike date before. Two points for creativity." I ring the bell twice for emphasis.

"Two points? That's it?" He opens the passenger door to the truck and pulls out a blue helmet. "I deserve at *least* five."

I laugh.

"You've gotta do a lot more than throw me on a bike to get big points with me."

His face shows the hint of a smile as he walks towards me and plops the helmet on my head, then clips the straps under my chin. He takes a step back and just looks at me, causing my face to flush.

"Perfect."

He steps back towards his bike, straddles the seat, and calls a 'let's go' as we take off down the road.

It has been a really long time since I've ridden a bike. At least since before I started driving, if not longer. I forgot how fun it is. We pedal next to each other down the road, and at this slower pace, I'm able to soak in details about the day that would normally race past me.

Like what an absolutely gorgeous day it is, and how the sun is high but not too hot. Or the leaves on the ground, when the abscission of leaves doesn't happen on most trees in my neighborhood. Or something less beautiful, like the fact the people down the road decided it would be okay to leave their stained mattress at the curb. Bleh.

It's a short ride, maybe twenty minutes total, and we don't

really talk. We just alternate between racing and riding at a leisurely pace. When we finally pull into the Atwater Village Fun Center, I ring my bell over and over as I race past Mack towards the bike racks.

"I beat you," I say with feigned innocence as I lock my bike into the rack and pull off my helmet.

Mack smiles.

"Congratulations. Now, have you been here before?"

I shake my head.

"Good. Because today we are going to have awesome kid fun."

"Mini-golf?" I ask.

"And bumper boats."

"You know if we ride the go-karts, I'm going to completely kick your ass."

He looks at me with a grin.

"Somehow, that doesn't surprise me at all."

After locking our bikes to the rack, Mack grabs my hand and loosely links his fingers in mine. It's easy. Natural. Like we've always done this. He squeezes my hand lightly and gives me a sweet smile before leading me inside.

He doesn't let go, not even when one of the employees asks us to hold onto golf clubs to help measure which ones we should use. He doesn't let go until we get outside and pick up a scorecard and golf pencil.

"Alright, so what are the stakes of this game?" I ask, crossing my arms as we look over the first hole.

"Ahhhhh, so you're a betting girl, huh?"

"Absolutely. I am *very* competitive."

"Oh that has become *glaringly* obvious," he replies, chuckling to himself. He puts his hand to his chin and looks me over, then makes a humming sound. "The winner plans the next date. Whatever they want."

"You're assuming there will be another date," I retort.

"Are you assuming there won't be?"

"I never said that. I just think you're getting a little ahead of yourself." I rest my golf club over both of my shoulders and hook my arms on each end. "What if this date is a miserable experience for you and then you're stuck planning some lame trip to Applebee's for next weekend. I mean, for all you know, I'm a totally insane, crazy person who sifts through Justin Bieber's trash looking for hair clippings."

"*Do* you sort through his trash looking for hair clippings?"

"Maybe."

"Are you a *Belieber* with Bieber Fever?"

The giggle that falls from me is relentless and I nearly drop the golf club.

"How do you even know those words?"

He grins.

"My sister has a daughter, which is where she places the blame for her ludicrous knowledge of his song lyrics, even though I *know* it's really her with the cardboard cutout." I laugh again. "And suggesting this bet doesn't mean I'm thinking there *might* be another date." He steps in close to me and lightly rests the palm of his hand on the back of my neck, his thumb tracing the edge of my jaw. "I'm *guaranteeing* there will be another date." His eyes flicker to my lips, then back up to my eyes.

I'm not sure how to respond. The laughter from just a moment before has been sucked out of the space around us and replaced with a weird tension that makes the hairs on my body stand to attention. I feel jittery and unsure what to do with my hands.

When he rests his forehead against mine and I can feel his breath on my face, I want him to kiss me. I don't really know him and I know it would be way too fast for a girl like me, but at the same time, I can't explain the way I feel right now.

The closest descriptor I can think of is that it feels like I've been shaken up inside, like the nuts and bolts that normally hold me together have fallen loose and I might collapse at any moment and melt into the ground.

After another beat, Mack steps back, releasing his hold on me, and it takes every effort I have to not show in my facial expression everything he just made me feel.

I let out a controlled breath even though I feel like gasping for air.

"Sounds like a good bet to me."

*   *   *   *   *

Two hours later, we've pretty much done it all. We've completed a round of mini-golf, which Mack won by a landslide, followed by three trips on the go-karts, one hard collision in the bumper boats, we each took a turn in the batting cages, and about twenty minutes playing Skeeball in the arcade.

"So, I know we are somewhere in the limbo between lunch and dinner, but are you hungry?" he asks as I feed his tickets into the ticket counter.

"Sure. What sounds good?" I snatch the receipt that spits out of the machine. "Eighty-five tickets! Nice job!" He takes the receipt from my hands and we start walking towards the prize booth.

"Well, I've been hearing pretty awesome things about a place called In-N-Out Burger, and I was hoping to try that."

I turn quickly and slap my hand flat against his chest, halting his forward movement.

"Woah, woah, woah. You've never had In-N-Out before? Where are you from? Mars?"

"Indiana, actually," he responds, raising an eyebrow. With a laugh, he adds, "and somehow I feel like I've offended you."

"Well, Indy, the fact that you've have lived in SoCal for - how long did you say? Nearly a month? - and haven't been to an In-N-Out Burger means you have been making horrible friends since you got here." He laughs. "Lets cash out your tickets and ride back. There's an In-N-Out a few blocks from my apartment."

After taking forever to decide on a prize, Mack finally picks a small stuffed animal and a few glittery jelly bracelets, which he quickly deposits into my hands.

"Make sure you wear those bracelets on our next date," he says, wrapping his arm around my shoulder and leading me towards the exit. Of course, I don't wait that long, and the bracelets are quickly slipped onto my wrist.

When we finally get to In-N-Out, the line is crazy long, per usual. Mack looks concerned.

"Do you want to come back another time when it isn't so busy?"

I laugh.

"This place is always busy. But it'll be worth the wait, I promise."

He just smiles and joins me in line, taking my hand and interlocking our fingers again. I peak up at him while he studies the menu. I might not date often, but I'm also not blind. I usually notice attractive men, but I usually try to get to know guys better before I allow myself to develop an interest. Who they are, what they value, how they approach the world. Why would I want to begin something with someone who I have nothing in common with or who makes really horrible choices? It sounds like a waste of time and energy.

My relationship with Mack so far is different. Yes, he has seemed nothing but genuine and thoughtful during our interactions, but I know almost nothing about him. We've laughed a lot today and talked non-stop, but our topics have remained fairly surface level, which I know is typical for a first date.

But I've never before felt a pull like this to someone I met less than 24 hours ago. And then there's the way he looks at me. I feel like I'm in a low-budget chick flick the way he makes me weak in the knees. And I'm a soccer girl - I have kick ass knees. It makes me feel idiotic, because my logical brain is telling me I'm too overwhelmed by the physical rush he gives me when he touches me lightly or looks at me like he can't get enough of me - the physical and hormonal parts of a new relationship.

I shake off that thought, though. I may not be able to put it into words just yet, but this thing with Mack feels special. Unique. My interest hasn't been guided by my logical brain, and maybe that's the issue.

Once we finally get to the front of the line and place our orders, we nab an open table outside and wait for our number to be called.

"So, we've spent the whole day talking without really talking," he says, taking a sip of his chocolate shake. "What's your story, RJ?"

I fold my hands under my chin and prop myself on the table with my elbows. Time for the get-to-know-you part.

"Not much to tell, really. I'm 21, and I'm in college studying to be a high school English teacher. I've lived in SoCal my entire life. That's about it, really."

"Why English?"

"I had a really amazing English teacher when I was in high school. I really enjoyed his class, but he also helped me deal with some personal issues and he really cared about me as a person."

"Very cool," he responds.

"Yeah. I spent my lunches in his classroom, usually reading. We had some amazing conversations and he showed me you can

35

use your position as a teacher to invest in people." I take a sip of my soda. "Plus he was my coach. So I'm hoping to do that as well."

"Oh really? What did he coach you in?"

"Football," I reply.

His eyebrows fly up.

"Seriously?"

"Yeah, I was the kicker on my high school team."

"Wow, that's really cool," he says, just as our number is called. "Be right back." Once he's back with our food, we pause so he can take in the gloriousness of the In-N-Out Double-Double. I just stare at him while he takes his first bite and then groans at the taste.

"Live up to the hype?" I ask.

He nods, then moves back to our earlier conversation. "So, you're a football fanatic?"

"Well, I'm not a fanatic. I really do enjoy football - playing and watching. One of the reasons I joined the team was to piss off my dad, though. He took huge issue with the fact his little girl was covered in sweat and dirt and getting slapped on the ass by fifty guys every day."

"Sounds like there's a story there."

"There is. But we can save that for next time."

"Next time?" He asks, with a quirked eyebrow.

I smile, slightly embarrassed, but move on.

"Anyway, the real reason I played was to keep my legs in shape for soccer during the off season," I say as I squeeze out some spread onto my fries and throw a few in my mouth.

He coughs, then takes a sip of his soda.

"Really?"

"Yeah, my soccer coach was a real bitch. And not that 'endearing bitch' you see coaching championship teams. She was just awful. I can only imagine how much better my team would have done at playoffs during my senior year if we'd had a better coach." I pause, taking a bite from my own burger. "Anyway, I'm hoping to teach English and coach soccer. But who knows if that will all work out."

Just as Mack is beginning to reply, I hear a squeal and a tiny voice shout "Uncle Mack!" before a little blur runs past me and plows into my date's legs.

"Hey, baby girl!" he says, wiping his hands and lifting the toddler up into his arms for a tight squeeze. "What are you doing here?"

"I should be asking you the same thing," comes a voice from behind me. I look over my shoulder and see a stunning brunette, all long legs and brightness. "I thought you had some 'unbreakable commitment' today. You're just getting food?"

Mack shifts in his seat and a look of embarrassment crosses his face, but he covers it by adjusting the little girl in his arms.

"Nice, Amy," he mutters with a sigh. "Amy, meet RJ. My unbreakable commitment."

Internally, I'm swooning and barely register as Amy's eyes glance quickly between Mack and me.

"Oh my gosh, I am so sorry."

"Don't worry about it," I say, reaching my hand out to her. "Nice to meet you, Amy," I respond.

She smiles at me, taking my hand in a firm shake.

"Nice to meet you, RJ. My little brother didn't tell me he had a date today." Her smile grows larger, practically taking up her entire face as she looks back at him.

"Oh, we aren't on a date," I say, grabbing my soda and taking a sip.

Amy's smile drops just a bit. "Oh," is all she says.

"Yeah, I mean, would *you* date a guy who screams from the top of buildings like a crazy person and brings you dead flowers?" I fake a creeped-out shiver. "No thanks. I'm just here for the free food."

Amy looks confused, but I can see Mack's shoulders shaking with silent laughter out of the corner of my eye.

Without giving her any further information, Mack interrupts.

"So, what are you up to today, Amy?"

Amy quickly recovers and focuses her attention back on Mack.

"Kevin and I are celebrating our anniversary tonight, so Anna and I are grabbing some food before I drop her off at the sitter's. I'm supposed to be there in," she glances at her watch, "twenty minutes and she lives in Pasadena, so I better hurry because I'm already at least fifteen minutes late."

"I'm sorry, Ames. I didn't realize it was your anniversary. I can watch her," Mack says, keeping Anna sitting in his lap, where she is happily stuffing a fry into her mouth.

"Oh, don't be silly," Amy responds, reaching out for Anna. "I don't want to interrupt your... non-date." She still looks slightly confused about it, which makes me want to laugh again.

"It's really not a problem," I pipe in. "I only live a few blocks from here. And we're heading back to my place soon. We can feed Anna."

Amy looks at me, a smile tugging at the corner of her mouth.

"You sure?" I glance over at Mack and see a happily perplexed expression on his face, but he just gives Amy a short nod. "Well, alright. I'll call Chloe and let her know I won't need her after all. Her mom practically forces her to babysit, so I'm sure she'd rather enjoy a Saturday night with friends anyway." She smiles again. "Thanks a lot. I'll walk over to get her when we get home?"

"Absolutely. I'll probably swing through your place to grab some of her stuff, but we'll spend the evening at mine. If something changes, just shoot me a text."

"Thanks Mack." She leans over and kisses Mack on the cheek, and then looks to me. "It was nice to meet you RJ."

I smile at her, and then she's out the door.

Over the next twenty minutes, Mack and I are wrapped up in Anna as he orders her food and we get her fed. She really is adorable, all cherub cheeks and chocolate curls.

"How old is she?" I ask Mack as we walk out the door.

"Four next month. Hopefully we're edging out of the terrible twosomes, which extended into the thrillingly terrible threesomes," he says as he swings Anna up into the air above his head. She giggles and my heart glows. "Sorry about our little date-crasher here."

"I'm not stressed. I love kids. I'm glad we were there to help."

"Yeah, me too."

After unlocking our bikes outside, he lifts Anna up to sit on his shoulders and we start the fifteen minute walk back to my apartment. Mack guides his bike in one hand, his other clasped firmly around Anna's leg, while I ride aimless circles around them as we make our way down the street of houses.

"Amy shot me a text last night asking if I could babysit. If I had known it was her anniversary I would have figured something out instead of just telling her I was busy."

"Correction. You told her you had an 'unbreakable commitment.'" I glance at his face as I circle him and I see that same flash of embarrassment. He's silent for a moment, his brows pulled together, and I worry that I've somehow made him think I'm mocking him for real instead of for fun.

"Yeah, well..." he starts, but trails off without finishing his thought.

The silence between us becomes uncomfortable for the first time. Everything up until now has been easy. Our conversation, our teasing, my shy glances and his bold stares. Even our silence has been easy and free from that awkward need to fill the space. After a minute or two I finally just blurt out the first thing that comes to mind.

"I've only ever had one boyfriend," I say, unsure exactly where I'm going with this. Mack looks up at me briefly, then back at the street in front of him. "We dated in high school. He was always uncomfortable with the fact that I hung out with the guys, that I could play ball. He was always on me about how I dressed and how I sat and how I joked around with the guys. He made it seem like I was defective because I played gritty sports with a bunch of meat heads instead of wanting to spend time at the mall."

"Sounds like he was more concerned about how you playing sports made him feel, rather than supporting it because you enjoy it," Mack cuts in.

I stop riding in circles around Mack and pull up next to him, not making eye contact, just rolling slowly next to him as he walks.

"He was a tool. He wound up cheating on me with a cheerleader. So cliché, right? For the rest of high school, I actually questioned myself as an athlete, wondering if I would have to quit the mud baths and sweaty, dirty behavior if I wanted to ever date again, as if there's something wrong with women who play sports. But when you're barely 16 and surrounded by girls who spend hours on hair and makeup and clothes, and *also* surrounded by a bunch of guys who had so much to say about the female body and what these girls would wear and how they looked... I just really struggled to see myself in anything but a negative light. You know?"

We turn the corner and I can see my apartment complex at the end of the block.

"I've only had the one boyfriend, and I think that negative attitude kept guys away for the rest of high school. But I've been on some dates here and there in college now that I finally have more confidence in who I am and what I do. Nothing serious, just random guys. And even though I'm comfortable with myself now, I've always played the casual card. My approach to dating has usually been to smack guys over the head with who I am. My therapist told me it was a way of weeding through the people who weren't worth my time to make sure that the shitty guys who care about superficial things don't have a chance to hurt me. I always wear the same clothes I wore that day. No effort. Just, 'here is me'." I pause, trying to sort through my thoughts quickly. There's a point, here, and I need to make it.

"Today, I was ready an hour early. I showered. I shaved. I put on mascara. I picked out a new outfit. And I realized as I was getting ready that sometimes, a guy can be worth the extra effort. Simply because they make your face flush, and you get butterflies when they look at you, and they take you on bike rides and win you jelly bracelets."

We stop in front of the gate to my complex, and I connect with his eyes for the first time since I started talking. He's looking at me with such intensity, I feel like I might burst into flames.

"I guess the point of that overly long and far-too-detailed story is that I just want you to know that today was an unbreakable commitment for me too."

My heart is pounding. So fast, so hard. I've never revealed that much about myself so quickly, so early. But I know it's worth it. Mack seems worth it.

Please be worth it.

Just as his mouth opens like he's going to say something, Anna lets out a wail and starts squirming frantically. Mack drags his eyes away from me and sets Anna down, where she promptly flings herself to the ground in tears.

"I think she's tired," he says, glancing at his watch. "I should probably get her home so she can lay down."

"Okay, yeah," I say, looking away from him and rolling my bike towards his truck.

Mack unlocks the door, then buckles a squirmy Anna into a car seat that is already set up in the back. After cracking the window, he shuts the door and picks up my bike, lifting it into the bed. When he's done strapping down both of the bikes, he hops down next to me.

"I had a really great time today." He reaches forward to take my hand, but instead of linking our fingers, he just holds my hand and rubs lazy circles against the inside of my wrist, under the bracelets. My stomach is jumping all over the place. He's looking at his hand on mine when I hear him say, "I really want to kiss you," then his eyes lift and stop at my lips, and my stomach launches itself into my throat, "but I have Anna in the car, and I don't think it's a good idea right now." I can do nothing but nod as he continues to rub circles. "But I'm gonna hug you goodbye, because just holding your hand today has been the most amazing torture I've ever felt, and I'm not ready to let go of that yet."

If I thought my heart was beating fast earlier, I had no clue. I can feel it racing a million miles an hour as he leans forward and wraps his arms around my waist, pulling me snug into his solid chest. My arms instinctively loop around his neck, our cheeks pressed together. We just stand there for a minute. An hour, maybe. I have no idea. But I know that no kiss in my life has felt as good as being wrapped in his arms. Damn, he smells good.

His head drops as he pushes his face into my neck, and I hear him inhale.

"You feel it too, right?" he whispers, his hands on my lower back playing with the edge of my shirt. His thumb sneaks under the fabric and strokes lightly against my skin. "Please tell me I'm not crazy and that you feel this connection too."

My eyes squeeze shut as I try to temper the flood of emotions rushing through me. "Don't worry," I reply. "I think we're both crazy."

He presses his face into the crook of my neck one more time before releasing me and taking a step back. He looks at me for a moment, his eyes soft.

"I'll talk to you soon," he says. And then he's hopping into his truck and driving down the street.

The minute he turns the corner, I lay flat on the ground on the sidewalk, letting the cold cement cool my flushed body.

Maybe Charlie was right about firsts, because if this is how I react to a hug from Mack, I can't imagine what my response would be if I were to have sex with him. And in that moment, I know that whatever happens between us is going to absolutely wreck me.

Chapter Three

When I wander into the apartment, I find Charlie still splayed on the couch, reading and snuggled under a blanket. Without a word, I crawl onto the couch with her, sneaking my body between her arms and wrapping myself around her, my head intentionally blocking her from seeing her book.

She folds down the corner of the page and lays the book on the coffee table, then wraps her arms around me. We just stay there quietly for a moment. I know she knows something is coming. I can't remember the last time I did this.

"So," she starts, breaking the silence, "that good huh?"

I let out a noise that sounds like a terrifying cross between an awkward laugh and an uncomfortable groan. I let my eyes fixate on the TV, which is on mute and set to ESPN.

"Yeah," I whisper.

"Well, my dear, it's about time someone knocked you on your ass," she says with a little giggle. "God, I don't think I've ever seen you like this."

"I've never felt like this," I respond. "I swear, Charlie. I can't even describe to you what this day felt like. We just laughed and talked and… *god,* he's just so great. I just really like him. No, I don't just like him. I *like* him, like him."

She pushes on my face until my head tilts up and I'm looking at her.

"You *like* him, like him? Jesus, RJ. How old are you?" Then she pushes me off her and I land unceremoniously with a thump on the floor.

And our tender moment is over.

Charlie hops up and stands on the couch.

"Mack and RJ sitting in a tree," she starts.

"Charlie, come on!"

"K-I-S-S-I-N-G!"

"Quit it!" I bark, remaining in a lump on the ground, tossing my arm over my eyes so I can't see her mocking me.

"First comes love, then comes marriage, then comes a baby in the baby carriage."

"Alright, you've had your fun." I stand and shoot her a scathing look intended to wither her into the ground. She just laughs. Apparently I need to work on my scathing face. "I'm going to study for my psych test."

"Would you rather study, or do something more productive like stalk your new love toy online?"

"That's *your* M.O., Charlie, not mine." I pause. "And I don't even know Mack's last name. I couldn't stalk him even if I was some creeper like you."

"You don't know his last name?" she says, her face contorting with confusion. "What if he's like, an escaped convict? Or a rapist? Or a Republican?"

I roll my eyes. "Glad to know you think all of those belong in the same sentence."

"But seriously, how do you not know his last name?"

"It never came up," I say with a shrug.

She sits back down on the couch.

"How old is he?"

"Uhm, he's like early twenties. I think."

"Where does he work?"

"We didn't get to that."

"RJ!"

"What!?"

She crosses her arms and hits me with a concerned look that I consider to be completely unnecessary.

"Did you guys just make out in his car the whole day? How do you not know any of those things? It's like, First Date 101. You get his last name to stalk him online. You get his age to make sure he isn't old enough to be a Sugar *Daddy*. And you find out where he works so you know he isn't a mooch who wants a Sugar *Mama*. You don't know anything about him!"

"Hi pot, I'm kettle. Lets turn this around for a second and ask which one of us is more at risk here by not knowing this information after meeting a guy. Me, who goes on a date with the guy? Or you, who goes down on the guy?"

"Hey!" Charlie's face isn't pleased, but I can tell she isn't mad about what I said, just the fact that I won the points from that argument.

"You don't get to make a bunch of judgments because I didn't get the information you suddenly think is important. The likelihood of Mack having a sordid past of looting gas stations is fairly low. "

She glares at me. I throw my hands up in the air in resignation and frustration.

"We just had a fun day! We played mini-golf and raced go-karts and ate In-N-Out. I met his sister and his niece." I pause to think if I picked up any other tidbits. "He grew up in Indiana," I add.

"He must be one amazing make-out buddy for you to get all googley over him when you don't know any of the things that *you* usually want to know about a guy."

"I'm not all *googley* over him. And we haven't even kissed yet," I retort, then avoid her wide eyes and walk into the kitchen to grab a water.

"*Excuse* me?" I hear the slaps of her footsteps on the floor behind me, which is actually really impressive, considering it's carpet. "You came in here twenty minutes ago practically shitting butterflies and unicorns and marshmallows." I roll my eyes again – apparently, I do that a lot. "And you haven't even *kissed* yet?"

"What do you want me to say, Charlie? First, you're upset that I didn't get to know more information. And now, you're upset because I didn't get physical enough? Make up your mind."

"I want you to tell me what happened today," she replies. "How can you get through," she glances at her phone, "almost four hours of a date without touching on the fundamentals?"

I slap my hand on the counter in frustration.

"Why does this feel like a fight? I just *like* him. We had a great time. I laughed really hard. *He* laughed really hard. We were just silly and had fun and the conversation was easy. He makes me feel like..." I sigh. "He makes me feel like I'm not broken."

Her face falls, and I think it's at that moment she realizes she may have pushed too far in regards to the first guy I've really gushed to her about.

"That's because you're *not* broken."

She walks towards me and wraps her arms around my shoulders, linking her fingers behind my neck and keeping me at arms-length so she can look at my face.

"You can't let what a handful of people have said in your past impact your ability to have a relationship now. You're *not* broken, Rachel. Carter cheating on you doesn't make *you* broken. Your dad being a completely useless bag of shit and pouring that out on his kids doesn't make *you* broken. It makes *them* broken."

I've never been comfortable with these kinds of conversations. I feel awkward. Like I'm begging for compliments.

"Thanks Charlie," I say, kissing her on the cheek. "I'm gonna go study for my test."

She squeezes my shoulders, then lets her arms fall. She knows me. She knows I need to be by myself after any mention of Carter. Or my dad. Definitely when both are mentioned at once.

"I'm heading out tonight," she says to my back as I begin climbing the stairs to my room. "You wanna skip studying and join me? Richie and Corbin will be there." Richie and Corbin lived next door to us freshman year. Charlie spends a lot more time with them than I do, but I would still consider them to be my close friends.

"Nah. I've gotta get this grade up or I won't be able to keep my scholarship next semester," I reply, turning to give her a smile. "But have fun. And tell the guys I miss them."

And with that, I close myself into my room and crack my textbook, even though I know I won't retain anything I'm about to read.

*   *   *   *   *

Beeping from my phone at nearly 10pm draws my eyes from my notes. My face breaks into a smile when I see a text from Mack.

Mack: I'm daydreaming about that burger

45

Me: You should be. In-N-Out burgers are the tits

Mack: Did you just say tits?

Me: You know you can still see the message on your phone after you've read it, right? It's not like it disappears

Mack: Nope. Not on my phone. The minute you read something it goes away. Into the void of messaging

Me: Yeaaaaaaaaa, that's not a real thing

Mack: You don't know

Me: I think I do, actually

Mack: ANYWAY. I've been thinking about our next date

I leave my desk and wander down to the living room to flip on Sports Center.

Me: Oh?

Mack: Yeah. I'm thinking Chuck-E-Cheese

Me: Only if you promise not to lose your diaper in the ball pit

Mack: Bad experience?

Me: A kid I was babysitting when I was in high school. That was NOT a good day for me

Mack: Sounds pretty glamorous

Me: Story of my life.

About five minutes goes by before anything else comes

through. My eyes glaze over the television, which currently sits on mute. Some asshole that plays college football in Texas is causing a stir. I love those stories.

Mack: I wanted to kiss you so bad today

My breath catches and I immediately begin to chew on my fingernails. I'm unsure how to respond. Do I make a joke? Is this one of those moments? I can tell him I wouldn't have wanted his burger-y onion breath in my face.

Even though it's a boldfaced lie.

I hit the sleep button on my phone and watch the screen go black, staring at it for a moment and allowing everything in my mind the chance to jumble around until the pieces fall in a way that makes sense.

I like that he said that to me, both in the text and earlier today. But I don't know what to say back. What's a normal response to someone saying they want to kiss you?

When he said it earlier today when he dropped me off, I stood like a statue until he hugged me and I was able to show him with my return embrace that I was feeling the moment too. But, I don't have the luxury of allowing him to read my body language. If I don't respond to his text, maybe he'll think I don't want him to kiss me. But if I tell him how I really feel...

What? What will happen if I tell him how I really feel?

Nothing.

Well, that's not true. I might die of embarrassment.

But apart from that, nothing.

Me: I wanted you to kiss me, too

I wait for a response, but my phone stays dark. I flip through the channels, not even sure what shows are on. I go into the kitchen and get a glass of water. I stand at the island, snacking on strawberries. Fifteen minutes go by and nothing.

When my phone rings suddenly, I'm so surprised I drop it on the ground. I'm immediately grateful for my phone case and screen protector.

"Hello?"

"Why are you all short of breath? Were you on a jog or something?"

My heart drops at Charlie's voice.

"No, I was just glaring at my phone, willing Mack to call me with my voodoo powers."

She laughs. "Girl, you have got it *bad*. He dropped you off five hours ago."

"I know. I feel ridiculous."

"It's not ridiculous, RJ. You have a crush. I used to be concerned when you *didn't* react this way."

I let out a huff.

"Whatever. Let's not talk about all of the strange things that make me special. What can I do for you?"

"I just wanted to make sure you weren't wallowing in self-pity, so it sounds like I called at just the right time." Her voice is bright and happy and I regret staying at home by myself to pretend to study. "Any chance you want to give your psych test the middle finger and head out to meet us at O'Reilly's? I know you didn't *actually* get any studying done tonight."

I look at my watch. If I leave immediately I can be there in fifteen minutes, enjoy some time with my friends, and take my mind off the fact that Mack hasn't texted me back.

"Yeah, okay."

I hear a whoop on the other end of the phone, followed by Richie's voice in the background, shouting "Get your fine ass down here, sweet thing!" I can't help the laugh that escapes me.

After ending the call, I pull my hair into a ponytail, grab my wallet and keys off the entry table, and pull my favorite gray Glendale College sweater from the closet. I'm tugging it over my head when I open the door and come face-to-face with Mack, his hand poised to knock.

I stop moving.

I think I nearly stop breathing.

Yup, I just had to remind myself to inhale.

"Hi," he says.

"Hey." I'm trying to sound unaffected by his sudden presence, but I'm pretty sure the sudden pounding of my heart in my chest made my voice waver. He just stands there looking at me. "What are you doing here?"

"I was driving around to clear my head when I got your text. And I just... drove here."

At the mention of my text, my moment of vulnerability feels foolish. My face flushes and I'm embarrassed at the fact I told him I wanted him to kiss me. I want to tell him I didn't mean it. I want to tell him that a robber stole my phone or I was drunk or something. This might be the first time I actually wish I drank alcohol. But I don't say anything. I just stare back at him. Because saying any of those things would be lying to him. And I like that we say strange and very honest things to each other.

"I'm heading to meet some friends at O'Reilly's," I finally offer, as I close the door behind me. "Do you want to come with, or...?" I let my voice trail off as he shakes his head 'no' and then takes a step towards me. He's inches away now. I could reach out and touch him if I wanted. And oh do I want to. I want to wrap my arms around him and let him hug me like he did earlier.

He reaches his hand to me and places his it on the back of my neck and traces his thumb along my jaw, like he did at the mini-golf course. His eyes drop to my lips and he stares. He just stares at them with such intensity and focus I begin to wonder if he's trying to read my emotion in the creases in my skin. Part of me wishes he could hear my heart shouting at him. *Kiss me, kiss me. Please kiss me.*

And then he does.

He presses his lips against mine. Softly. Delicately. Like my lips are fragile and he doesn't want to break them. He kisses my top lip, sucking on it lightly. Then he kisses the corner of my mouth, and the side of my jaw, and my neck. His mouth opens against me and I feel his tongue on my skin. A moan escapes from deep in my chest.

Suddenly everything moves from slow and languid to full speed. He's back at my lips, and our mouths part, our tongues seeking entrance. His hand is still behind my head, his fingers gripping my hair, his other hand at my lower back. He pulls me against him. I can feel just how much he's enjoying this kiss, but I know there is no way he could possibly be feeling as riotous and reckless as I do.

I snake my arms around his neck, letting my fingers tangle in his hair as our kiss deepens. When I tug slightly, he moans into my mouth, and his hand at my lower back drops lower to my ass and he squeezes. He takes a step into me, and with nowhere to go, I find myself backed up against the door. He presses himself against me and my stomach muscles clench. We are nothing but a pile of moans and kisses and tongues and heavy breaths.

I feel something brewing inside. I've never been kissed like this, like my next breath can only come from this connection, like if we pulled apart something inside of my soul would tear in two. This one kiss puts all of my other youthful fumblings to shame.

Our hands are everywhere. On shoulders and arms, gripping skin and clothing, pulling and tugging to get our bodies closer, closer, so much closer. We are fused together, my body soft and pliant, his body hard and firm. He grips my thigh and lifts my leg just slightly, pressing into me with a roll that has the space in my lower belly tightening and shivers skittering through my body.

I can barely breathe and suck in a long breath through my nose and inhale his warmth. His scent is familiar. Comforting. I breathe him in as deep as I can, to try and imprint the essence of who he is into my veins, burrowing that comfort into the lining of my lungs.

And just as quickly as the kiss became frantic, I can feel it slowing down. He leans further into me to kiss my neck, and then my jaw, and then the corner of my mouth, before kissing me one more time on the lips. Softly. Delicately. Our foreheads are resting against each other. Our eyes our closed. Our breathing ragged.

"Wow," I whisper, sure that there has never been a bigger understatement.

"Wow isn't enough," he whispers back, bringing words to my unspoken thoughts.

I smile as I try to catch my breath.

"So, what now?"

He pulls his forehead away and looks me in the eyes.

"Now, I head home and take a cold shower, and try to think of an amazing second date to knock your socks off."

I laugh, taking his hand from where it still rests on my shoulder and interlocking my fingers with his. "Trying to get into my socks already, huh? I knew you were only after one thing."

He tugs on my hand and wraps his free arm around me, snuggling me in for a quick hug and a kiss at the crown of my head. Then he's releasing my hand and taking a step back. His smile is small but genuine. I can't help but return it with my own.

"I'll hear from you soon?" I say, as I open the door to head back into my apartment.

"Count on it. You're not going out anymore?"

"No need," I say, shaking my head. He looks at me in

confusion, so I try the honesty route since it worked so well last time. "I was going out to distract myself from thinking about you. Now, I know any attempts at that tonight will be a complete failure."

His face breaks out into that breathtaking smile of his, nodding his head in understanding.

"Okay then. Night, RJ."

"Night, Indy," I say with a wink.

I close the door to the sound of his light chuckle, walk straight up to my room and collapse on my bed. It's the second time in just a few hours that interacting with that man has made me want to lay down and replay every word, every touch. My fingers graze over my lips, still slightly swollen from being thoroughly kissed. And then I'm laughing, and laughing, and hugging my arcade teddy bear to my chest.

* * * * *

Through most of Sunday, I ride a high only a mind-blowing kiss can give, plowing through my homework with lightning speed and getting my laundry and grocery shopping done in just a few hours. I ride it until mid-evening when I get a text from Piper.

Piper: Did you hear the news about Coach Walker?!

Me: No. What's going on?

Piper: She got picked up by Washington. She flew up today and starts with their team tomorrow.

My heart plummets and shock rolls through my body. I love Coach Walker. Is she really leaving us to contract with another team mid-season? Is that even allowed? I thought the NCAA had rules about this or something. Don't get me wrong, Coach Johnson is great. But he's the Assistant Coach and this is his first college-level job. Can he really manage our team this close to playoffs?

Piper: Coach Johnson is bringing in someone else to co-coach for the rest of the season

Me: Are you serious?! Do you know who the new coach is?

Piper: Haven't heard anything

Me: Let me know if you do

I grip my phone in my hand. How can this be happening? I mean, I know I'm not pro material like Jeremy. But there are some girls on the team who *do* have what it takes, and making it to playoffs is helpful for exposure to scouts. A new coach will disrupt everything we have going for us so far.

And I can't help but feel the tiny sting of rejection. Coach Walker recruited me. I've been with her since I started playing at Glendale freshman year. She's one of the only people here that knows about my home life. She really gets why playing is so important to me, apart from just the scholarship. And she always took the time to check in with me on a personal level. She wasn't just a coach. She was a mentor. A friend.

And now… she's just, gone? No goodbye? No explanation?

I try to distract myself by flipping through a book I told myself I would read for pleasure but never got around to opening. I settle on reading the first paragraph of each chapter and then reading the final page of the book. Much easier than wasting my time on all the drama, but surprisingly unsatisfying.

An hour passes before I hear from Piper again, and when I hear my phone beep, Charlie startles next to me with how I lunge at the table to grab it.

Piper: Okay I just heard from Ruth-Ann. We won't know who the coach is until tomorrow. They're still narrowing it down tonight and have to sign someone

Me: Do you think they'll be at practice in the morning?

Piper: Maybe. If Coach J and the AD can get everything squared away by then

Me: This is ridiculous. How can she talk to us about our strategy for the season YESTERDAY and then quit today?

Piper: I know. I hope she enjoys the weather

I laugh. Coach Walker *hates* the rain. But just as quickly, I feel bad for feeling ill will towards her. As frustrating as this is, I guess you have to take the next step for you when it comes along. Not everything can wait for convenient timing.

I try to relax the rest of the evening, but I end up taking too long of a jog, too hot of a shower, and get very little sleep. My body is restless. My mind is restless. And when I drag myself out of bed on Monday morning to get ready for practice, I feel like I have a hangover. Or at least, what I assume a hangover would feel like.

An email sent to the team at 3:30 this morning from Coach Johnson clarified that we would be meeting together in the athletic offices to 'discuss Coach Walker's departure and the new direction for our team.'

The only thing that alleviates my nerves about our meeting this morning is the text that pops up on my phone as I'm heading out the door, eating my pre-practice banana:

Mack: Morning beautiful. I was thinking about our second date. I'm putting the kibosh on Chuck-E-Cheese. How do you feel about the Atwater High School football game on Friday night?

Me: Only if you guarantee me an unlimited supply of M&Ms and popcorn

Mack: Well obviously

Me: Okay then count me in

Mack: Great. I might even try to sneak you behind the bleachers for a few minutes

Me: Oh Indy, you trying to put your sweet pre-pubescent moves on me?

Mack: Perhaps

Me: Well we have to be careful. I don't want any rumors about us impacting my bid for Prom Queen

Mack: No worries there, sweetheart

My heart soars as I drive to practice. I'm pulling into the parking lot at the school when his last text comes through:

Mack: Heading into an important meeting so I won't be able to chat much today. But I'll call tonight to hash out details for Friday?

Me: Can't wait

Mack: Me neither ;)

I smile and close out the screen, then chuck my phone into my duffle and practically float across the parking lot and into the building, allowing my excitement to wash over me for a few minutes.

When I reach the fourth floor, my excitement is replaced with trepidation. I find most of our team in the small banquet room just off the entryway. The chairs have all been lined up in rows to face the front, where I'm assuming Coach Johnson will be introducing our new coach. I drop down in a chair next to Piper and notice that everyone is whispering animatedly in little groups.

"What's the deal?" I ask Piper, elbowing her lightly on the arm to get her attention.

"We found out who the new coach is!" she replies in a sing-song voice, and I can tell that she wants me to play the guessing game. Normally I would appease her, but my nerves are off the charts and I am definitely not in the mood.

"Well?"

Before Piper can say anything, Ruth-Ann leans over her and quickly whispers, "Andy McIntosh!"

My jaw drops, my eyes going wide.

"Seriously?"

Ruth-Ann and Piper nod vigorously, huge smiles on their

faces.

Andy McIntosh.

I definitely knew him. Well, knew *about* him. If memory serves, he was ranked the number one NCAA soccer player in the country about five years ago, got drafted his junior year to play for the Chicago Fire, and then shot his entire career to hell when he got into a car with a drunk driver and ripped apart his body. I think the rumor was that he was paralyzed in that accident, though, so I am blown away by the news.

"How is he going to be our coach? Can he even play anymore?" I look back and forth between them and lower my voice. "Can he even *walk*?"

"Don't you know the story?" Ruth-Ann asks. When I shake my head she launches right in with the little snippets she remembers. He was partying with a bunch of guys from college who came to visit him. When they left the party, there was a lot of ice on the road, and the driver, who was totally plastered, lost control of the car and plowed into a freeway overpass. A handful of cars crashed in behind them, including a mother of three who was paralyzed. One of Andy's legs was crushed into dust, and just like that his career was over.

"Do you know what happened afterwards?"

Ruth-Ann shakes her head.

"I tried Googling him when I found out this morning but all I could find were the same articles about the crash and his release from Chicago, and then a bunch of recent playboy stuff."

"And his fine ass picture," Piper adds, fanning herself dramatically. "That man fell out of the sexy beast tree and hit every fucking branch on the way down. Sexy. Ass. Beast. I swear I've never seen someone so ridiculously good looking."

I giggle and roll my eyes.

"So is he gonna be here today?"

Ruth-Ann shrugs.

"I'm assuming so. Why else would we be meeting here? We probably aren't gonna get in any real practice time this morning, which is the exact opposite of what we need."

"What do you mean?" I ask, my brow furrowing.

"I just mean that before I transferred from Vandy, we got a new coach and she wanted to do individual meetings with us on her first day. They were a total waste of time and were supposed to *set us at ease* about the team." Ruth-Ann rolls her eyes and begins picking dirt out from under her fingernails. "You know what would set us at ease? Getting on the field and seeing that things aren't shot to hell because Coach Walker did a runner."

"Seriously," I grumble, then sit back in my chair and rest an ankle on my knee.

Just then, the door opens behind us. Every voice in the room falls silent as all thirty of us turn to look at the former soccer star following Coach Johnson into the room. And when my eyes find him, I feel the air whoosh out of my lungs.

Andy McIntosh.

My eyes blink rapidly, trying to will away the face of the man in front of us. But it does no good. I'm still left looking into the face of the man who has occupied my thoughts so thoroughly over the past few days.

Mack.

"You okay?" Piper whispers. "You look super pale all of a sudden."

I just nod and slump down lower in my chair. Maybe if he doesn't see me...

But there isn't anywhere that thought can go. Because I already know he'll see me... he *has* to see me. And when he does, I will break apart when I see the look in his eyes that means whatever we shared over the weekend is over. How is this possible?

"Alright ladies," I hear Coach Johnson start speaking, but my eyes are trained on Mack. "I know most of you are aware that Coach Walker got a job at Washington and left over the weekend. The Athletic Director and I have been working tirelessly over the past twenty four hours to find someone to join our humble team as an interim head coach for the remainder of the season. I am excited to introduce you all to the man who will be stepping into that role. Please welcome your interim head coach, Andrew McIntosh."

A light applause and a smattering of giggles. I look around suddenly and notice my teammates eyeing Mack with various shades of flirtation, appreciation, and downright lust. I glance back up at the front at Mack, standing comfortably in his track pants and Glendale Soccer shirt, a thick black band around his wrist and a whistle hanging from his neck.

He's gripping a clipboard to his chest, posing his arms in a position to show off his flexing muscles. His eyes are trained on Coach Johnson, who is continuing to talk, although what I'm hearing sounds more like the adults in Charlie Brown. *Waah,*

waah waaaaah, waaah waaah.

When I finally snap out of it, I realize it's because Mack has started talking, his rich voice cutting through the room.

"... excited to be here. I've been looking for an opportunity to get back into the game, and think working at Glendale is going to be an excellent chance to challenge what you think you know about yourself, both on and off the field. Coach Walker and Coach Johnson have done an excellent job in moving this team in a great direction, and I am looking forward to the chance to help you all continue your playoff hopes." His eyes are glancing around the room, and as I see them flit towards me, I bend over and grab my water bottle from my bag. I can't let him see me.

Not yet.

I need to brace myself for the look I know I'll get when he sees me. I just need a few more minutes to prepare. Just a few more.

When my head pops back up, he's talking about meeting with us individually. He starts at the beginning of the alphabet and then heads out the door with midfielder Gina Brown. When she gets to the door, she turns back and looks at the other midfielders and gives them a quick up-and-down with her eyebrows and bites her fingernail before sashaying out of the room after him.

The *slut.*

As soon as everyone starts talking again, I'm pulling my phone out of my duffle and Googling Andrew McIntosh. I'm pretty sure my brother has talked about him before but I can't place the memory. When I pull up his bio online and his soccer history is displayed on my phone, I see why.

Mack and Jeremy were invited to the same U-18 National Team camp when they were in high school. I click quickly to Jeremy's Facebook page. He and Mack definitely know each other, and there are at least a dozen photos of them together over the past few years, looking pretty friendly, like more than just acquaintances.

How has this never been on my radar? Why did it never occur to me that Jeremy and Mack were friends? I met him at Jer's party.

I click to Mack's Facebook page and begin looking through his pictures. His profile picture is a shot of him and sweet little Anna, but he has uber-intense privacy settings. The handful of visible photos are of him and his sister, a man I am assuming is

Amy's husband Kevin, and Anna.

But when I go back to the page where I searched his name, I see the link to his Facebook fan page. It's fairly outdated, since Mack hasn't been in the spotlight much, at least to my knowledge, in the past few years. But when I click on photos, I feel like I'm looking at a completely different Mack.

I don't even bother studying the images as I scroll through photo after photo of Mack and a gaggle of girls. I can't help but notice that the majority of girls look like the stripper wannabes from Jer's party. I feel like I'm looking at a bang book, where his conquests upload photos once they'd gotten what they wanted.

He looks different, too. Rougher. Darker. His eyes are always hooded and brooding, his face remaining in that same lifeless expression with no hint of happiness or smile.

And then I get to photos I can tell are of Mack pre-accident. When his career was still bright in front of him. When his future still had promise. When he wasn't stuck watching his teammates play from the sidelines. *Before*. His eyes light and excited, his smile present in every photo.

Suddenly it occurs to me that Jeremy *must* know about the job. But does he know that Mack asked me out? I quickly fire off a text to him.

> **Me: Did you hear that Andy McIntosh is our new coach?**
>
> **Jeremy: He got the job? Sweet! He's great, Rach. You're gonna love him**
>
> **Me: What does that mean? Did you know he was applying?**
>
> **Jeremy: He didn't apply. I recommended him to Coach J**
>
> **Me: I didn't realize a coach could get hired on just a recommendation**
>
> **Jeremy: Ya. Coach J loves me**

I forgot that Coach Johnson played on the Glendale team with Jeremy. It would make sense for him to take Jer's recommendation so seriously.

Jeremy: We still on for MM tonight?

Mexican Mondays. Our tradition. When I was a freshman in college, we met at the quad for lunch. Once Jeremy went pro, he turned it into Mexican Mondays and an opportunity to treat my poor ass to dinner. Even with all of the craziness of his life as a pro-athlete, he still tries really hard to be available every Monday if he isn't traveling so we can catch up and bitch and moan about how terrible his fabulous life is.

Me: Absolutely. See you there

I spend the next hour staring out the window of the conference room, and half-heartedly listening to Piper and Ruth-Ann gossiping about Mack before moving on to talk about other male pro players they think are 'totally hot'.

When I finally hear Coach Johnson call my name, my stomach drops. I stand up slowly and head out of the banquet room, then down the hall to Coach Walker's old office. Mack's new office.

His *office.*

Where he will work from as my *coach.*

The open door at the end of the hall looms in front of me, and I feel like I'm moving in slow motion as a part of some horrible Hallmark movie. When I finally reach the door and take a step in, Mack looks up from his clipboard, where he's taking notes. The professional smile on his face quickly shifts, with something a little more heated passing through his eyes. I stand immobile at the door, soaking that look in for the last time.

He stands, cocking his head a little to the side. "RJ, what are you..." but he stops talking when I shake my head quickly.

Coach Johnson is behind me, standing at the door with a smile on his face.

"Alright, Coach. This is our starting goalkeeper, Rachel Jameson. I'll leave you to it and be back with Desiree in a few." And then he closes the door, leaving Mack and I to stand and stare at each other.

This can't be happening. I mean, logically, I know it's happening. I can see it happening. I know that the man who was at my door on Saturday night is the same man in front of me.

But at the same time, I don't want to let myself believe it. Because if I do, that means that the universe is actively working against my happiness.

Mack closes his eyes and squeezes the bridge of his nose. Without looking at me, he says, "You're Jeremy's little sister."

"Yes." My voice is a whisper.

"You're the goalie on the team I'm coaching."

"Yes."

He opens his eyes and the look of sadness I see in them reflects every piece of disappointment rattling around in my soul. He sits in his chair and rubs his hands over his face. I follow suit, sitting across from him, just staring at him, aware that this might be my last chance to look at him unabashedly without feeling self-conscious about it. I won't get that luxury again without fear that someone will see my feelings written on my face.

"RJ," he starts.

My head drops and I stare at my hands clasped tightly in my lap.

"I know," I whisper.

And when I look back up at him, I see the look. The look I was anticipating.

It's over.

It doesn't surprise me. Both of us could get in serious trouble if there was even a *hint* that something was going on between us.

"How is this happening?" I ask.

He shakes his head and exhales a heavy breath, taking a seat back at his desk.

"I've been talking with Jeremy about trying to get back into the soccer world. He called me a few weeks ago. Told me he'd heard word that Coach Walker might be moving on and a coaching job might come open here. That I should head out to be available for an interview." He shrugs. "I've been here about three weeks. I didn't even know if it was going to work out until last night."

"So it's Jeremy's fault," I say with a small smile.

He laughs. A small laugh, but it's still better than the desolate look he was wearing a few minutes ago.

"Yeah, I guess it is." He picks up his pencil and starts twirling it in his fingers. "So that's it then."

"We barely know each other." I try to brush it off, but even I can tell there's no conviction behind my words. "We went on one date. This shouldn't matter."

"You're right. It shouldn't."

And then we stare at each other, each of us silently acknowledging the fact that whatever was blooming between us would have been something special. Something more. Sometimes the loss of what might have been can feel just as intense as the loss of what is. We're in the process of losing both.

"We can't just sit here and stare at each other." I finally say with a sigh. "Treat me like the other girls. What questions do you have for me?"

His eyes drop to his clipboard.

"Tell me about yourself." But before I can answer he draws a line through the question and reads the next one. "What are your long-term soccer goals?" And then he scratches through that one and moves on. "Why are you a part of this team?"

There's a silence and I realize he's going to let me respond because it's finally a question he doesn't know the answer to.

"As you know, my brother plays soccer. He always made it sound like it was a way to escape from his life. So I joined the team in high school and I was hooked, just like he was. My dad had his own idea about what Jeremy and I should do with our futures, and it didn't involve soccer, or Glendale. I had to get a scholarship if I wanted to go to school, because my dad sure wasn't going to help. Half of my tuition is an academic scholarship, but the other half is covered by athletics."

"So you're a part of this team because it pays your way?"

"That's not what I said."

"Then what did you say?"

I pause, trying to find the right words.

"There are a few people in my past who have intentionally tried to make me feel like I had no value." I see Mack wince slightly, and I focus my attention out the window behind him instead of at his face. "It was important to me to be able to leave that behind and create a better life than what those people think I deserve. I knew my only way to get free was to go to college and I needed some sort of scholarship. I was lucky enough to fall in love with a sport when I needed it. I took that love and channeled it to learn and improve and kick ass so that I could get that scholarship. And now I'm using that scholarship to get my degree and be the person I think I'm capable of being."

When I finally look back at him, his eyes are roaming over my face. "You're going to do amazing things, RJ."

"I'm not sure about amazing things," I respond with a small shrug. "But I'll try my best to do something with my life that's more than getting drunk and ruining other peoples' lives."

Mack's nostrils flare and his eyes narrow. His posture has gone rigid, and I see him clenching his fist around his pen. Then he looks at his watch.

"Our time is up," he says curtly, rising from his chair.

I'm confused about his suddenly gruff response for a brief moment before it hits me – he thinks I'm talking about him, about his past. Without the context of my family he couldn't know what I meant.

"Mack, I didn't…"

"It's Coach McIntosh, Rachel. Please remember that in the future." His eyes have turned glacial, and he's looking through me, not at me.

"Please, if you would just let me explain I can…"

"I don't need an explanation, Rachel."

"Stop calling me Rachel!" I shout. Then I drop my voice and glare at him. "So this is how it's gonna be, huh? Now that there's some sort of power dynamic, you're going to use it shut me out before letting me explain? You have to…"

"I don't have to do anything," he cuts me off again.

I grab my duffle bag off of the floor and sling it around my body with a huff, holding the strap at the front. I see Mack's eyes drop to my wrist, to the jelly bracelets that I haven't taken off since Saturday. His shoulders drop.

"If you would have let me finish," I spit out, "I could explain to you that I was talking about the destruction my drunk of a father left in his wake. It had *nothing* to do with you." His eyes fly to mine and I see the shock in them. My nose prickles as tears begin to build in my eyes. "See you this afternoon at practice, *Coach McIntosh*."

And then I'm out the door and rushing down the hallway.

Chapter Four

"Aren't you supposed to be at practice?"

I ignore Charlie's question and bolt past her up the stairs, slamming the bathroom door closed, then stripping quickly and stepping into the shower. Placing my palms flat on the tile, I lean forward and let the hot water hit my face and cascade down my body. Warm water on the face has always been the quickest way to ward off tears. I haven't allowed myself to cry since freshman year, and I'll be damned if I let a guy ruin that record.

Five minutes later, I barely hear the soft knock at the door. I know Charlie wants to ask questions and I'm not really sure I want to answer them. The sound of the toilet lid dropping and a soft *thunk* indicates that she's taken up her usual spot and won't be leaving. Ignoring her isn't going to work.

"He's my coach, Char," I finally sputter out, the tears brimming even though I've been willing them away. "He's the new soccer coach for Glendale. And I know, I *know* that it's way too fast, way too soon to let my heart get this emotionally involved. I don't let my heart get involved. I'm not this person. We went on *one* date. We kissed one time. But *God,* there was something special there. Something really special. And you know I don't say something like that lightly. I don't know what to do with myself now. I don't know…" I take a shuddering breath. "I don't know if I can go to practice every day and have him watching me and critiquing me in some cold, robotic manner, like we aren't anything. Like it didn't mean anything."

There's silence, and I know Charlie's trying to put together

her response. For someone as quick witted as her, she takes an awfully long time to formulate a response to something important.

"Hey, what do you…" I start to draw back the shower curtain, and all of the color drains from my face when I don't see Charlie sitting in the bathroom. It's Mack. His forearms rest on his knees, his hands clasped together, his eyes trained on the floor.

I slam the shower curtain closed. "What the *fuck*, Mack! You can't be in here! Get the hell out!"

"RJ, I just wanted to…"

"No!" I shout, cutting him off mid sentence. "You do *not* get to show up at my house and sit in my bathroom while I take a shower." I bring my hands up to my face and press the heels of my palms into my eyes. "*God,* I thought you were Charlie!" I take a deep breath. "You need to leave, *now.*"

I hear him stand and open the door. "I'll be waiting downstairs when you're done," he says softly, and then the door closes behind him.

I can't even formulate a physical or emotional response to the fact that Mack was just sitting in the bathroom while I essentially poured my heart out to him. I said that stuff. All of the… feelings. He heard them. And now he's going to wait downstairs? I feel like I'm watching emotional table tennis. My head is flying back and forth as the emotions change. Anger, sadness, anger, sadness.

Right now, it is *definitely* anger. I roughly switch off the water and rip back the shower curtain, wrap myself in a towel and storm out of the bathroom. Walking down the hall, I see Charlie sitting on the floor of her room on the phone.

Her face pales when she sees my expression. "I gotta go," she whispers into the phone, then quickly ends the call.

"What the hell were you thinking?" I growl at her through gritted teeth.

"I didn't realize you were in the shower, RJ. I thought you just went up to your room. And then he shows up all puppy dog face and I thought he was here to make you feel better. I told him to head up. I'm so, so sorry!"

I just glare at her, dripping all over her carpet.

"What happened?" she whispers.

My face falls and the emotional table tennis is back. Sadness consumes me. "He's my new coach," I whisper.

Her mouth drops. We stay there in silence for a moment before I see her mouth split into a shit-eating grin. "That is without a doubt the *sexiest* thing I have ever heard."

My brows furrow. "Excuse me?"

"Oh my god, RJ. A forbidden romance? All that angst? It's like one of those bodice ripping romance novels my mom used to hide under her bed. Imagine... you're gonna be all sexed up and sweaty after playing with balls for hours and he's gonna be there with his clipboard and whistle and his amazing muscles. You could sneak off to the locker rooms for hot, steamy..."

"Charlie!"

"What? It sounds hot."

"You are literally the worst right now."

She frowns. "I was just trying to point out the positives."

"There aren't any positives. He is my *coach*. If anyone found out we even went on a date, I could be kicked off the team, lose my scholarship, and I'd have to drop out of Glendale and get a job working at Hooters."

"One, that is incredibly dramatic. Two, you couldn't get a job at Hooters. The qualifications needed for that job are in the name. Sorry, honey."

I let out a huff at her not so subtle jab at my underwhelming chest. "That is *so* not the point. And I'm not being dramatic."

Charlie just shrugs, her expression now sympathetic. "I get that you're in a rough spot. But you should at least talk to him. I mean, I doubt this is how he saw it playing out either."

Part of me thinks Charlie's right. But the other part of me is incredibly irritated that Mack cut me off in his office, spouting his 'it's Coach McIntosh' to me, but then thinks there isn't anything wrong with showing up at my house and sitting in the bathroom while I shower.

What a hypocrite.

"I'll talk to him," I start, but then quickly continue when her eyes light up, "but don't think this is going to end all sunshine and rainbows. This is a shitty situation." Charlie just nods her head. "I need to throw on some clothes. Can you go downstairs and let him know I'll be down in a minute?"

"Sure thing, girl." And she's hopping out the door and down the stairs.

I take my time getting changed, taking the extra effort to put on my vanilla scented lotion. As I'm poised to add a swoop of lip-gloss, I look at myself in the mirror. "What the hell are you doing?" I mutter to myself, then toss my gloss haphazardly on my dresser, unused, and throw my hair into a hasty, damp knot at the top of my head.

When I finally head down to the living room, I find Charlie sitting alone watching TV. "He's waiting out front," she says after catching my questioning look.

When I step outside, I'm immediately assaulted by the incredibly warm October morning. Just when I think things are starting to cool down, LA gets hit with a heat wave. Eighty degrees at 8am is not my idea of a good day.

Mack is sitting on our front stoop. The Glendale Soccer shirt he's wearing is stretched taught across his back. I want to run my hands across his back and wrap my arms around him. But I don't. He doesn't turn to look at me, and I don't sit next to him. I just stand, leaning back on the front door.

"I shouldn't have gone into the bathroom when I got here. It was inappropriate," he says, his voice smooth but professional. "When I showed up, your roommate was on the phone and just pointed me upstairs. But that's not really an excuse for why I made the decision to go in when you were obviously showering."

"I get it. You wanted to talk. The line was kind of blurry already. If you weren't my coach, who knows how that situation could have been different. It probably would have made me more fluttery than angry. But it is what it is, I guess."

Mack stands and turns to look at me, his hands stuffed in his pockets. "Fluttery? Where do you come up with these words?"

I shrug a little, letting my mouth turn up into a small smile, but I focus my eyes on his shoes. "So why are you here, Mack?"

When I finally get the nerve to look at him, his hands are clasped behind his head, pulling his shirt up to reveal just an inch of his toned stomach. His eyes are brimming with an apology, but I'm not sure I want it. "If it's to apologize or smooth things over, it isn't necessary." I look past him to the street, letting the words fall from my mouth, but they don't feel true. "You don't owe me anything."

He drops his hands from his head and then crosses his arms across his chest. "I just wanted to make sure you were okay. That we're okay."

"But we're not okay Mack. *I'm* not okay." I kick off the door and take a few steps towards him. "You're my coach. I'm your student. Not just your athlete. Your *student*. I have less than a year left before I graduate, and half of my world rests on the scholarship I get for playing on this team. Playing for *you*. Do you not see how that makes us not okay?"

"Of course I see it," he barks in frustration. He lets out a deep breath and drags his hands up and down his face, which I'm beginning to recognize as a sign that he's trying to find the right words to say. "What I meant was, are you going to be okay to play? Are you going to be able to play with me as your coach?"

I give him a short nod. And he nods back.

"Jeremy thinks you can go pro," he says suddenly, and I'm a little thrown by the topic.

"Jeremy also thinks the Black Eyed Peas are The Beatles of our generation. He's been known to think stupid things."

Mack just smiles. "I've been listening to him rave about you playing soccer since you were just starting to play in high school. He said you had the natural ability where he always had to work hard at it."

"He has that backwards," I say, shaking my head and looking down at the ground as I roll a small rock around with my shoe. "Jeremy's the star. He's good at everything. He's confident, smart, attractive, popular, an *amazing* athlete. He's the golden child." *And even* he *couldn't satisfy my dad. What chance did I ever have?* The thought is fleeting, but it immediately settles over me like a dark cloud.

"To hear it from your perspective, it sounds like you think you aren't any of those things. And I can tell you that from my point of view, that is the farthest thing from the truth."

"Thanks." My response is quick, my brief smile disingenuous. I don't react well to compliments as they typically make me feel more inferior rather than lift me up. I was barely okay with Mack's tendency to lean towards me and say something about my eyes or my smile.

Damn, that man can lean.

"Anyway, he's always had wonderful things to say about you. I've been hearing about the infamous 'Rachel Jameson' for years. I'm excited to see what you can do on the field."

I plaster on a fake smile. "Well, you'll get to see me in action this afternoon."

"Don't do that."

"Do what?"

"Don't force a fake smile." My face immediately drops as he closes the distance between us. He isn't inappropriately close by any means, but I can feel the tension radiating between us. "That's two times in just as many minutes that you've done it. Your real smile is too amazing for anyone to believe you when you aren't being completely sincere."

I feel confused and I'm sure it's probably reflected on my face. He's complimenting me. Again. I feel confused because maybe I *do* want him to say these things. But I know he shouldn't, and ultimately that is the feeling that takes control.

"Yeah, well, sometimes you just have to smile, even when you don't want to. Even if life deals you a shitty hand. You grin and bear it."

Mack just looks at me. "So, earlier, in my office," he starts, but I quickly cut him off.

"Did you seriously leave to chase after me as soon as I left?"

He's silent for a moment, looking out to his right with a hint of a smirk. "Yeah, that might not have been the brightest thing for me to do on my first day. I'll need to reschedule meetings with all the girls I didn't meet with."

I shake my head slightly. "Meh, they won't care. Just let that one go." I pause, wondering how to broach the conversation from earlier. "I wasn't making a slight at you or your past. Earlier, I mean."

His head bobs in a short nod. "I know. It was a knee-jerk reaction."

"Well if your knee-jerk reaction is to assume that I would make an off-handed comment at your expense, you obviously don't think very highly of me based on our previous interactions." He frowns, but doesn't say anything. I let out a sigh and look back at the rock I'm still playing with on the ground. "Mack, you don't need to do this. You don't need to come here and try to fix things or make us 'okay.' If you're worried I won't play, you don't have to worry." I look up at him and try to give an unaffected shrug. "I'll be totally fine. No big deal."

His frown slowly morphs into a scowl. "You'll be totally fine." He says it like a statement, not a question.

I give him another shrug and just stare at him blankly, willing him to leave so I can go lay down on my bed and pretend the past few days never happened. And as I stare at him, I can feel the shutters begin to close in my body. My need to explain myself, my desire to ensure that he and I are 'okay', my wish that we could navigate whatever this is in light of our new relationship as coach and athlete... they're beginning to fade to the periphery. I don't want to have these feelings, and shutting them out is easier than dealing with them.

It's always easier.

It's how I deal with attention from men when I don't want it. Apathy.

It speaks volumes more than dislike or snappy responses or frustration or any other emotion. Keeping my face unaffected and neutral, as if I couldn't care less. Because apathy demonstrates a complete lack of care, as if the person doesn't even mark a blip on the radar.

But I also know apathy is destructive. And Mack's facial expression is a clear demonstration that my apathy is impacting him.

When he doesn't say anything else, I take his silence as an invitation to end the conversation, maintaining my calm demeanor. "I'll see you at practice this afternoon, Coach McIntosh."

His scowl deepens and he flexes his fists at his sides, then spins abruptly and stalks down the path to his truck. He doesn't look back, and I'm thankful. Maybe if I pretend I'm fine for long enough, I actually will be.

I just wish I could get my heart to agree.

*   *   *   *   *

Piper and Ruth-Ann are running alongside me when I hear the whistle blow, indicating that practice is about to begin. I jog quickly over to the bench and pull out my water bottle, splashing a quick swig into my mouth before turning and focusing on Mack and Coach Johnson.

"Alright ladies, I don't want to waste a lot of time talking at you," Mack says, focusing on the women standing in the front of the group.

Of course, Gina is front and center wearing what I can only assume are hot pants and a sports bra. My eyes roll so hard they might detach from my body.

I keep my eyes trained on my water bottle, not hearing a lot of what he says until he mentions that he'll be working with the goalkeepers.

My head snaps up and our eyes collide. Coach Johnson has always worked with me directly. Why the sudden change?

I look over at Erin Thomas and Kristal Agnes, the two other keepers on our team.

"Did you know about this?" I whisper. Both of them shake their heads. "What's the deal? He shouldn't be making changes like this without at least talking to us about it." Erin shrugs, but I can see that Kristal is as irritated as I am.

"Did you have something to share, Rachel?" I hear from the front. I look quickly up to the front and see Mack looking at me.

I clear my throat, suddenly nervous as all eyes turn to look in my direction.

"We were just wondering why we're making a change to GK training so late in the season."

My reply is cautious, as I want to ensure I don't implicate that Mack is doing anything wrong. He *is* the coach, after all. But I also suspect that he's doing this on purpose. There's no reason for Mack to focus on our training. Coach Johnson and I have a system, a schedule, a plan. I don't want to throw a wrench in it right now.

"Coach Johnson has expressed an interest in focusing more on offensive training and strategy, as that's where his interest lies. I'll be focusing more on the defense. We can talk more about it when the four of us hit the gym in a few."

His reply, while answering my question, is like a slug to the gut. I'm surprised and slightly disappointed to know that Coach Johnson asked to change his focus. Did he not like working with us?

"Alright ladies, let's get started."

Everyone disburses into groups on the field while Erin, Kristal and I turn and head to the training room, talking softly about the change on the way there.

We normally only work out in the gym in our free time, as Coach Walker always wanted us to feel cohesive as a team during actual practice. It made sense to me. It spoke of her having a vision. Splitting the GKs off on our own feels wrong. But I know I can't risk voicing my opinion, especially when things with Mack are so tentative.

When Mack walks in fifteen minutes later, we're jogging lightly on the treadmills with weights around our ankles.

"I like the weights," Mack says, standing with his arms crossed in front of our machines. "It plays perfectly into what I want to do with the three of you over the next few weeks." He reaches over to his bag and pulls out more weights, walking over to each of us and strapping them to our wrists. "From now on, I want you to wear these as often as possible."

I glance quickly at Erin and see her face break out into a smile. Erin read online over the summer that a lot of pro players wore light weights around to increase their speed and reflexes. If you could move quickly and accurately with an extra twenty pounds on your body, imagine how fast you would move once those weights were removed. She put together a bunch of research and took her findings to Coach J, but ultimately Coach Walker didn't like that method and told Erin it wasn't going to happen.

"I can see from Erin's reaction that I won't get much of a fight from you on this. It's a technique used in the professional level in a lot of different sports, and I've heard great feedback so far." Mack is standing in front of us again. "But I do mean as often as possible. I know it isn't fashionable..."

"We aren't concerned about that," Kristal cuts in. "We spend a lot of time covered in sweat and dirt."

I let out a little laugh, picturing our practice last week after the one day it poured rain in California. The three of us were basically standing in pits of mud. Once practice was over, we spent a good twenty minutes in a mud fight. Jeremy had refused to let me in his car when he picked me up for dinner that night.

"Sweat and dirt," I breathe out, with a smile. "The glamorous life of a keeper."

I look back to Mack and see him watching me intently. My smile quickly drops and I replace it with an unaffected expression. Mack clears his throat, averting his eyes. After giving us further instructions and pulling us off the treadmills, he heads back out to the field, leaving us to train on our own.

"Damn that man is a fox," Erin says, once he's finally out of the gym. "Think he has a girlfriend?"

I let out a snort of laughter.

"Laugh all you want," Kristal pipes in, "but Gina said she wants to hit it. Hopefully he's taken so we can throw her off his scent." She sits on the ground and begins doing sit-ups while throwing a medicine ball at the wall at the same time, catching it before it drops. This bitch is a tank and I *wish* I could train as hard as her. She might be a backup GK, but she's one of the ones who will go pro, without a doubt. She just needs a little time to develop more.

"Fucking Gina." Erin slams her ball to the ground, picks it up, and then slams it down again. "If that bitch tries to crawl into Coach's pants, we could have a huge issue, and our team doesn't need that."

"If he's really as much of a ladies man as he looks online, she won't have a hard time getting him between her thighs," Kristal adds.

"He's a ladies man?" I ask, my stomach turning just a bit. I remember the pictures I saw on his Facebook page, but those weren't very recent. I thought maybe he had grown out of the nameless hookups phase, unlike my brother.

"Oh yeah," Kristal says through heavy breaths, lying on the ground, still throwing the medicine ball at the wall. "Ruth-Ann said she couldn't find anything about him online. But I did a little digging. His last thing was that Victoria's Secret model with the sexy body. What's her name?"

Erin lets out a bark of laughter. "The Vic model with the sexy body? You're really narrowing it down, there, Kris."

Kristal makes a face but continues with her workout. "You know who I'm talking about. She has those huge boobs and recently did a movie."

"Ooooooooh," Erin says, recognition hitting her. "Are you talking about Ronnie Kade?"

My stomach plummets and I hear a slight ringing in my ears. His last girlfriend was *Ronnie Kade*?

"He dated Ronnie Kade?" My voice comes out a little harsher than I had planned, but neither of them notices.

"He didn't *date* Ronnie Kade. He *fucked* Ronnie Kade. They're like, friends with bennies or something."

I stare at Kristal, unsure how to process that information. How did this not register for me? I went on a date with a guy who was so sweet. I remember how affected he looked by our kiss, how connected we seemed over bullshit texting. But there's no way I even clock on his radar if Ronnie Kade is sexing him up on the regular.

"How do you know that? Is it still going on?" I grit my teeth as I throw the medicine ball against the wall. I don't want to be affected, and I *definitely* don't want to seem too nosey.

"There are a lot pictures of him leaving her house early in the morning, looking rumpled and thoroughly sexed, but both of them say they're just really good friends," Kristal replies. It sounds like she has done a thorough check on his dating history. "Supposedly she's dating a B-list actor, but there was a photo of her and coach together in *People* just a few weeks ago at a movie premiere in Hollywood."

"Hopefully Gina can't sink her claws into him if he's used to hooking up with people on that level," Erin says, swigging from her water bottle.

Erin and Kristal shift away from Mack and instead begin discussing one of our other teammates' recent flings with a player on the men's soccer team. But my mind is firmly entrenched in picking apart my interactions with Mack in light of what I'd just learned.

I'm a confident woman. I'm comfortable with who I am. It has taken me a long time to get to a place where I don't judge my life or my worth based on a man's perception of me, in spite of my father's constant barrages of insults aimed at my choice of clothing, body type, or anything else I do.

But knowing I'm following Ronnie Kade is messing with my stomach. She's everything I'm not. Everything I told Mack I wasn't. And what blows my mind is that he seemed to *like* that I wasn't one of *those girls.* Was that all a lie? Was I just a girl that he thought would be easy to play with when he was bored?

My thoughts roam all over the place during the remaining ninety minutes of training. When practice ends, we join the team back on the field, and I know I'm in a sour mood that's visible on my face.

As hard as I work to be unaffected, sometimes the Jameson attitude drips from my every pore and I can't help the sass.

I keep my eyes from Mack's as he addresses the team, letting us know we'll be playing with the men's team tomorrow in our regular pre-game day scrimmage.

When we finally wrap up, I turn quickly towards the parking lot. Hopefully some distance from Mack and a happy dinner with my brother can sort out my mind and help me get back to where I was before.

Comfortable. Calm. Confident.

I don't need to measure myself to any model. That type of thinking is a recipe for disaster. Not to mention the fact that it will get me nowhere. *And you're not even dating him!* I roll my eyes at myself.

A quick honk yanks me from my thoughts, and I turn to see Jeremy's SUV pulling up. My face breaks into a smile and I run to the passenger door.

"Hey Rach," he says as I climb inside. I lean across the center console and land a smooch on his cheek. "Thought I'd pick you up for dinner instead of meeting you there."

"As long as you don't mind my funky sweat smell," I reply with a smile.

About forty five minutes later, after sitting in traffic and shooting the shit about how things are going with the Galaxy and catching up on our favorite TV show - *Fixer Upper* is literally amazing - Jeremy and I pull into Ricardo's. We rotate between our favorite restaurants every Monday, and Ricardo's is this delicious little taco shop in Hollywood taking up a tiny lot space at the end of a long line of ritzy restaurants. It is literally twenty feet wide and only has about a dozen tables inside. But they have some of the most legit tacos ever. After placing our order, we take a seat by the window.

"So," Jeremy starts, rubbing his hands together, "tell me about your first practice with the new coach."

I groan internally. I need this dinner with Jeremy to *distract* me from Mack, not to sit and gab about him. "It was fine."

"That's it? It was fine?" Jeremy's eyebrow lifts up and I immediately realize my mistake. I keep my opinions guarded for the most part, except with Jeremy and Charlie. They've been witness to some of my most ridiculous rants over the years. Not having an opinion on Mack as my new coach is equivalent to telling Jeremy that I'm hiding something, so I scramble for a response.

"Okay it wasn't fine. Coach Johnson doesn't want to work with us anymore and we were split off from everyone else. I don't like feeling segregated. It's a dick move." I grab my soda cup and begin chewing on the straw.

"Maybe that's just his style," Jeremy says with a shrug. "Coach Mitchell used to split off the goalkeepers, but Coach Norman wanted us all together. It's just a difference in philosophy."

I think back to Jeremy's high school and college coaches, nodding my head with his statement.

"I get that. I just wish Mack's philosophy wasn't different from what I'm familiar with. It's just a little much to take in at once and I don't know how I feel about it." To be honest, I'm not entirely sure I'm only talking about his coaching style.

"He lets you call him Mack?" His eyebrow lifts again, and I'm instantly aware that I've misspoken again. Coach Walker and Coach Johnson were rigid about having us call them by their last names with 'coach' attached so as not to breed familiarity. Its unlikely Mack's approach would diverge from that.

"No, no." I stutter quickly. "Erin and Kris were all '*Mack this*' and '*Mack that*' during our workout. They were stalking him online or something."

"Thank you," Jeremy says to the waitress as a tray of tacos is placed before us. As he's squeezing lime onto his carnitas, he looks up with a tiny grin. "So they're already flocking?"

My face scrunches in confusion. "Flocking?"

"The girls on your team," he replies. "Your new coach can be quite the lady killer. It doesn't surprise me that they're already trying to get more information about him. Has Gina tarted herself up yet?"

Even with the uncomfortable turn of conversation, I still can't help but let out a snort at his comment about Gina.

"You should have seen her today," I respond between bites of delicious Mexican goodness. "I swear, her shorts were so short, her booty was winking at me."

At that, Jeremy laughs and coughs through his tacos. "Holy shit. Where do you come up with these descriptors?"

I smile as Jeremy continues to chuckle to himself, but it doesn't feel completely natural. Twice in the span of a few hours I've been confronted with this idea of Mack as some sort of sexual busybody. It makes me want to get out my cell phone and Google the shit out of him with the word *date* attached instead of *soccer*. But I know it won't do me any good.

It won't change anything either. Yesterday he was a man I was interested in, and in that reality, I could have asked him the million questions racing through my mind. But today, that reality is different.

Still, as I stare out the window at Ricardo's and listen to Jeremy ramble on, I can't help but wonder: a lady killer, ladies man, man whore, *whatever he is...* what the hell was he doing playing mini-golf with a 21-year-old virgin?

*   *   *   *   *

One hour, fifteen tacos and four sodas later, and the

Jameson siblings are nursing enormous food babies.

"I can't believe I ate six of those tacos," I say, leaning back in the booth with my eyes closed, tempted to give into the food coma. "You're a horrible influence."

Jeremy lets out a loud belch and rubs his tummy. "Obviously."

I smile at him and dig through my purse for my phone, switching the sound back on. My face falls when I see the missed call and voicemail.

"Something wrong?" Jeremy asks, leaning forward and searching my face with concern.

"Dad called," I respond softly.

Jeremy's face contorts into a hard expression. "Ignore it."

"He left a voicemail. He never does that. What if something's wrong?" I say the words quietly, but I know in my heart it isn't true.

"You know that's not what it is. No matter why he's calling, he's going to play mind games with you, Rach. Don't give him the satisfaction. If you listen to it, you'll be letting him suck you in."

Jeremy has always been incredibly protective of me when it comes to our dad. He knows first-hand what it was like to grow up with Frank Jameson, and he felt incredible amounts of guilt when he moved to Glendale and left me at home for three years by myself. We've always been honest with each other about dad's... *difficult* behavior, but there are a few things from those years that I haven't told Jeremy about.

Regardless of those things, though, I've always felt this sense of obligation. I am constantly at war with myself. I know interactions with him will always be negative and horrible and result in either tears or a few days of self-reflection to get past it. But he's my father, and as much as I know he will always let me down, I can't help this niggling desire at the back of my head that he might change. Someday.

I slowly click the screen and lift the phone to my ear. Jeremy lets out a resigned sigh and leans back, draining the rest of his soda and glaring out the window. When I hear my father's slurred words, my heart constricts, and I know that today is not 'someday'.

Rachel, it's your father, but I guess that doesn't mean anything to you. I ran into Colin Lincoln yesterday. Carter's home from Princeton, visiting his family. Apparently he's heading to Harvard Law next year. He's really turned into something. But you were just too much of a dyke to hold onto something good. Anyway, I'll be at your game on Wednesday.

The voicemail cuts off there, like he couldn't even waste his time to finish the statement and say goodbye. I stare blankly at Jeremy, feeling all of the blood in my body rush to my face in embarrassment at my father's words.

Jeremy grabs the phone from me and quickly listens to the voicemail before deleting it and taking my hands in his.

"This is why you shouldn't ever listen to a word that man says," Jeremy says softly. "He's fucking wasted, thinking only of himself. The *nerve* of him to bring up Carter Lincoln as if he's someone you should... I can't even..." Jeremy stops, unable to finish his statement. I can feel the rage rolling off of him in waves.

"Thanks Jer, but I don't want to talk about it. Can you just take me home?"

Jeremy searches my eyes before nodding. We load our trays with our trash, shove it in one of the trashcans, and head for the exit.

My brain feels fuzzy, like it always does after seeing, speaking to, or hearing from my dad. I still feel the twinge of embarrassment, but also the beginnings of anger and frustration, at the idea that my dad is going to grace me with his presence on Wednesday. I've gotten through all of college without him humiliating me like he did when I was in high school, showing up blitzed at my matches and causing such a problem that he was eventually banned from the games. I can't imagine what it is that's made him want to come to this game.

Why now?

We're walking out from Ricardo's, my mind still trudging through the fog, when I see him. At first, I'm so confused that I'm sure my mind is playing tricks.

Mack, dressed in a suit, walking down the Avenue of the Stars.

My body betrays me as my heart begins to race. For just a brilliant moment, thoughts of my dad and the impending game vanish. He looks so handsome, his tailored suit showing off his trim hips and broad shoulders. I'm surprised he was able to get showered and changed after practice so quickly. I'm surprised to see him in Hollywood at all, considering how large this area is and the fact we could have missed each other if either of us had left moments earlier.

But mostly, I'm surprised to see him strolling down the street without a care in the world, hand-in-hand with Ronnie Kade.

The fog clears quickly and I feel like my heart has slammed into a brick wall. My eyes, still slightly glassy with the tears I had refused to let fall over my dad's callous voicemail, begin to water again as I take them in, laughing together in an easy way as they walk in our direction.

Damn, they look like they're in a movie. All they're missing is a soundtrack.

But his relaxed smile vanishes and his steps falter when he sees me. His eyes flicker from me to Jeremy, who seems oblivious to the riot of emotions currently rushing through my body.

"Mack!" Jeremy shouts in jovial greeting. "How are you, man?"

Mack and Jeremy approach each other and do that bro-hug handshake combo thing that guys do.

"Jeremy. Rachel." Mack nods at both of us, his face nearly expressionless, though his eyes stay rooted on me.

My gaze, however, strays to the right. To the absolutely breathtaking model who has snuggled herself into his side, still clutching his hand. She wraps her other arm around his, her head leaning comfortably on his shoulder like she's done it a thousand times. She's an amazon, her gorgeous pitch-black hair shining in the fading sunlight. She oozes sex and confidence in a tight, short, red number that clings to her amazing figure and huge breasts.

Suddenly, I realize the four of us are standing in silence as I stare at her. My eyes shoot to Jeremy, who is looking at me expectantly.

"I'm sorry, what?" I ask, feeling like an absolute idiot.

"Mack just introduced you to Ronnie," Jeremy says softly.

"Oh, I'm sorry," I nearly trip stepping forward, my hand extended. "I've had a really long day. It's nice to meet you," I say, forcing a smile that feels anything but genuine.

Ronnie beams a megawatt smile at me, oblivious to my discomfort, accepting my hand in a light shake. "You too, Rochelle."

"It's Rachel," I hear from Mack, but I refuse to connect my eyes with his again.

"So, what are you two up to tonight?" The question is out before I can stop it, and I wish I could reach out and grab the words and stuff them back into my mouth.

"Just grabbing a quick bite, catching up on life," Ronnie replies, "and getting in some quality time." She glances up at Mack with what I can only imagine are her bedroom eyes.

My mouth goes dry and I feel like my stomach has dropped three feet.

There it is.

Confirmation that my fears about Mack and Ronnie aren't entirely unfounded.

I quickly try to shake the unsettling feeling that Mack thought I could be a quick bang between models and actresses. But the image before me doesn't leave room for much else. Mack and Ronnie, out on the town, dressed to the nines, before heading home for what will probably be mind-blowing, loud, sweaty, dirty sex across the kitchen island in what is probably a mansion on the beach.

When my eyes dart to Mack, I see he's staring at me unabashedly. His eyes are glued to mine, pleading with me. I can only assume he's hoping I won't spill the beans now that I know our kiss was... nothing compared to whatever he shares with Ronnie.

"Well, we won't keep you from your... quality time," I choke out the words. "We're just heading home. See you tomorrow, Coach." I loop my arm in Jeremy's and practically tug him away with me.

"Fucking Ronnie Kade," Jeremy says as we make our way around the corner to the lot. "Of *course* he's fucking Ronnie. That dick."

I glance up at Jeremy and I'm shocked to see a smile on his face. "Why do you look so happy if you sound pissed?"

"Why would I be pissed? Jealous is more like it," he answers, flashing his charming smile at me. "That guy gets so much ass, and he doesn't even try." My mouth drops open. "I know he's your coach, so I shouldn't say stuff like that. But, damn. Ronnie Kade."

I chew on my lip as we walk, wondering if I should ask any questions or if that's too obvious. Ultimately, my curiosity gets the best of me.

"The girls made it seem like they've been together a while." It isn't a question, but I know it's enough to get Jeremy talking.

"I always suspected something was going on 'cause they've known each other since he was playing in Chicago. He's never been one to chat about who he's banging, but with the number of chicks he's pulled since he's been here for all of a month, I just assumed they'd called it off."

"What?" My voice is a slightly higher pitch than I wanted it to come out.

"Don't get me wrong. If he wants to sleep around while he's living in LA, more power too him. I'm just surprised he was able to keep *her* in his bed when he's been inviting so many other ladies into it. Like I said, he's been here under a month, and he gets *way* more play than I do."

I grit my teeth, trying to hide my frustration and confusion, and if I'm honest with myself, sadness. We walk the rest of the way to Jeremy's SUV in silence.

"You okay?" Jeremy pulls me from my thoughts after we've been on the road for a bit. When I look away from the window, I see him looking at me with concerned eyes.

I nod. "Just thinking about everything," I respond, my tone low and distracted, a perfect reflection of my mental state. I know by saying it that way, he'll think I'm talking about dad, our rocky and uncomfortable relationship, the game on Wednesday.

But my thoughts are stuck on Mack and his date. And I wonder how I ever could have misunderstood.

Chapter Five

"I appreciate the thoughtfulness, Jeremy, but you don't have to babysit," I say with a sigh.

Jeremy's offer to attend my game on Wednesday is sweet, but unnecessary. He has his own life, his own practice schedule to contend with. He doesn't need to concern himself with our dad's need to embarrass me.

"It isn't about babysitting," he replies as he pulls up into the lot at the college where my car is and shifts into park. He runs his hands through his hair, then grips the steering wheel again. "I just know he's going to be an absolute fucking nightmare. I don't want you to have to deal with it on your own."

"I love you Jer, but you're not coming. I've dealt with him before. I can do it again." I lean across the console and kiss him on the cheek. "Thanks for dinner. I'll see you next week." I quickly grab my bag and hop out of his SUV before he can argue with me any further.

He stares at me for a moment before nodding. "Let me know if you need anything," he says.

I nod and close the door, walking off to Trusty Rusty. I wave as he drives off, then turn on my car and begin the short drive home, reviewing the day.

How has everything that has happened today happened in one single day?

I woke up from my dream about Mack with such high hopes. Our date had been so perfect, so sweet, so real. And that kiss. *That kiss.*

Warmth had radiated through me, cracking some frozen piece inside I didn't know existed. Contrast that with the heartbreak of finding out he's my new coach, followed by our uncomfortable argument in his office and at my house. Then the drama of practice and hearing about Mack's relationship with Ronnie. Then *seeing* him with Ronnie. I just can't wrap my head around it all.

And the shit with my dad. Frank Jameson is a mess, and if I'm not careful, he's going to drag me back to an emotional place I don't want to be.

How am I ever going to get through the game on Wednesday?

My stomach turns over as I think about the certainty of my dad showing up wasted and belligerent, causing problems and hassling people in the stands, shouting out at us while we play.

His antics caused a heap of problems for me in high school. Parents didn't want their kids to be friends with Frank Jameson's kid, even though we were old enough to have friendships that didn't involve parents facilitating play dates. My relationship with Carter was strained partly because of him. My soccer team gossiped about me behind my back. When your dad is seen as the trash of the town, the assumption is that the apple is rotten too, no matter how far it has actually fallen from the tree.

I don't want to see that happen again.

When I get home, I park and quickly call his home number.

"This is Frank," his voice comes through the phone in a slur.

"Hi dad," I say, trying to muster up my confidence. "It's RJ."

"Rachel." Even the way he says my name, with such disdain and hatred, causes my head to ache. "What the hell do you want?"

"I'm just calling you back. You know. Because you called earlier?"

There's silence on his end. I'm unsure whether he has fallen asleep, or doesn't remember why he called me, or if he just doesn't know how to respond. I never call him back. He leaves nasty voicemails and I torture myself by listening to them. But I always muster up the strength to call on holidays and his birthday. Even then, he rarely answers. I haven't actually spoken to him since Christmas.

"You mentioned coming to the game on Wednesday." I'm fairly sure he's forgotten, the memory just a blur in his whiskey-addled brain. "I just wanted to thank you, but you don't have to come. I know it will take you a long time to get there on the bus, and I'm sure you have better things to do."

I'm trying to make it seem like I'm looking out for his best interests. But I already know he's going to find a way to turn this around on me.

"Listen up, you spoiled shit. I don't need you doing me any favors. If I say I want to come to the game, I'm going to be there. And you can't do anything about it."

I try hard to keep my tone light, placating. "I know, dad. I know. I just wanted to make sure you weren't putting yourself out."

"Putting out is more your style, right Rachel? Always around all those boys, lettin' 'em slap your ass. You just couldn't be a normal fucking daughter, could you? You don't think I know you were lettin' those boys fuck you?"

"Which one is it dad?" I grit out, my anger from the day suddenly boiling over, shocking me slightly. "Am I a whore who spreads her legs? Or a dyke who can't keep a decent man?"

"*Don't* talk to me like that you worthless piece of shit. No wonder your mother abandoned you. I just wish she hadn't left you with me, ruining *my* life too."

I squeeze my eyes shut, as if that could block out his words. But of course it doesn't work. "If you come to the game on Wednesday, stay the *hell* away from me."

I hang up the phone and use all of my self-control not to chuck it into the street. Then I rest my forehead on the steering wheel and cry.

*   *   *   *   *

Soft knocking wakes me from my place in front of the TV and when I glance at the clock on the wall, I see it's after 11pm. I sit up on the couch and rub my face, unsure if the knock is coming from the show currently airing or the front door. After sitting still and listening for a minute, I hear another knock, this time a bit louder.

I wrap the soft blanket around my body and shuffle into the entryway, catching a view of my face in a mirror in the process. Bloodshot eyes, hair in a ratty bun at the top of my head. To say tonight was rough is the understatement of the century.

I pull the door open, and to say I'm shocked to see Mack standing outside is an understatement. I quickly try to backtrack and shut the door in his face, but his hand flies out to hold it open.

"I'm not in the mood, Mack, for whatever you're selling."

"You have to let me explain," he says, his face an interesting combination of determined and pleading. "I know exactly what you thought when you saw me with Ronnie, but I promise you it isn't what you think."

"What I think doesn't matter, Mack. You're entitled to fuck who you want." My words are short and clipped, betraying my internal conflict.

"Damn it, RJ," he starts, letting out an exhausted breath.

"So now I'm RJ again? Funny, because just a few hours ago I was Rachel," I tug the blanket tighter around me, slowly shaking my head as I look at him. "The only thing I'm sure of with you is that I'm definitely no Ronnie Kade."

He rubs his hands on his face in frustration. "I need you to let me finish a sentence RJ. I know I didn't provide you the same courtesy in my office this morning, and now I understand what that feels like. Will you *please* let me explain?"

I assess him for a moment. His hair is mussed, as if he's been running his hands through it too much. His eyes are tired, his suit wrinkled. I give him a stiff nod, but make no move from the doorway. He can say whatever he wants, but he is *not* coming in.

"You have five minutes. After that, whether you're done or not, I'm going to bed."

He wastes no time jumping right in. "Ronnie and I have known each other for a few years. But we are *not* together." I roll my eyes. "Ronnie got back from New York on Saturday night and called me. She always wants to hook up when she gets back from an extended trip, and we made plans for tonight."

My anger suddenly morphs into a dull ache in my chest, and my face falls.

"So our date on Saturday was, what? A cock-tease? Had it been over for more than five seconds before you immediately scheduled time to hook up with her? At least I finally understand where I fall on the bang-list."

I tuck my face into the blanket and crouch to the ground. The reaction is juvenile and to be honest, a bit of an overreaction. But I feel like my emotions are a piece of twine stretching thin by too much weight. I'm at an emotional low after my dad did his best to obliterate my self-worth. Mack's statement is just icing on the cake.

I immediately feel his hands on me, tugging on the blanket. When I finally let go and look into his eyes, I see him crouched next to me, one knee on the ground.

"So tell me, Mack," I continue, "did you set that up before you came back to see me or after."

"Before."

It's just one word, but my face bunches up in reaction as tears begin to fall.

"So you made plans to get together with her and then drove over here to... to what? See if you could bang a random no one to round out the evening?"

It's the only real possibility, and I shouldn't be shocked. My life is a series of unfortunate circumstances and hurt. I just feel like I finally had something good, even for just one day, and now it's tainted too.

Mack's response comes quick. "RJ, when I talked to Ronnie on Saturday, I only agreed to meet up with her because I wanted to tell her in person. I wanted to tell her that I met someone I was interested in, and that she and I just needed to go back to being friends. *That's* why we made the date."

I'm shocked by his revelation, frozen in place, unable to move. Is he saying he was going to call off hanky-panky with *Ronnie Kade* after one date with me?

"What?"

It's only a whisper, but his response isn't much more. His hand comes to the side of my face, his thumb sweeping under my eye to wipe away the few traitorous tears that have fallen free. Unbidden, I lean my face into his hand, reveling in the feeling of closeness in this moment.

"I called her back on the drive over to see you."

My eyes are glued to him, and all I can do is whisper back, "But we hadn't even kissed yet."

"I didn't need to kiss you to know that you were a person who was going to change everything. And if I could see that within just a few hours of knowing you, I wanted to make sure nothing would get in the way of whatever was going to happen next." His thumb swipes again, catching the last tear that's tracked down my cheek. "I want whatever is next."

We sit like that for seconds, minutes, I'm not sure. But I can feel the air in the room shift and crystalize with tension. His attention drops to my lips, only for a second, before his eyes flash up to mine.

Before I can even internalize his glance, he leans forward and plants his soft lips firmly on mine. I let out a breathy sigh as my lips part for him, inviting his tongue to explore my mouth. His other hand moves to my side and grips me tightly. I quickly release the blanket and wrap my arms around his neck, tugging him close.

Suddenly I'm on my back and he's hovering over me, resting his strong, muscular body between my legs. My hands dig into his hair as he leaves my lips to lick and kiss my neck, my head tilting back to give him better access. My body shudders, my physical response to him so strong.

"*God*, Mack," I whisper. I feel his fingers slipping under the bottom of my shirt, his cool hands gripping the warm skin on my sides.

I feel consumed, like my body has been zapped with a warm sizzle of electricity, and the resulting tingle is radiating from the middle of my body to the tips of my fingers, to the tips of my toes. I can't get close enough. He can't get close enough. Our bodies are melded together and I've never felt so *right* being this close to someone.

He pulls his mouth from mine and stares into my eyes as he rocks into me, letting out a husky moan. I gasp raggedly and clench my eyes shut at the overwhelming feeling of lust rushing through me.

"*Fuck*," he whispers, his lips coming back to mine for a heated kiss. Deep and passionate.

I can't get enough, can't get close enough. I want to press every inch of us together and bind us there, because this feeling... oh this feeling. This depth of passion, being so lost in the moment, is something I've never known before.

But when he pops the top button on my jeans, my eyes fly open as if I've been doused with ice water. The gravity of this moment has rushed into my bloodstream, eradicating the desire and longing almost completely.

What am I doing?

This is my coach and we're grinding on the floor inside of the entryway of my apartment.

Fuck.

The *door* is still open.

My body flushes again with heat, but this time out of a sudden and very shocking jolt of embarrassment. His haste to remove my clothes is a swift reminder of *my* innocence and *his* lack of.

"Mack, stop." My voice comes out strong and sure, masking my confusion and sudden nervousness.

His hands instantly come off of my body, but his body is still connected to mine from knee to cheek, his mouth next to my ear and his breaths ragged. I give him a tiny push and he rolls off of me, laying flat on his back, staring up at the ceiling.

"You need to leave."

He remains unmoving on the floor next to me for a moment before his head turns and I see him looking at me. When I turn to meet his gaze, I see the longing in his eyes.

"Please know, I didn't come here for that. I wasn't expecting anything."

I turn my head away and roll onto my stomach before elevating into a kneeling position, my butt resting on my heels. I give a slight nod, giving myself some time to collect my thoughts.

"I know, I just..." I pause, unsure what to say. "I don't really get... physical... with guys. And that was just..." a breath of air leaves me, "... really fast."

When I look at him, I can see the surprise written on his face.

"Are you...?"

But he doesn't finish the question when my eyes dart away in embarrassment, heat creeping up my neck into my face. And what the hell? Why am I embarrassed about my decision to wait until it's right?

I lock eyes with him again, choosing to be unashamed. "Yes. But ultimately, that's not what we should be talking about. We should be talking about us and the fact that you're here." When he just continues to stare at me, I continue. "Part of me is glad you came by, to clarify about Ronnie. To know I meant something."

"Meant something?" he interjects, his voice slightly incredulous. "You can't be talking in past tense, RJ. You have no idea..."

"It doesn't change anything, Mack," I interrupt, squeezing my eyes shut in effort to block out his pained expression. "Does it make me feel better? I guess." I exhale a breath. "I feel less pathetic, and I'm glad to know I wasn't one of the many girls you just bang and move on from." He starts to interrupt again but I put up my hand in a silent request to let me finish. "I realize now that's not the truth, but it doesn't change the fact that we can't continue whatever this is. So I am asking that you don't come by my house again. I am asking that you don't concern yourself with making me feel better about this fucked up situation. You don't owe me anything. You don't belong to me."

He stares at me for a long minute, but eventually gives me a sad nod and stands. The urge to hug him and bring back the smile that I was so captivated with when we first met is overwhelming. But I remain seated on the floor, watching as he steps towards the open door.

"I'm sorry, RJ." I barely hear the words, but they resonate deeply.

It isn't until he's gone, the door closed, that I let out an exhausted breath.

"Me too."

Chapter Six

"Shit, who killed your puppy?"

I roll my eyes and ignore the jab about the lack of sleep reflected on my face. I'd stayed up well into the evening, thinking about what had happened with Mack, and couldn't have gotten more than three hours of sleep before I had to race to get ready for our early morning conditioning followed by my 10am class. I normally love going to class, but I had my psychology test today and that is one subject I absolutely detest.

The last thing I need this afternoon is Thomas Moore, the captain of the men's soccer team, making comments about my appearance.

It is my unfortunate luck that he and I share the same sport as well as the same career goals, placing us in the same traveling buses and a significant number of the same classes. He's kind of a dick to me. Needless to say, I do my best to avoid him whenever possible.

"I don't have a puppy. But if I ever buy one that someone plans to kill, I'll be sure to name it Thomas."

He smiles, unaffected by my response, and settles onto the bench next to me, adjusting his socks over his shin guards.

"I've been thinking about Markson's class," he says, pulling out his water bottle and taking a quick swig. "You're going to focus your paper on Edith Wharton right?"

I nod, unsure how Thomas would already know the author I'd been strongly considering for the focus of my thesis. I hadn't shared that information on our discussion board.

"Yeah, how'd you know?"

Now finished with his shin guards, Thomas grabs a scrimmage jersey from the box next to me and pulls it on.

"You tie her into almost everything we discuss in class. I'm pretty sure you've brought her up in almost every small group discussion you and I have been a part of."

My eyebrows furrow as I try to recall our recent conversations in small group. If I'd been mentioning Wharton in class on a regular basis, I was unaware that I'd been doing so, and surprised that Thomas had noticed.

"Anyway, I've been thinking about centering my paper on Henry James. I was thinking we could ask Markson about doing overlapping presentations in December, and incorporate some components about their relationship and how it impacted their writing."

"You're focusing on Henry James?" I ask, a small smile popping onto my face.

Thomas palms a soccer ball and drops it to his right foot, bouncing it back into his hands, then repeating the move.

"You sound surprised."

"I don't know... I figured you for more of a Dickens man."

"Well since you referred to him as, and I quote 'sexist, patriarchal and derogatory' in class last week, I'm pretty sure I should take offense to that statement."

I let out a short laugh.

"You remember that, huh?"

"Yes, ma'am."

I drop to the ground in front of the bench and begin stretching. "I'm not sure Markson would go for that. She might see it as cliché or something. And I don't want her to think we're looking for some gimmick for a grade."

Thomas gives a little shrug, his eyes trained on the ball he is bouncing from knee to knee.

"Couldn't hurt to ask. Besides, I think it would only benefit us to work together, even a little bit."

I spread my legs and do my best to lay my stomach flat on the ground between them, stretching the muscles on the inside of my thighs and lower back. Out of the corner of my eye, I can see a group approaching through one of the tunnels at the bottom of the stadium. Time to get this scrimmage going.

"How do you figure?"

Thomas catches the ball and looks at me, tucking the ball in against his hip.

"Verbally sparring with you is my favorite thing about the classes we've taken together over the past few years. I always take something new away from discussion groups when you're there."

I smile slightly at the compliment. I'd never thought about it like that before, but reflecting now, I usually did enjoy those classes the most. Even if I usually wanted to wring Thomas' neck.

"Yeah, I guess I know what you mean."

I hear the voices of our teammates behind us, as they drop their duffle bags and begin to get ready. Thomas smiles again.

"Besides, I've been looking for a way to spend some one-on-one time with you for a while."

My mouth falls open and I'm unsure how to respond. He wants to spend time with me? Since when? But before I can formulate a coherent thought, I hear a laugh behind me.

"Finally putting the moves on our girl after pining away for too long, huh Moore?"

My head whips around and I see Thomas' co-captain, Will Steiner, grinning ear to ear just a few feet away. My face flushes as I take in the fact that everyone standing around us may have heard what Thomas said, and most definitely heard Will's comment. I stand quickly, hoping that moving away from the physical space I was just inhabiting will remove the feeling of uneasiness settling into my body.

It doesn't.

"Cut the shit, Steiner," Thomas grits out. I quickly glance back at him and see him glaring at Will. "Sorry, RJ." His face has morphed into something akin to relief and embarrassment at the same time.

"It's cool," I mumble, turning away and grabbing my water bottle.

As I take a sip, I spot Mack a few feet away, his mouth in a thin line as he stares at his clipboard. Hopefully he isn't going to allow our interactions yesterday impact today, but the look on his face as he scribbles angrily doesn't bode well.

I try to push the question away and take a quick lap around the track to get warmed up and clear my head. The comments from Thomas and Will have completely blindsided me.

Part of me is flattered that a guy as stunning as Thomas Moore would be interested in me. He's classically handsome.

Short blond hair, strong jaw, baby blue eyes. He's really smart, too, and we always *did* get into little arguments in class that left me riled up. Apparently they left him turned on.

Men are so weird.

If this had happened last week, before I met Mack, I might have felt something apart from just flattery.

Maybe.

Would I have entertained the idea of getting to know Thomas better? Spending more time with him? Can I even objectively answer that question now that I know how it feels to have my heart pound so hard it feels like it might slam out of my chest?

And probably the most difficult question that I don't have the answer to: am I using the idea of my emotional connection with Mack as just another way to push away a guy?

When I make it back to the bench where everyone has gathered, I'm no closer to answering any of those questions. But I do know that I can't allow my interest in Mack to impact other relationships, platonic or not. I like Thomas' idea of teaming together for our presentations in December.

The more I think about it, I decide it is a thoughtful approach, and pairing our work together will provide a depth our other classmates might not be able to reach, possibly something that will get Markson to write me a stellar letter of recommendation for grad school.

I see Thomas chatting with Will and a few of the other guys from his team at centerfield. I take a quick jog out, calling out to Thomas as I approach. He takes a step away from the group and meets me.

"I'm sorry about Will," he starts. "I don't want you to feel uncomfortable. He doesn't know how to keep his damn mouth shut and you don't have to..."

"Will you shut up a second?" He stops talking and just looks at me. "I really like your idea about Wharton and James and the intersecting presentations. Lets talk to Markson about it."

His smile comes out full force.

"Really?" I nod. "Sweet. Okay. Yeah, I'll start putting together a proposal after the game tomorrow and I'll send it your way so you can incorporate your thoughts."

"Sounds good." I smile back at him.

He reaches out and puts his hand on my shoulder. "This is going to be great, RJ. Really."

I nod again with a smile, then turn to jog over to where my teammates are meeting as a group.

Its time for a little fun.

*   *   *   *   *

After we divide into co-ed teams, we get started. Playing soccer with the guys is one of my favorite parts of playing soccer in general. It reminds me of playing football in high school. The camaraderie is just different. More relaxed and playful. A little more rough and tumble.

Jeremy used to brag about me to the guys on his team when I was a freshman. How I wasn't fragile and could take anything that came my way. That mentality has stayed with the guys' team over the years, because *damn* do they come at me full force.

It's thrilling though. To take the risk of charging out from the goal and be able to grab a ball when it is just inches away from your opponent's feet. The rush of meeting another player's eyes as you both power towards the same object, both so sure that you'll be the first to make it, is like nothing else. However, there's also the risk of getting a foot to the face, a cleat in the hand or other body part, or the ball kicked into your nose.

Which is how I find myself flat on my back, clutching my side, attempting to recover from having the wind knocked out of me.

"Holy shit, RJ! I'm so sorry!"

I can hear Will's voice, but my eyes are clamped shut as I hold my hand against my abdomen. I hear someone drop to the ground next to me.

"Are you okay?"

I want to respond but I'm taking large gasps, trying to bring in enough air.

"Is this the only place it hurts?"

Tender hands take hold of mine and remove them from my side, touching lightly over my clothes. I grunt in pain when the wounded area is poked a little to hard.

"Don't touch that spot again," I say, finally opening my eyes and finding Thomas on his knees next to me. I try to hike up onto my elbows to see, but pain radiates through me and I

93

remain flat on the ground.

"Such a tough one," Thomas jokes, smiling as he pushes my sweaty hair out of my face. "You know, you can acknowledge the pain and no one will judge you for it." I give him a playful roll of my eyes.

"Rachel, you okay?" I look quickly away from Thomas towards Mack, who is now standing next to us but slightly behind me. I'm unsure how long he has been standing there. His mouth is in a thin line again, but I don't think it's out of concern for me. When I find his eyes, I realize they are trained on Thomas' hands, which are resting on my stomach and my thigh.

"Yeah, I'm good. Thomas was just…"

"Well if you're fine, get up and we'll keep going. Please don't waste time laying around on the ground. This isn't the pros, and I don't accept dramatic, overinflated pretend injuries."

His tone is clipped, a clear demonstration that Mack doesn't know how to accept our circumstances without blowing everything out of proportion. He turns quickly and walks back to the sidelines.

"What a prick," Thomas mumbles as he and Will help me to stand. "Maybe you should have Erin stand in for you for the rest of the game. You know, so you're all good for tomorrow."

"Yeah, that's a good idea. We don't have much time left anyway."

As I turn to head towards the sidelines, I hear Thomas call out after me.

"You're a total badass, by the way!" When I turn to look at him, he and Will are still standing there looking at me. "The last guy to take a cleat in the rib from Will was carried off the field." I shoot him a huge smile. "Total. Bad. Ass."

I smile and turn to jog over to the sidelines, but slow to a walk after I feel the stab of pain that shoots through me.

Janice Grange, our athletic trainer, comes over to where I'm seated after a few minutes and lays me back on the bench to get a better look at the damage. When she pulls my shirt up slightly, I can see that there are dark grooves above my ribs where Will's cleat connected with me. Several of the indentations are bleeding from deep scratches.

"Coach," Janice calls to Mack after inspecting me and prodding me for a moment.

Mack looks irritated as he gets closer, but I see his steps falter a little when he eyes the bruising that is already evident on my skin, as well as the other cuts and marks.

"I doubt that a rib has broken, but the cuts and bruising are pretty extensive. I want to see how she feels tomorrow before deciding whether she can play or not."

My breath catches when I consider the idea of not playing tomorrow. My dad is coming to the game. How would he react if he manages to get there and I don't even go on the field? Part of me wants to see the bastard as irate as can be, but the other still clings to the idea that watching me excel at something might make him proud. Or at the very least, keep me from incurring his wrath.

"I, uhm…" Mack starts but pauses. "… yeah, we can wait until tomorrow to decide." And again, he turns and walks away abruptly.

Janice rolls her eyes and gives me a sweet smile.

"So moody, that one. Keep it iced today, alright? If you can keep the bruising at bay and you don't swell up, I'll feel better about the idea of you putting your body through the ringer tomorrow."

"Thanks Janice," I reply, half-heartedly. "Although, I won't be too fussed if I can't play tomorrow, so just make whatever decision you think is best."

Janice frowns slightly, probably unsure that she heard me correctly when I've been a 'total bad ass' for the three and a half years she's known me. I've had a few small injuries and have always fought tooth and nail to stay on the field.

"Since when is my best decision the decision you agree with?"

I shrug, but Janice keeps her eyes trained on me, waiting for a response. She's always been pretty motherly with us, even though she's only in her early thirties. My first year playing for Glendale was her first year with the men's and women's soccer teams, and she requested to stay with us instead of moving when it was time to rotate to football or basketball. I think she secretly loves the girls that started with me freshman year and wanted to see us all through our college careers.

Janice doesn't know about my issues with my dad.

Well, not everything.

During my freshman year, I went home to pick up the last of my belongings on a day when I thought my dad would be at work.

He wasn't.

Not only was he home, but he was absolutely plastered and ready to extract his rage wherever possible. When I returned to campus with a split lip and some extensive bruising on my torso, I was able to explain away the lip pretty easily. But my attempt to get changed after a game that week was another story.

I had taken my time until everyone started to head out to the bus, then tried to change my top really quickly. But Janice walked into the locker room and saw the shoe and fist marks that had begun to fade from deep purple to a yellowish green.

We talked for a few minutes about it, and I told her that the 'problem' wasn't a part of my life anymore. It had been that trip home that solidified my decision to extricate him from my life as much as possible. Jeremy was thrilled that I cut ties, although he never knew about the physical abuse, or the horrible things that happened before I finally left.

He also didn't know that I still called my dad every so often on holidays. He wouldn't understand. Hell, I don't even understand.

"Why don't you want to play tomorrow?" Janice asks, sucking me back to the present and away from the drama I'm constantly trying to leave behind.

When I don't say anything, Janice leads me away from the game that's coming to a close, and walks me to the athletic facility that houses her office. Once inside the athletic training room just off of the locker room, she turns to me with a concerned look on her face.

"Jeremy mentioned that your dad might be coming to the game tomorrow."

I suck in a sharp breath. I'm sure the look on my face demonstrates my surprise that Janice is in contact with Jeremy. I know they've met before, but had no idea there was enough camaraderie that they would be sharing information.

"Since when do you talk to Jeremy about me?"

"We run at the same park," she states nonchalantly.

"Why did my dad make it into the conversation? Jeremy hates talking about him."

I can see that Janice is withholding something, but for the life of me can't figure out what it is.

"You should talk to Jeremy about it. My point in bringing it up was just to tell you that I could put you on the injured list if you want me to. You don't even have to travel with us if you don't want to go down to San Diego."

I glare at her.

"I don't need anyone making assumptions about my life, Janice. If you think I can't play, bench me. If I can, I'll be on the field in my gear when the whistle blows."

I hop off of the table I'd been sitting on, ignoring the jolt of pain in my side, and plow out of the room. I throw the door open so fast I don't see anyone in the hallway and run smack into Mack, sending me to the ground with a hard thud.

"Jesus, RJ." Mack kneels beside me, trying to help me up.

"Get your hands off me," I growl at him, pushing his hand away and standing on my own.

"I just wanted to make sure you were okay." His response, quiet and concerned, speaks to his regret for his curt words on the field. But I'm not having any of it.

"Oh, so *now* you want to know if I'm okay? You know what? Fuck. You. You need to sort out your shit, Mack, because I am sick of this Jekyll and Hyde crap you're pulling." I lean in close and stare into his eyes. "Less than twenty four hours ago, you had me on my back and your tongue down my throat, then this afternoon you're barking at me like I'm an absolute idiot." Mack's expression rolls between heated at the reminder of last night, and remorseful at his recent behavior. "Don't talk to me again unless you have feedback about my game."

I brush past him and prowl down the hallway, trying to get away from everything about this horrible, horrible day.

*   *   *   *   *

My mood hasn't improved much by game time the next day. I'm grouchy with my teammates as we load into the bus and claim two seats for myself so I don't have to talk to anyone. Instead, I opt to glare out the window and blast some kind of horrible screamy music that Jeremy added to my phone.

The three-hour bus ride passes slowly, and my only solace is that I at least don't have to be in an enclosed space with Mack for the ride. He drove down to USD in the morning for some sort of meeting, so it's just Coach Johnson and Janice with our team, and the men's team and coaches, on the bus.

I'm lost in thoughts about my dad and today's game when one of my headphones is popped out of my ear, and Thomas plops down next to me.

"How's the wounded party doing today?"

"I'm fine. But I'm not in the mood to talk, Thomas." I take my headphone in hand and begin to place it back in my right ear when it's snatched out of my grip. "I mean it. I'm not trying to be a bitch, but I'm really not in the mood. I need you to leave me alone."

Thomas nods, holding his hand out for me to take back the single headphone. "Whatever it is, let me know if you want to talk about it. I'm a pretty good listener." He gives me a small smile, then stands and walks back towards the front of the bus.

My eyes turn back outside, but my thoughts remain on my dad. What dramatics will he pull at this game? When he came to the first game I started in during my sophomore year of high school, he kept screaming that we were all a bunch of 'fucking dykes'. Families were literally moving away from him in the stands, and I was mortified. That was the first time security escorted him out.

Jeremy had driven down to watch the game, but traffic held him up, and he got there late enough to miss dad's tirade. He told me he was so proud of me and how I played, took me to dinner, and then dropped me off at home. He had taken a shitty day, a shitty first game, and completely turned it around.

But that evening was the first time my dad's abuse turned physical.

I came through the back door of the house, hoping he would be passed out in the den in the front. As I crept through the dark kitchen and rounded the corner to the stairs, he came out of nowhere, wrapping his hand around my throat and slamming me against the wall, knocking the wind out of me.

"Where the fuck have you been?"

I clawed at his hand as it squeezed tighter, unable to get out the words to explain. I felt suspended in time, both seconds and hours going by as I remained pinned to the wall, unable to breathe. In reality it was probably less than thirty seconds. When he finally let go, I collapsed to the floor on my hands and knees, drawing in large, shaky breaths.

"Jeremy."

Inhale.

"Came."

Inhale.

"Dinner."

Inhale.

"You lying sack of shit. He doesn't give a shit about you. You can't sneak this past me. Which of those boys were you fucking? Huh?"

He emphasized his last word with a swift kick to my gut, and I crumpled into the fetal position on the floor, crying out in pain. I struggled to get out my words, but finally managed to catch my breath enough to choke out an explanation.

"I didn't. I swear. We grabbed a burger. I didn't do anything."

"I didn't ask for your lip, you fucking cow. I know what you girls are like, whoring your way through school. How many of those guys' dicks have you sucked? Don't you know how pathetic you are?" He crouched down and grabbed the back of my hair, yanking back until he could see my face. The scent of alcohol hit me like a wall. "I've seen you with them. But I also see how they look at you. Like you're worthless, because you are. You're a worthless piece of trash."

With that, he finally let go of my hair and stood up, stumbling back down the hallway to the den. I remained lying on the floor at the bottom of the stairs for at least fifteen minutes, curled in a ball, focused on breathing.

Maybe your life really isn't worth anything, I thought. It was only fleeting. But it was there. And it scared me.

That interaction dictated my every decision from there on out. I did everything Frank asked me to. I never talked back. I never made excuses. When he called me worthless, I agreed. When he said I was a whore, I didn't say a word, allowing him to come to whatever conclusions he wanted to. I kept my head down when I was home and stayed out of his way.

It was horrible.

It was degrading.

It made me feel as worthless as my dad believed I was.

I lived through that for another two and a half years before escaping. I hid the bruises on my skin from my teammates in the locker room. I didn't tell Jeremy.

It was *my* burden to carry.

The fact I believed anything my dad said is what made me

think I had to hide it. Something about the abuse was my fault, so I had to deserve it, right? It wasn't until my world fell apart that I really understood how destructive his fists and words were to me... and not just on the outside.

My memories shift away from the past and bring me back to the present, to the game looming closer as the bus speeds us along the freeway to San Diego.

My past is coming back. I haven't seen my dad in-person since my trip home during freshman year of college to collect the last of my things. He had been drunk, alone in his chair, staring at the TV. When he realized I was home, he took his last chance at beating the shit out of me. I choose regularly to push that night to the back of my mind. I'd done everything I could to avoid having to see him again after... well, *after*.

As we pull into the USD parking lot, I stand and stretch, wincing slightly at the reminder of the injury on my torso, trying not to let my concerns and fears show on my face. I give a small smile to Erin as she grabs her backpack off of the overhead shelf and walks past me. I follow her out and grab my gear out of the carriage, scanning the people wandering around the area.

And that's when I see him, standing outside of the gates to the soccer field, glaring in my direction.

I quickly turn my eyes away, refusing to acknowledge him, and follow the team through the parking lot to USD's athletic facilities. We split off from the men to go into the ladies locker room, each of us throwing our bags down next to empty locker stalls.

As the girls begin to change, I head into the restroom and into a stall. Once I've locked the door, I take a seat and bend forward, dropping my head between my legs, willing the calmness to return.

My old therapist told me that I am the only one who gives him power over me. He can't take it away anymore. I am independent, and free. I am strong and he can't touch me. *I* decide who gets to put their hands on my body, always.

After a few deep breaths, I step into the main locker room and begin changing with the team. The words of my teammates are muffled in my ears, my mind still unable to fully focus on the immediacy of my surroundings, instead staying firmly rooted in my past.

The breathing helps with my anxiety attacks, but not with focus.

I catch a few curious stares as I stand in the back of the group while Mack and Coach Johnson address the team, but I don't catch any of what they're telling us. I nod when everyone else does and follow the hooting and hollering girls out of the locker room and onto the field, where I keep my eyes averted from the bleachers.

The game moves quickly, and I can't stay on point. Several of my teammates ask if I'm okay, and I just nod and give them tight smiles.

I don't even know the score or how we're doing when halftime arrives, apart from the fact that I've let in two goals and botched the majority of my saves in one way or another.

As we exit the field for halftime, I do myself the disservice of looking up into the stands, allowing my eyes to roam the dozens of jovial friends and family of my teammates and competitors.

When I spot him, sitting on the bleachers front and center, a paper bag covered bottle clutched in his hand, the same war wages in my brain as every other time that I've seen my dad wasted in public.

I want to go to him and help him out of the stands and into a car so that I can drive him straight to a rehab facility. But I also want to slap him, and kick him, and scream at him for how he has failed me and hurt me in so many different ways.

I do none of those things, though, as I jog behind my teammates to the locker room. I'm drinking water, leaning up against a wall, still mentally checked out, when I realize everyone is looking at me.

Wiping my mouth with the back of my hand, I scan the group, unsure what I missed.

"What?"

"Are you going to join us? Or are you going to continue to stare off into the distance like you don't give a shit about this game?" Gina's voice cuts through the group and my eyes whip in her direction, where she stands next to Mack.

"Gina, language." Mack's response is firm and controlled. "Rachel, your head is obviously not in the game today. I'm pulling you out. Erin, you'll GK for the second half."

My head drops, my eyes stinging. I've never been pulled mid-game. I've had to sit out before. Injuries happen. But I've never fucked up and been benched. I hear Mack give a few encouraging words to the team, then everyone is walking out of the locker room, but I sit briefly on a bench, staring at my cleats.

"Looks like the golden girl isn't so shiny and perfect today," I hear from above me. I know the voice is Gina's. No one else can pull off that particular brand of bitchy as well as her. I hear her laugh before she follows everyone else out.

After taking a few deep breaths, I stand and head back to the field, trailing about fifty feet behind everyone else. Getting benched doesn't mean I get to sulk in the locker room.

When I arrive on the sidelines, I take a seat and try to get my head in the game. I'm still a part of this team, even if my worth on the field has been minimal today. I still have to focus and show support.

But within just a few minutes, it starts.

My shoulders tense instinctively when I hear the first jumbled shout from the bleachers just fifteen feet behind us. It isn't incredibly loud, and I don't think anyone on the sidelines hears it, as I only catch clips of it myself.

"... fuckin' piece of shit..."

"... can't even finish a game..."

I keep my head straight forward, refusing to acknowledge him, and when a few minutes pass without another word, my muscles unclench and I begin to rotate my neck in an attempt to relax.

But my relief is short-lived, as it isn't long before it starts again. This time, I can feel the other players' reactions. I know they hear the words being shouted in our direction. I see many of them turn their heads and look into the stands, trying to find the person responsible. I just pray they don't know that the jumbled and sometimes incoherent shards of glass are aimed at me.

"... absolutely worthless..."

"... come out here and you're not even playing? Couldn't keep your shit together..."

"... loser dyke."

All of the blood in my body rushes to my face and I flush in embarrassment as the horrible words continue. I feel like I'm climbing through a barbed wire fence. If I focus on something else, I might be able to push through and get to the other side, but the marks left behind won't fade quickly, gouging holes until I'm bleeding secrets for everyone to see.

I stare blankly at the field where the game continues, and will the tears that brim at my eyes to keep from spilling over.

But when I hear the slurred shout of my name, and I hear several gasps next to me, I feel them slip free and trail down my cheeks.

I remain seated and staring blankly at the field, refusing to catch the eyes of any of my teammates. I don't need to see their faces awash in pity. So I glare at the ball and allow the rest of the world to blur away until all I see is the small white and black orb moving rapidly between feet.

When the whistle blows, I hear my teammates shouting with glee, but I don't even look in their direction. I walk straight off of the field and into the locker room shower. I rinse off so quickly that I'm fully clothed in my tracksuit just as the rest of the team enters the room. I feel eyes on me as I press past them, but I walk quickly from the room and down the hall towards the front. Hopefully I can get on the bus early and stay there until the men's game is over.

Unfortunately, the buses aren't in sight, so I take a seat on a planter box and stare into nothing.

"So you're sitting out here like a fucking loser by yourself, huh?" I hear from behind me, about ten minutes later.

My hands clench into fists and I continue to stare at the ground.

"Why did you come today?"

My question isn't more than a whisper, but I know he hears it. He ambles around me, swaying slightly, and I wonder absently what happened to the drink in the paper bag, as he's now clutching a black water bottle that is very likely housing Jack Daniels.

"No one else comes to see you play. I figured, why not go see what Rachel is really wasting her life on. And fuck if it wasn't an absolute waste of my time." His words are a slurry mess. He leans in close and the smell of liquor overwhelms me. "Everything about you is a waste."

I stand quickly and try to side-step him, but my movements throw him off balance and he tumbles over to the ground, shouting out in pain. My natural instincts come out in full-force and I bend over to help him up, but he shrugs my hands off of him and rattles off a string of curses and insults loud enough for those passing to hear.

Once he's finally righted himself I rest my hand on his upper arm. "Are you sure you're..."

But my words are cut off when he grabs my wrist and twists,

hard. I shout out a little in pain and bend at an awkward angle to release some of the pressure, then whip my other hand around and slap him hard in the face.

He steps back in shock, releasing my wrist, but his eyes are murderous. I've never hit back before.

"Hey!" I hear the shout from behind me, and my eyes close in defeat. I know that voice, and it is the last one I want to hear right now. "What the hell is going on?"

I keep my eyes trained on the ground, unwilling to look at Mack or my dad. Neither man would be able to soothe or assuage the feelings of embarrassment roaring through my body.

"Mind your own business, kid," my dad slurs out. "Turn around and walk away."

"I don't think so," Mack responds. "I'm Rachel's coach and whatever is going on here is a bit concerning, so if it's all the same to you, I don't plan on going anywhere."

His hand comes up and rests on my shoulder. I know it's meant as a sign of support, but I know instinctively how my father will interpret the move. I very quickly step to the side a bit and twist my body so Mack's hand falls away, but not before my eyes flicker up. My father's face has maintained the same harshness, but it has now latched onto Mack's small sign of affection. His eyes look from me, to Mack, and then back.

"You worthless little shit," he finally says. "You're spreading it for your coach? Is that the only way you can get him to put your disgusting attempt at playing soccer on the field?"

I ignore the comment, choosing instead to focus on the best thing to do moving forward, which is to get my dad out of here.

"It's time for you to go home, dad." I say in the sternest voice I can muster.

"Yes, Mr. Jameson, I think it is time for you to go home," Mack's voice pipes up from beside me. He sounds like ice, cold and brittle. "In fact, we will make sure you get there safely." Mack suddenly takes my father by the neck and begins pushing him forward.

"Get your hands off me you little..."

"I wouldn't finish that sentence, sir. Rachel and I will escort you home. Now. Any attempts to struggle out of this and I will call the police regarding your public intoxication and the assault I witnessed you commit against Ms. Jameson a few moments ago." When my father says nothing, Mack pushes him forward again.

I follow in silence, unsure what to do. Part of me is embarrassed that Mack is involved in this situation at all, that he's seeing my dad this way. But another part of me is flooded with relief that I don't have to shoulder this one interaction on my own, that I have someone to help me.

I feel less likely to crumble.

We make it to Mack's truck and he shoves my dad into the back seat. Once the door is closed, I look up at him and whisper, "You don't have to do this."

Mack's eyes roam over my face for a moment, but then he simply says, "Get in the truck, RJ," before turning and walking around to the driver's side.

Chapter Seven

Two and a half hours later, we've left my dad asleep on the couch in the living room of the house I grew up in, and Mack is driving me back to Glendale. Other than arguing about driving me home instead of returning to USD for the men's game, we haven't said anything to each other in the past two hours. And there is still another thirty minutes left until we make it back to town.

I can feel the tension and frustration rolling off of Mack in waves. His hands are clutching and releasing the steering wheel with such force, I'm surprised he hasn't been able to crack all of his knuckles.

When my phone begins to ring, I lunge for it, desperate for anything to alleviate myself from the dark silence dripping from Mack's truck.

"Hey Jer," I say, my voice tight. I was trying to sound light-hearted, but alas.

"Hey Rach! How was the game?" Jeremy's warm voice wraps around me through the phone, making me feel safe.

"It was fine."

Silence comes from the other end of the line and I know what's coming next.

"What did he do?"

I let out a sigh.

"I'll tell you about it later, okay? I'm almost home and I'll call you when I get back."

"Wait, you're almost home?"

"Yeah, Ma... uhm... Coach McIntosh is driving me back."

Silence again.

"Put him on the phone."

"What? No. Look, we're almost back and I'll just..."

"Rachel, put Mack on the phone."

I look over at Mack, expecting his eyes to be facing forward. But I find him watching me, his eyes soft as they go back and forth between me and the road.

I extend the phone towards him.

"It's Jeremy. He wants to talk to you."

Mack takes the phone and puts it to his ear.

"Hey man, I'm driving so make it quick. Don't wanna get a ticket."

I can't hear what Jeremy is saying, but I can hear murmurs through the phone that make it clear his tone is far from happy.

"I'll let RJ fill you in, but it wasn't pretty. I didn't feel comfortable making her wait around and then putting her back on the bus with everyone. I already had my car, so I figured I'd just take her home."

More murmuring from Jeremy. I wish so much I could know what he's saying.

"Yeah, sounds good. See you in a bit."

Mack hands my phone back to me and I put it back to my ear.

"Hey."

"Look, I don't know what happened or what's going on, but I'm leaving practice and I'm on my way to you. With traffic, I should be there about twenty minutes after you get back."

"Jer, you don't have to come over. I can just call you and..."

"Not now, Rachel. I'll see you in a little under an hour." And he hangs up.

When I pull the phone away and look at the screen, I can feel the tears building in my eyes again, partly from the conversation and partly from frustration that my emotions have been so haywire over the past week or so.

Jeremy sounded angry. The rational part of me is aware that he's mad at our dad and not me, but I'm upset with his reaction. I have enough on my mind and don't need Jeremy's emotions mixing in.

"So," Mack says, clearing his throat, "it seems like you and your dad have a complicated relationship."

I can feel his eyes on me. I can feel the desire coursing

through him to understand what he saw. But I can't bring myself to return his gaze or give him the information he wants, so I keep my eyes out the window.

"Yeah. I guess complicated could be a word used to describe it."

"Has he... I mean... it looked like he was getting a little bit physical with you. Is that something that... or, uhm... does that happen a lot?" His words are a jumbled mess as he tries to tactfully ask if I'm used to being tossed around.

Unfortunately for him, there isn't really a tactful way to ask.

I'm unsure how much I want to share, so instead of answering right away, I lift my feet to rest on the seat and hug my legs, tucking myself into my knees. In a split second I realize I am literally curling myself into a ball in embarrassment. Or maybe sorrow.

Sharing this part of my past isn't something I do. Jeremy knows some of it because he was there growing up. But the true heart of it, the actual physical and verbal abuse I've lived through and what it did to me... just the idea of sharing makes my stomach twist. I don't want anyone to know how terrible it was. I don't want Mack to know what my father thinks of me or the ways he practically tortured me for years. Or about what happened before I finally left.

I let out a sigh and keep my eyes averted. Lying isn't an option, but that doesn't mean I have to be an open book.

"It's not really something I talk about."

He's silent for the remainder of the drive.

As we pull up in front of my apartment, I'm already preparing my bag, ensuring I can be up and out of the car as quickly as possible. I mumble a quick 'thanks for the ride' and hop out as soon as we come to a stop.

I know luck isn't on my side when I hear his door close and the sound of footsteps behind me walking up the path to my door. My one mistake was not keeping my keys easily accessible, and I have to drop my bag to the ground to dig around for them at the door. When I finally stand back up, keys in hand, my eyes lock with Mack's.

"Did you need something?" I ask in an attempt to push him back to his car without any more conversation. "Because I'm really tired and just want to relax."

His eyes search my face, and I see the moment his decision is made.

"Yes, I do need something. I need us to talk about what happened today. Because what I saw? Shouldn't be something you don't talk about, RJ." He lets out a rush of air, scratching the back of his head before bringing his hand forward to rub his face in that way he does when he's nervous. "If you don't talk about the things you're ashamed of, you'll never get past them."

My head jerks back in response to his statement.

"Ashamed?" He nods, but stays silent. "You think I'm *ashamed*? Of what exactly?"

Mack shrugs.

"I don't know. But whether you deserve to feel ashamed or not, it's important to talk about it. Otherwise, that shame becomes your whole world."

I stare silently at him. Yes, we are absolutely talking about me. But we are also talking about him. Him and his past and the accident and the fallout. The paralysis of the woman driving the other car. The crash and burn, both literally and figuratively, of his career and the future he had likely envisioned for himself.

"Like it became *your* whole world?"

My question is soft, but I know he hears it. His eyes are sad as he slowly picks through whatever he has of those memories, shifting and sorting, trying to determine what to share and what to keep to himself.

"I ruined several lives because of a foolish mistake. And I held it in and didn't talk about it for years, until the weight of my shame became like a vice gripping me so tightly I was afraid my chest would be crushed."

"But it wasn't your fault."

He exhales and crosses his arms over his chest.

"Look, RJ. I was drunk, and so was my friend. Yes, he crashed the car. Yes, there was ice on the road. No, we weren't the only people going too fast, which is one of the factors in the pile-up. But ultimately, we both played a part in what happened to Cherise." He swallows hard, appearing to choke on his words before forcing himself to continue. "She will *never* walk again. She will live in a chair for the rest of her life. If I hadn't made a few poor choices that led to me and Darren getting in that car, she would get to do those things."

The silence between us is heavy as he leans sideways against my door, playing with the black band on his right wrist. But before I can step in and say anything, he continues.

"I let my shame consume me until there was hardly any 'me'

left. When my sister finally talked me into seeing someone, it was like tearing my insides out. Because if a bone heals incorrectly, you have to re-break it to set it right. And talking about what happened was almost more painful than experiencing it."

He pauses and runs his hands across his face.

"But I was finally able to sort myself out, forgive myself and make amends for what I did. Everyone talks about 'moving on' from things, as if you can forget and start over. I don't believe that anymore. Now, I focus on moving forward, accepting the choices I've made and the consequences that came from them, and doing my best to live the kind of life I'm proud of."

I stare at him, overwhelmed with emotion and understanding about his past. But I'm not sure what his story has to do with me.

"I know you're probably wondering what this has to do with you," he says, voicing my unspoken question. "RJ, whether or not you are to blame for whatever you've been through... and let me be clear that I am entirely certain you are not, not, *not* at fault... that doesn't mean you aren't experiencing your own form of shame. Wondering what other people will think of you if they know your secrets. Unsure about diving back into the source of that brick wall you're carrying. Talking about it, and I'm not saying you have to talk to me, but talking about it can help you move forward and not stay rooted in the past."

One tear slips from my eye, and before I can move, Mack has stepped forward and wiped it away with his thumb. His hand rests softly on my cheek, and I give into the urge and close my eyes, leaning into his touch. He steps forward and places his other hand on my face, bringing our foreheads together, and for a moment, everything is forgotten.

He moves slightly, bringing his mouth close to my ear. "You're precious, and special, and you don't deserve to walk through your life carrying this burden," he whispers, lightly kissing my temple.

I take a deep breath, inhaling his scent. Our eyes are closed, but I feel like we are really seeing each other, broken bits and all, for the first time.

"Rach?" I hear from my right, and I quickly step back and turn my head, seeing Jeremy standing at the curb. His eyes flick back and forth between me and Mack. "Everything okay?"

I clear my throat and clutch my keys more firmly in my

hand. Nodding, I finally get out a terse, 'yup' before I turn and unlock the door to my apartment.

Before I walk through the door, I look back at Mack. His eyes are glued to me and I find myself wanting to get lost in his eyes. Those warm, brown depths that make me feel safe.

"Thank you, Mack," I whisper. "For everything."

And then I walk through my door and close it behind me.

*   *   *   *   *

Jeremy is still not in my apartment when I come downstairs fifteen minutes later, post-shower. Even though I showered at USD, I felt like I needed another rinse to wash away the shitty afternoon.

I might have also wanted to sit on the floor of the shower, because that's pretty much the best place to sit and think when you're upset.

When I step towards the door, I can hear the murmur of their voices outside. Jeremy sounds angry. Mack sounds apologetic.

Both of them make me want to roll my eyes.

The 'emotional depths' I was feeling after my conversation with Mack have passed, likely dripping down the drain with my body wash.

Thankfully.

As earnest as Mack was in his speech outside, I truly don't want to take the time to sort through the muck of my past. It's easier to shove it away and focus on something else.

I stroll into the kitchen and pull the orange juice from the fridge. As I drink down half of the glass, I hear the door slam closed and harsh, booted footsteps in the entry. I continue staring at the fridge, unwilling to look at my brother as he enters the kitchen.

"Please tell me you're not totally fucking up your life," are not at all the words that I expect to come out of his mouth.

My eyes whip to his.

"Ex*cuse* me?"

"You heard me. Tell me I didn't see you out there with your coach, who bangs everything in sight. Tell me you are not risking your scholarship and place on the team for that piece of shit."

His hands are gripping tightly to the kitchen island separating us, his eyes piercing me with a stare so intense and laced with frustration that I have a hard time maintaining eye contact. His tone is oozing with a bitter nastiness I don't think I've ever heard from him before, or at least definitely not had aimed my way.

But his comments fuel me.

"You wanna start throwing stones, Jer? I suggest you take a nice long look at the glass house *you* live in first."

He scoffs.

"This isn't about me, Rachel. This is about you and whatever you think you're doing with Mack."

I set the glass of orange juice down on the island as delicately as I can, mostly because I don't want to risk chucking it at Jeremy's stupid face. I lay my hands flat on the island, staring at the granite and willing myself to a calm place.

"You have no idea what you're talking about. So don't you dare crawl up on the high horse you think you deserve to be on and begin to judge me."

"Rachel, you are making a colossal mistake. You have no idea what you're getting yourself into."

"Jeremy, you need to quit while you're ahead. I don't want to hear your..."

"Do you know about his time in a mental hospital?"

I take in a deep breath and flick my eyes to his in shock.

"What?"

"The guy is fucking crazy, Rachel. The Chicago team released him from his contract at his request when he was institutionalized."

My insides are warring with my mind, but I know Jeremy is just baiting me. Mack went through a lot after the accident. It isn't our place to say he's crazy. We don't know what that time was like.

"When he finally got back on his feet after the accident, he started fucking any pussy that walked his way. I've never seen *any*one go through women the way he did. This one time, he was out here visiting his sister, and he had a threesome with two strippers. *At* the strip club. It wasn't even in a private room."

I suddenly feel sick to my stomach and I lean on the island for support.

"He was doing drugs and drinking like a fucking fish. And then he was thrown in the loony bin."

"If you think so poorly of him, why did you help get him the job at Glendale?" My tone is short, my teeth grinding together as I get out one question.

But I can't help the million new questions cropping up in its wake.

"We've known each other for a long time. I thought it would be a good fit, something to help him get back on his feet. But if I had thought for even *one* second that you and he would have started something up, I never would have told him a thing about it."

I glare at Jeremy. I'm upset at hearing about Mack's history on top of what I've already heard. But right now, my anger with Jeremy is taking precedence.

"You have a lot of nasty things to say about someone bed hopping. Like I said, Jer. You shouldn't judge when you've got your own shit to shovel."

He rolls his eyes and my temper flares further. "My life is different."

"Why?!" I scream.

Jeremy is so startled by my outburst that he actually takes a step back.

"Why is your life so different than mine? Or Mack's? Why do you get to fuck all of my friends, and do whatever the hell you please, but I'm supposed to be a do-gooder, happy pants, innocent forever?"

Jeremy stays silent, so I continue, feeling the pent up anger begin to roll off of me in waves.

"You slept with and pissed off so many girls when I was in high school and college that I had a hard time making any friends. You would call me when you were wasted and needed a ride from whoever's place you were at. So you want us to start throwing stones? How about this, Jer? How *dare* you fuck my best friend after I *specifically* asked you to stay away from her!?" Jeremy's eyes widen and his face blanches. "Yeah, I found out about that little gem the other day. Way to be such an upstanding guy."

"Rachel, it isn't what you think..."

"Cut the bullshit Jeremy. You don't get to excuse your behavior while vilifying someone else. Mack is imperfect. But so am I. And so the *fuck* are you."

Jeremy lets out a sigh and adjusts his weight from foot to foot, looking a bit sheepish. His hand goes up to his face and pinches the bridge of his nose.

"This isn't the way I wanted this conversation to go. At all."

"Yeah, well neither did I." I step forward. "*I'm* the one who had to deal with dad screaming out that I'm a worthless dyke in front of a crowd of people. *I'm* the one who had to deal with the embarrassment of my coach and someone I care about seeing dad on the verge of smacking me around. *I'm* the one who had to be carted home like a child. And then apparently, I'm *also* the one who had to be scolded and reprimanded by her brother, who is without a doubt the biggest asshole on the planet."

His mouth drops open just a bit in response to my continued outrage.

"Did you even think about what it would feel like to have you shout at me on the phone while I was still dealing with seeing dad? How about an 'is everything okay, Rachel?' or an 'is there anything I can do, Rachel?' No. Instead, I got a 'shut up, I can't deal with this, I'm coming to check up on you'. Well thanks, but no thanks. I don't want your help. I don't want *anything* from you right now. Except for you to leave me the hell alone."

I've never, ever talked to my brother this way before. And his reaction is a reflection of that. He doesn't say anything for a few minutes as I turn and begin rooting through the cabinets for a granola bar. When I finally turn around to look at him, his face has morphed into the perfection of contrition.

"I'm sorry you had to deal with dad today, Rachel. I can't imagine how embarrassing it must have been to go through that." His words are thoughtful, and more along the lines of what I was expecting from someone with a heart like his. "I'm glad you had Mack there to help you and bring you home… make sure you're okay. I wish I could have been there to do that for you so you didn't feel so alone in this."

I nod.

"Thank you."

"But I still think this thing with Mack is a mistake."

I growl in frustration.

"God, Jeremy, why can't you just…"

"I'm not trying to make you angry," he says loudly enough to interrupt me, putting both hands up. "I'm not trying to get involved in your life in a way that makes you feel like a child. I just want to do right by you and make sure you're really thinking things through. You could lose your scholarship and you wouldn't be able to finish your degree. Mack could lose his *job*. These are not insignificant problems, Rachel. How are you going to continue your new, happy life without a job to take care of yourself if you can't graduate?"

My nostrils flare and I cross my arms.

"I've already thought of these things. Which is why Mack and I aren't pursuing a relationship."

"Really? Could have fooled me. That scene outside sure looked like you've gotten pretty close."

I re-cross my arms and continue to glare.

"We are. Or, we did get close, I guess. But we're not doing anything about it. He already knows I can't risk anything."

"Good. I'm glad he knows that. And that you do too. But knowing you shouldn't do anything, and actually having the fortitude to keep yourself from acting on how you feel are two very different things. I should know. That's what happened between me and Charlie."

He pauses and steps forward, taking a sip of my half empty glass of orange juice.

"I just want to make sure you're making choices that are right for you, and not letting yourself get swayed or pulled in a direction that can screw up your life. Especially not for a guy like Mack."

Chapter Eight

The awesome thing about the day after a game is that we don't have conditioning in the morning, so I'm able to sleep in until my 10am class on Thursday. The shitty thing about this particular Thursday is that I get my psychology test back, and I'm almost entirely sure I bombed it. Even though I put a lot of time and energy into studying for this particular exam, I wasn't at my best on Tuesday after the exhaustion of the most manic Monday I'd ever experienced, and I'm certain my grade will reflect my emotional state.

As I cross the quad from the parking lot and make my way towards the lecture hall, my phone beeps with a text. Part of me wants to ignore it, knowing that I'm not in the right mood to talk to anyone in my life right now, but curiosity gets the better of me and I pull it out of my bag. My stomach churns when I see the sender.

Mack: Can we talk?

How am I supposed to answer that? Deciding to ignore the text and deal with it later, I begin to place the phone back in my bag when it dings again.

Mack: I know things are weird right now, but it's important

I sit on a bench outside of the Mueller psychology building, soaking in some sun while deciding how to respond. Do I want to talk to Mack? My brother practically insinuated he was insane, although I'm sure there's more to the story. Mack is a good guy with a kind heart. He cares about me, regardless of his past. If he thinks we need to talk, I should give him the benefit of the doubt.

Me: I'm just about to start a class. Can we meet after?

Mack: Sure. You done at 11?

Me: Yeah.

Mack: Any other classes today?

Me: I have a break from 11 to 1.

Mack: Can you swing by my office?

Me: Sure.

Mack: Thanks. See you in a bit.

I place my phone on silent and move quickly into the building, heading up to the third floor. When I enter my classroom, I spot Piper in the back row where we normally sit and make my way towards her. It isn't until I'm pulling my notebook out that I can feel her gaze on me, and I realize she's probably brimming with questions about my dad's scene at the game yesterday.

Without looking at her, I let a soft statement cross the space between us.

"I would really appreciate it if we can just not talk about it."

Thirty seconds pass before Piper's hand reaches out and she squeezes mine. I don't look at her, but I see her pull out her laptop and begin fiddling around on Facebook like she normally does. A few more minutes pass, and I hear her whisper, "Did I ever tell you about the time Gina shit her pants during a game?"

My eyes fly to hers, my shock evident on my face.

"Serious?"

Piper lets out a contained laugh. A Los Angeles native, she

and her older sister, Peri, went to high school with Gina in Laguna Beach.

"No joke. It was Gina's senior year, so I was still on the freshman team. Her family was doing some weird juice cleanse or something. Coach told her she needed to eat differently and she ignored him. Said her 'holistic nutritionist' guaranteed a more athletic body or some shit."

"Please, please tell me every detail of this story," I whisper, a crooked grin on my face.

Piper's smile keeps getting wider as she continues.

"Peri said that Gina was in the process of kicking the ball when she heard a loud fart and saw Gina freeze, then grab her ass."

Tears are literally streaming down my face. I've never been one to revel in someone else's shit, no pun intended, but Gina is such a dick sometimes that this opportunity is too good to pass up.

"She ran off the field and straight to the locker room. She took a week off of school and then had a week off for Thanksgiving. I think she was hoping no one would hear about it or everyone would forget if she was gone for long enough. But Peri said no one let her live it down for the rest of the season. Having the last name 'Brown' also didn't help the situation. She likes to pretend people called her 'Brownie' in high school because she was 'so sweet', but that's complete bullshit."

I'm laughing full out, my face buried in my arms on my desk as my body shakes violently. When I look up, I catch a few glares from the students around us, most of them freshmen. The professor isn't even here yet. They need to relax and let me enjoy this fleeting sense of elation.

"Oh my god," I say, wiping my eyes and taking deep breaths. "Thank you for telling me that. You've completely redirected my day."

Piper smiles at me.

"Everyone has their own shitty days," she says. "Some just have ones more obvious than others." And with that, she goes back to her Facebook page.

I watch her for a minute, my heart swelling with how sweet she is. I was a little worried at the start of the year when I realized I had to enroll in Psychology 101 as a senior. But General Education Requirements are actually required, hence the name, so I didn't have an option. I was thrilled to see my young teammate when I entered the classroom that first day, and we've sat next to each other every Tuesday and Thursday, without fail.

Piper is new to our team this year, a fresh-faced, 18-year-old with a killer leg and an amazing sense on the field. I give it another two games before Mack sees her potential and puts her in as a starter. Her force on the field doesn't translate to real life, though. She has a huge heart and is incredibly sensitive. Her story about Gina is her way of letting me know she doesn't judge, and she found a funny way of breaking down whatever barrier I thought I would need to put up between us.

I lean over and give her a noisy smooch on the forehead just as our professor walks in the door.

"Thanks, Pipe," I whisper, then lean back in my chair and turn my attention to the front of the room.

An hour later, Professor Nguyen has just finished giving us our homework for the weekend when he pulls a sheet of paper out from his briefcase.

"As all of you know, I pride myself on returning exam grades in the class directly following the exam." The moment he indicates he has grades in his hand, the classroom becomes completely silent. "I've organized your grades by student ID number. I will be posting them on the board by the door. Please check it on the way out, and feel free to swing by during my office hours if you have any questions. Have a wonderful weekend, everyone."

The students sitting in the front make a mad dash after him as he steps out of the door, and I can hear a few groans and subdued cheers of excitement. Piper mentions something about seeing me at practice and bolts to the board, while I pack my belongings and trudge slowly down the steps, as if by moving slowly I can change my fate. When I finally make it to the doorway, almost everyone has already made it out of the room, and students from the class after ours are already trickling in.

I take a deep breath and let my eyes scan the grades, looking for mine. I'm currently on academic probation because second semester last year I missed the GPA minimum for my scholarship. I had a 2.9, and the minimum is a 3.0. My academic advisor and I have a very clear plan for this semester in place, and it doesn't really allow for any deviation or else I'll lose my scholarship one semester away from graduation.

Psychology is the only class I'm allowed to get a low grade

in, since I'm almost guaranteed A's and B's in my other courses, but I still have to pass. So when I spot the C- next to my ID number, my stomach turns over. I needed at *least* a B-. I'm not failing psych, but I've heard over and over that Professor Nguyen's finals are the hardest in the department.

My advisor and I agreed that I will need to make a C+ or better on everything so that my inevitable horrible grade on the final won't ruin my attempts as passing the class. My last few grades have been in the C- range, so I'm still currently safe. But I'm not really setting myself up for any flexibility on the final.

With the weight of my grade just another worry on my mind, I begin my trek across the campus towards the athletic facility, not eager at all to see Mack or add anything else to my list of concerns.

*   *   *   *   *

When I'm just outside of Mack's office, I take a moment to peer through the open door. He's standing at his one small window, looking outside, seemingly lost in thought. His hands are tucked into the pockets of his tan slacks, his stance relaxed. It's in this moment that I realize I'm seeing him this way for the first time, as a young professional.

He's in a blue button down shirt and dress shoes, his slightly too long hair just a shade darker than normal, hinting at the gel he's likely used to keep it from disarray. He shifts where he stands, his right hand coming out to scratch his jaw. His hand rubs back and forth a few times, as if this motion can alleviate whatever weight sits on his shoulders or solve the problem on his mind.

It's that back and forth motion that reflects his true mental state. His stance, that at first appeared easy and casual, now appears taut and tense. His arm and back muscles flex as his hand moves from his face to grip the back of his neck.

I knock lightly on the doorframe, ignoring my desire to continue staring at him without interruption. His head whips towards me, his hand falling from his neck to rest at his side.

"Hey," is the only thing I can think to say, and I offer him a small smile. "You wanted to see me?"

For just a brief second, I see something flicker across his

face. But just as quickly as I see it, it's gone, and I don't have the time or mental fortitude to decipher it.

"Yeah, thanks for coming." He steps away from the window, moving towards me at the door. "Come on in. Take a seat."

He closes the door behind me as I drop into the pleather chair across from his desk. Was it just three days ago that I took a seat in this very spot and stumbled through our first conversation with Mack as my coach? It feels more like three months has passed.

"You said it was important," I say to him, popping my left ankle onto my right knee.

The way I sit is 'unladylike', according to a bunch of people I don't care about. But it's comfortable, and something tells me I need to try to be comfortable right now, and ladylike isn't really my style anyway.

"What's up?"

"A couple of things, actually." His tone is professional, which instantly allows me to relax. Thank god. The last thing I want to do is rehash our conversation at my apartment yesterday. Or his moody behavior. Or our kiss. Scratch that... *two* kisses. Those things need to just remain taboo topics that we don't address.

"Okay, shoot."

Mack clears his throat and stares at me, his eyes assessing. "I want you to be an unofficial coach for some of our upcoming practices."

My head jerks back in surprise, my eyes narrowing in confusion. "You want me to what?"

His reply is to tilt his head and tap his pen a few times on the pad of paper in front of him. He sits back in his chair and crosses his legs in a way that mirrors mine.

"I said that I want you to be an unofficial coach for a few practices."

"That's what I thought you said. But I don't understand why."

"You told me you want to be a coach some day. I can tell you from personal experience that getting a coaching job without any experience can be rough. This way, Coach Johnson and I can provide some critique that will allow you to have some reflective experiences to draw from in the future.

His offer is so thoughtful, and so supportive, that my mouth drops open and I can't think of anything to say.

"After the Cal game next week, we have a bye week. I'll give you my notes about the things I want us to stay focused on for the practices we have between Cal and the next game. I'll explain to you how and why I lay out practice structures so you can piece things together as you think is best." His voice is calm, his tone almost teacher-like. "I think this could be really good."

I continue to just stare at him. If I want to coach someday, this will be an amazing opportunity. Which is what I should be focused on. But instead I am trying to wrap my mind around the amazing consideration and investment Mack is making in my life.

Suddenly, I realize that I'm nodding without saying anything.

"Sure," finally bursts from my mouth. "I can do that. Thank you so much."

Mack smiles, then, and for a brief moment, I'm lost in it. How it lights up his face and eyes.

"Great! I'm excited. Coach Johnson thinks some of my philosophies are a little nuts, so it will be good to have someone I can laugh with on the sidelines."

My laugh is small, but genuine. "Well, I'll definitely be laughing *at* you." My phone starts buzzing and I drop my eyes to the bag at my feet.

"You need to get that?"

"Yeah, sorry." I bend forward and snag my phone from the front pocket, flicking the screen to see a missed call from Thomas. "Missed it. I'll call him back later," I say out loud, more for myself than him.

"Jeremy?"

I shake my head and look back at him after my phone is dropped back into my bag. "No, Thomas."

There's a brief pause and his eyebrows draw together, but they quickly smooth back out. "Moore?" I nod. Mack picks his pen back up and begins tapping it again. He clears his throat once. Then twice.

"You said there were a few things you wanted to talk about?"

He shifts in his chair, his discomfort clear.

"Look, RJ, I know I'm your coach. But I obviously care about you," he starts, and I know he's moving away from the professional chatter and onto the personal. Something I don't want him to do. "Well, at least I hope it's obvious. I mean, not to everyone else, but to you." He clears his throat again. "I just want you to know you can talk to me. About anything."

His eyes on me feel like lasers, as if he's trying to burrow himself under my skin and into my DNA. I don't say anything to him, just nodding at his words.

He looks away then, his fingers now twisting his pen nervously in that way drummers twist their drumsticks.

"I still want you to come with me to the football game tomorrow night," he says, his voice slightly above a whisper. When his eyes cut back up to mine, he adds, "just as friends."

I lick my dry lips and softly chew on the inside of my cheek.

"Are we friends, Mack?"

He expels a heavy breath, dropping his pen and running both hands through his hair, causing the smoothed down pieces to stick up slightly in disarray.

"I'd like us to be. Just because I'm your coach doesn't mean we can't care about each other. Spend time together, on occasion. We can figure it out." When my head falls to the side a bit and my eyes narrow at his naivety, he smiles sheepishly. "Okay, so maybe being actual friends is pushing it. But, there's someone I want you to meet. At the game."

"Who?"

He just shakes his head slightly.

"Will you come?"

I assess him from across the desk. It hasn't escaped my notice that he's gripping his pen tightly, as if my response really means something. He must really want me to go to this game.

I sigh.

"What time am I meeting you?"

His face blooms into that grin I love so much, and I immediately wonder if I'm making a huge mistake.

Chapter Nine

The Atwater High School parking lot is packed when I pull in and I spend nearly ten minutes scouting for a space. Once I've pulled in at the end of the lot, I sit in Trusty Rusty for a few minutes in an attempt to calm my nerves. I don't understand why Mack wants me to be here. But even worse, I don't understand why *I* want me to be here.

It's a bad idea.

And yet, I find myself slipping from my car, tucking my card and keys into my front pocket and my phone into my back, and walking towards the stadium entrance.

I see him almost immediately, leaning against the chain link fence that separates the parking lot from the field, and my breath catches. He's in dark wash jeans and a gray henley, the sleeves pushed up slightly to reveal his forearms. His hair is loose today, the ends curling slightly behind his ears. In a word, he looks phenomenal. His casual stance resting against the fence makes him look like a model, and as I continue to walk towards him, I see a group of high school girls giggle and smile as they walk past.

He runs one finger absentmindedly under that same black wristband, then slips his phone out from his back pocket, checking the screen. He's tucking it back into his jeans when he looks up and sees me approaching. I couldn't see his eyes from farther away, but they are glued to me as I get closer. I see them flick from the signature red Chucks on my feet, over my favorite pair of faded jeans, to linger on my black screen print tee that says 'Fries Before Guys.' When his eyes finish their shameless perusal of my body and finally reach my face, my stomach flips and my cheeks burn.

"Mack," I say, as I come to a stop just an arm's distance away from him.

I internally curse myself at the slightly breathy tone of my voice. I clear my throat and glance around nervously. I don't think I'll know anyone here, but the goody-two-shoes inside is secretly terrified that someone will see us together.

He steps away from the fence and rests a hand on my arm. "RJ, you look…" he trails off and removes his hand, running it through his hair. "I'm glad you came. Ready to go in?"

I nod once, and follow him as he leads the way to the entrance. He passes ten bucks to a woman at a table in front of the entrance, palms the two tickets and reaches an arm back to usher me first through the gate.

Once we're inside, he slips his hand into mine, twisting our fingers together. My eyes travel to our hands, then up to his face. But he doesn't look at me, instead just giving my hand a small squeeze and leading me forward to the bleachers.

We're ten minutes into a fairly decent game of high school football before either of us speaks. And it isn't my pansy ass that breaks the silence.

"I don't want things to be awkward."

I keep my eyes trained on the field, following the snap and quick hand off with too much focus. When the running back is tackled to the ground, I look down at my shoes resting on the bleacher below.

"Me either, but I don't know how to fix it."

"Well," he starts, leaning forward and resting his arms on his knees, clasping his hands together, "maybe talking about it will help. You know, get everything out in the open. We can get on the same page and hopefully start over. Or something."

I nod. "Okay, you first."

When I glance over, I see him smiling slightly. "Chicken."

I smile back. "Yup. I'm as chicken as it gets."

He's silent for a moment, likely collecting his thoughts. Two more plays get the AHS team within field goal range, but their kicker misses, and there's a groan from the crowd.

"I like you, RJ." His statement startles me, and suppressing my smile is nearly impossible. "I like you a lot. And I know I said we should be friends, but I don't want to just be friends. You're smart, and funny. I laugh a lot more with you than I've laughed with anyone in a long, long time. And you're beautiful. Like, stop me in my tracks gorgeous."

I look at his profile and see him swallow hard.

"I hate that I'm your coach. And I hate that the timing is wrong. But more than that, I hate that you've closed yourself off from me over the past week. I felt like I got to see the real you at Jeremy's party and on our date, but that isn't who talks to me anymore. The woman at practice, sitting next to me now, is not the woman who beat my ass on the go-karts, who calls me Indy. I really, really like that woman, and I'm afraid I'm never gonna see her again."

After another minute or two, he stands up, and I'm worried he's leaving since I haven't said anything back.

"I'm gonna grab us a snack. Want anything specific?"

I shake my head and give him a small smile before he turns and walks down the bleacher steps towards the concession stand. As I watch his shape disappear around a corner, I allow my blank mind to begin sorting through everything he just said to me.

First of all, his honesty kills me. The guys I've gone on dates with, not that there have been many, have always seemed evasive. As if getting them to share too much would be pushing too far.

And then there are the actual words he said. Yes, he called me beautiful. But his first words were about my mind and my humor, things that are far more important in a relationship than looks. His comments hit the mark when he said I'm not myself around him. Which makes me sad, because for the first time, I feel like I've met someone who actually gets me and makes me feel like *being* myself is something special.

When Mack gets back, he's carrying a soda and a small box of popcorn. He hands the popcorn to me and pulls a bag of M&Ms from his back pocket before he takes a seat.

"You remembered," I whisper.

He just nods and takes a sip of the soda before placing it on the bench between us, allowing a comfortable silence to pass for a few moments.

"You scare me," I say, loud enough that he can hear me but soft enough that we don't have any eavesdroppers.

His head jerks slightly as he takes in my words. "I scare you?" I can hear in his tone that my words have hurt him, and I know instantly that I need to clarify. "Is this because of what happened with your dad? Or because of the kiss in your house? I swear I wasn't trying to push you too far, I just..."

"*No!*" I say emphatically. "No, no, no. That's not what I mean."

"Well, can you tell me? Because I want to make you smile and laugh and feel happy. The last thing I want to do is scare you."

His sweetness impresses upon me how important it is that I get this right. He needs it. I need it.

"You scare me because I barely know you, and I feel like I'm falling for you harder than I ever thought would be possible."

When his eyes fly to mine, I swear I feel a current of electricity shoot between us.

"I really like you too, Mack. And trust me when I say that having feelings for someone is *not* something that happens to me. Ever. But when I'm with you, I alternate between feeling like I can breathe deeper, and wondering if I will ever be able to catch my breath again. I want to know everything there is to know about you, but I'm scared that when you see my broken, you'll turn away. I'm afraid that the wrong person is going to be able to see how I look at you, or know how I feel when you're around. And I'm scared that this feeling is all on me, like this connection I feel with you is somehow in my imagination. *That* is what I mean when I say you scare me. I am not a person easily scared by much, but I am *terrified* of you, and me. Of us."

We haven't looked away from each other through everything I just said, and watching his face while I spoke made me feel naked. Vulnerable. But I feel like something has passed between us. Something rare, and true. His eyes are bright, his lips quirked up in the tiniest smile.

When he reaches between us and takes my hand in his, I relish in the warmth that sinks into my skin. Mack lifts my hand to his mouth and rests a soft kiss on my knuckles before releasing me and turning his head back to the field.

We pass the popcorn and M&Ms back and forth between us, not saying a word as the players on the field trudge back and forth. When the clock finally runs down, the team runs off the field for halftime, replaced quickly by the school band and color guard. When Mack stands, I assume he's going to the bathroom or concessions again, but he takes my hand and pulls me to stand.

"Come on," he says. "This is why I asked you to be here tonight."

He leads me down the bleachers and towards concessions, but stops at the swag table that looks like blue and green monsters have thrown up all over it. Foam fingers, streamers, t-shirts, sweaters, beanies. My high school definitely didn't have this kind of gear.

"Mack!" A cheerful voice from my left draws my eyes from the table itself to the woman sitting behind it. "Hey, sweetie!" Mack releases my hand and walks around the table, bending over to give her a hug. "I didn't realize you were coming tonight. Dean will be so excited to see you after the game."

She's in her forties, with bright blue eyes and short, choppy, chocolate hair. She's absolutely beautiful, and I wonder how she and Mack know each other. Apart from similar hair coloring, there doesn't seem to be a family resemblance.

"You know I love watching Dean play," Mack says, his smile easy and his eyes warm. "Sorry I couldn't make it last week. I was talked into watching a game over at my buddy's place."

"Ah, well friendship is important. And Dean knows you can't make it to *every* game." She reaches out her hand and places it on his arm in a reassuring gesture.

"Well, I do my best." He shrugs slightly, his grin still light and easy. "I wanted you to meet someone," he says, his eyes lifting to mine. "This is Rachel Jameson. Rachel, this is my friend Cherise."

She beams at me. "Hi Rachel sweetheart. So nice to meet you." She leans forward over the table and holds out her hand. I step forward to take it.

"Nice to meet you, too." I smile back at her because, well, because I can't not. She has those lines next to her eyes that always make me happy.

When I was really young, before she left us, I used to sit and watch my mom put on her makeup. She used to pull at her face and make comments about her wrinkles. "Be careful how much you smile," she would say. "There's no ridding your face of these lines once they're there."

That always struck me as strange, and as I grew up, even with my shitty life, I've always believed that the little crows feet people get next to their eyes from smiling so much are a good thing. It means they've lived a life where they laugh a lot, they smile a lot. Hopefully they've *loved* a lot. And I'll take that over a smooth face in my forties and fifties any day.

Cherise has those lines next to her eyes. So I continue to beam back at her. Her smile is infectious, and she looks like one of the happiest people in the world.

"How did you two meet?" Cherise asks, looking up at Mack and snapping me back to present.

"We met at my friend's last week," he responds.

"Introducing you to a beautiful girl? Sounds like a great friend," she says, her voice bright and happy.

I cringe internally, thankful that neither Cherise nor Mack are aware of the things Jeremy said to me at my apartment a few days ago.

"Well, we didn't want to take up too much of your time. I just wanted to swing by with Rachel. But we'll make sure to say hi to Dean before we take off after the game." Mack looks around as if he's lost something. "Where are Theo and Max?"

Cherise laughs.

"Probably running rampant around the parking lot like the fools they are." She looks to me. "Twins are a lot to handle. Sometimes it's easier to just let them fly around until they tire themselves out."

I laugh as well.

"How old are your kids?"

"Well, Dean is 16. He's the one playing in the game. And Theo and Max are 14 going on 3." I laugh again. "What are you gonna do?" She shrugs lightly then looks back up to Mack. "Good to see you, sweetie." She lifts her arms and he bends down for another hug. When she turns back to me, she says, "It was great meeting you Rachel."

"You too," I say, lifting my hand to shake hers again.

But she waves her hand wildly in front of herself, as if to say, *put your hand away.*

"If you're friends with Mack, I'm sure we'll be friends as well soon enough. Come 'round here and give me a proper hug."

I step around the table and my eyes fly immediately to Cherise's wheelchair, which I hadn't seen behind the piles of school gear. I quickly catch myself, raising my eyes back to hers, sure to keep the genuine smile on my face. I lean down and give her a hug.

"He's a keeper," she whispers. "And if he likes you, I bet you are too." When I step back, her face has a small smile, as if she knows a secret. "I'll see you again soon, Rachel."

I nod my head, then follow Mack away from the table and back up to the bleachers.

*　　*　　*　　*　　*

"Hey Mack!"

A teenager in full uniform comes barreling towards us after the game. I can only assume it's Dean, and my heart sings when the two embrace in a full hug, Mack leaning over the short fence. If I remember correctly, guys in high school aren't big on hugs. But when Dean steps out of the hug and looks up at Mack, I can clearly see the admiration in his eyes.

"Awesome job, man," Mack responds, clapping Dean on the shoulder pads. "Proud of you."

"Thanks! Hey, I'm heading to grab burgers with some friends. We still on for tomorrow?"

Mack nods.

"Absolutely. I'll pick you up at four."

"Sweet. Later!" Dean jogs back along the field, following behind the rest of his teammates.

"Ready to go?" Mack asks, and begins to lead me out to the parking lot. "Where are you parked?"

"In the boonies," I say, with a hint of a laugh. "I think I may have been the last one here."

We continue to walk towards Trusty Rusty, the silence at once both comfortable and alight with underlying tension.

After meeting Cherise, we'd walked back to the bleachers and spent most of the game just watching, not really talking apart from commenting on the game. It seemed like Mack wasn't ready to talk about it, even though I was fairly certain that Cherise was the woman from his car accident. I'd been bursting with questions, but decided to let Mack lead the conversation at his own pace. That pace just happened to be standing completely still, because he hadn't said a word about it for the entire second half of the game.

When we get to my car, Mack whistles.

"Wow. Didn't realize you were driving a legend."

I laugh.

"Yeah, well, Trusty Rusty was what I could afford when I got to college." I run my hand along the top. "I love my baby.

Jeremy and I fixed it up and it runs great." I look back up at him with a smile. "Nothing like that swank truck of yours, though."

"Nah, my truck's nothing special. Just a ride when I need one."

I nod. When he doesn't continue, I take that as my cue and pull my keys from my pocket.

"Alright, well, I'm gonna head off."

"You didn't ask me about Cherise." His expression shows he's not angry or upset, just confused.

I shrug and twiddle the keys in my hand.

"It's your story to tell. I didn't want to pry." He doesn't say anything, just continues to assess me. "I figure she's important to you, since you talked me into watching two hours of high school football so I could meet her for five minutes."

I want to ask more questions. How long have they known each other? Did he move to California to be closer to her family? How are they on speaking terms when he played a part in her current wheelchair-bound state? But as the stream in my head continues, I keep my verbal filter firmly in place.

Mack exhales loudly, resting his hands on his hips. He looks around, then turns to lean back on my car, looking out at the emptying parking lot.

"I went through some stuff after the accident. Some personal stuff. As soon as I got my head on straight, I tracked her down. I met her boys, her mom. We just clicked. I'd spent hours driving to Chicago, rehearsing what I was gonna say to her, but she barely let me get out one word when we met. She just gave me a big hug and asked if I wanted some coffee. Brought me into her kitchen and sat me down," he laughs. "Pretty much pulled my entire life story from me."

He clears his throat and looks down at me.

"She didn't judge me for one minute. She's always got a positive attitude, and since the day we met, I've wanted to be a part of her life. I do whatever I can for her and her family since I took such a huge part of her away from them."

I nod.

"You have a lot of character. So does she. It doesn't surprise me that you'd find each other and develop a friendship." I smile, thinking of Cherise's bright, positive attitude. "She seems like someone who doesn't let anything get in her way."

He chuckles slightly at that.

"No. She definitely doesn't. I always feel like I don't do

enough, but she always reminds me that I can't be a crutch for her. That she still has to live a life where she's capable of doing everything on her own."

"Self-reliance is an admirable trait." In the moment, I'm talking about Cherise. But my response is heavily rooted in the importance I place on being able to take care of myself.

"Being able to accept help and care from others is also an admirable trait," he responds.

I turn my head to look at him next to me, leaning back against my car with his arms crossed, his eyes focused in the distance. His jaw is tight, a frown on his face.

"It frustrates you that she won't let you do more." When he doesn't respond, I continue, unsure of where the boundary is. How much I can say. But if what Mack and I feel for each other has any chance of lasting, our streak of honesty will need to continue.

"You have to remember that she wants to feel capable. Stepping in and doing things for her might feel good for you, help assuage whatever guilt you still feel, but it probably makes her feel helpless. Like she's a charity case."

"That's not how I feel about her," he clips.

"I know that," I say, my voice soothing. "I never said you did. It's just important to make sure you understand that she might *feel* that way." I step away from the car and stand directly in front of him. "You're a good person, Mack. Regardless of the things that have happened. You have a great heart, you've done everything you can to make amends for the damage you believe you've inflicted. You obviously care about learning from the past rather than repeating it."

His eyes search my face, his words escaping his mouth as if he's unsure whether they should be spoken.

"What if the things I've learned make me feel like I have to go after things that are important, even when it might be wrong?"

I don't know how to respond, so I don't.

He reaches out and puts a hand on my hip, his eyes watching his own movements as his thumb slips under my shirt to rub small circles on my hip. I let out a shuddered breath as he steps into me, his other arm wrapping around me to bring me into an embrace that I can't help but return, my hands resting on his muscular back. His warmth seeps through my thin shirt, his breath tickles my temple. His words are a whisper.

"This is something important. I can feel it. I've never, *ever*, felt like this before." He brings his hand up and tilts my chin so I'm looking at his handsome face. "Tell me we can figure this out, RJ. Tell me that meeting you a few months too early doesn't mean either of us are going to miss out on something amazing."

I take a deep breath. And hold it. Rational Rachel wants to say it can't work. She wants to stay rooted firmly in logic and what she can control. There are just too many things in the way. His job, my scholarship, both of our futures.

But it isn't Rational Rachel who lets out the deep breath. "We can figure this out."

The words are barely from my mouth when his lips are on mine, his hand slipping back to twist into the hairs at the nape of my neck. I grip his shirt, giving it a slight tug, before sliding my arms fully around his waist and holding myself as close to him as I can.

I expect the kiss to be hard and punishing, a reflection of the frustrations we've both felt over the past week. But his arms hold me reverently, as if I'm a treasure. His hand in my hair twists around playfully, massaging at the base of my neck. And his lips are soft, sweet.

Our kiss feels like a drunken haze, as if we have all the time in the world. And while I'm not sure exactly how we are going to 'figure this out,' knowing we have time to try makes all the difference.

Chapter Ten

Drop, kick, kick, kick, knee, knee, knee, knee.

The ball bounces around, my eyes trained on it as it pops back and forth between my knees and feet. This is one exercise I've never been very good at, keeping the ball in motion without letting it touch the ground. But today I'm doing pretty well.

Kick, kick, knee, kick, kick, knee, knee.

My eyes feel like lasers on the blue and yellow orb in front of me. My mind is clear. My focus is sharp. The whistle finally blows and I let the ball fall to the grass at my feet, my eyes shooting up to the person responsible for my current state of mind.

Mack.

I've felt his eyes on me all morning. Watching me run, critiquing my time at the net, encouraging my saves. I'd assumed that our conversation and kiss last night would make today weird. I was sure that I would be wrapped up in watching him, or focused on *not* watching him for fear of someone else seeing the affection in my eyes.

In an unforeseen turn of events, this morning has been an education of sorts. I've been focused, sharp, tapped into my team like I've never been before. I'm unsure whether this is because Mack is watching and I don't want to look like a fool, or whether our decision to try and figure things out has just calmed me to the point that I feel like I can be completely present at practice.

While I *could* focus on the fact that we don't really know what we are doing, I've instead chosen to accept the fact that I get to enjoy this with him now.

When practice concludes, I grab my bag and begin walking towards the locker room. A quick shower, and then I'm off to StubHub Center, where Jeremy and the LA Galaxy play. I hate that name. StubHub. But I guess it's better than some of the other MLS stadiums.

I'm looking at you, Dick's Sporting Goods Park.

Just as I am about to clear the field, I hear my name called out. Turning, I see Mack walking my direction, clipboard in hand, a mesh bag of soccer balls slung over his arm. I give him a small smile and wait as he walks closer. He looks delectable in his black and white track pants and sleeveless Glendale shirt, his muscles flexing with each step. His typical practice outfit is much different than Coach Johnson's, who is always wearing khakis and a polo. But Mack wears those cutoff shirts like they're going out of style.

And damn does he look good in them.

My smile grows as I remember him from last night, his hands tight on my waist as we... well, okay, we had a crazy romantic make out session and it was amazing.

Once we'd finally gotten our fill, he kissed my forehead, opened my car door, and told me he'd see me at practice. I promptly went home, snuggled up in bed, and spent over an hour replaying our conversation, the implications of a relationship, and the two of us trying to figure things out.

A small sigh escapes my lips, almost startling me out of my memory, reminding me that I'm still on the soccer field and there are other players around. My eyes dart around quickly, but I don't think anyone caught me ogling him.

"What's that smile for?" he asks, once he's an arms length away from me.

I purse my lips and narrow my eyes, teasingly. "I don't know what you're talking about."

He chuckles. "I just wanted to ask..." he pauses, looks around, clears his throat, "... if you wanted to get together this afternoon. Hang out or something."

"I'd love to, but I can't today. Charlie and I are going to Jeremy's game." He nods, his eyes flicking again to my teammates who are trickling off the field and heading to the locker room. "Tonight? We can watch a movie?"

He shakes his head. "I'm taking Dean to do 'guy stuff' tonight - whatever that means." He laughs. "Tomorrow?"

I also shake my head. "I'm meeting with Thomas so we can begin preparing for a presentation." I see his jaw tense just slightly, and it sends a strange feeling rippling through my body. "Are you...?" I laugh lightly, shifting my bag up higher on my shoulder. "Does that bother you?"

"No. Why?"

I shrug. His demeanor has shifted slightly, his eyes a bit more brooding than before. But just as quickly as I see it, it passes.

"So you're busy all day tomorrow?"

"Not all day, but I've got other homework and stuff too, and laundry and grocery shopping. Sunday's normally my 'catch-all' day."

"What about Monday?"

I shake my head again.

"Practice, class, practice, weekly date with Jeremy."

He sighs with an exasperated smile.

"So we finally get our shit together and then can't get our shit together."

I laugh.

"Yeah, I know. It doesn't feel fair."

"Here's what I think," he says, stepping just a bit closer. "I think when you're done with dinner on Monday, give me a call. Even if I just swing by for a little bit... I want to see you. Not around others."

My face flushes as his eyes skate over me, and I'm suddenly a bit more conscious of my sweaty, exhausted appearance. Suddenly I remember Charlie's joke about being sweaty and sexed up and sneaking off to the locker room with Mack for a little hands-on *practice*. I feel my flush spread down my neck and I break out into nervous laughter.

Mack's brow crinkles with confusion.

"What did I miss?"

I swallow my laughter and adjust my bag over my shoulder, looking away from Mack for a moment to collect the nerve to tell him. But my shit-eating grin is still plastered to my face.

"Just something wildly inappropriate that Charlie said to me."

He raises his eyebrows in question. I purse my lips.

"Lets just say it involves this exact scene, but ending with us in the locker room. *Alone*."

His eyes become just slightly hooded at the idea and he

bites his lip.

"Oh really?"

I nod, still surprised that I shared that little story with him.

He leans in towards me, his words a whisper.

"Let Charlie know I love her idea and might have to make sure that particular scenario happens sometime."

My eyes widen and I can't force myself to maintain eye contact. I let out one more uncharacteristic giggle, then bury my face in my hands. Peaking at him through my fingers, I manage to squeak out an, "Alright, I've gotta go. Bye."

And I take off towards the locker rooms, Mack's hushed laughter sounding from behind me.

*　　*　　*　　*　　*

"As much as I wish MLS games were better attended, there really isn't anything better than plenty of arm space and propping your feet up in front of you."

Charlie smiles and shakes her head.

"Missed you this past week, girl. Where you been?" She sits a bit sideways on the seat, tilting her body towards mine to give me her attention.

"Just busy," I reply, taking a massive bite of my hot dog. "You know... doing... stuff."

She snorts.

"Thank you for the insight into your life. That wasn't vague or evasive at *all*."

She waits while I swallow down my food and take a sip of the water next to me.

"Mack and I are trying to figure it out."

I nearly drop my food at the sound of the squeal that comes from Charlie's mouth. Swear to God, this girl has some pipes on her to rival an opera singer.

"I *knew* it. I *so* knew it." She's now bouncing up and down in her seat.

Part of me wants to roll my eyes at her excitement. The other part of me loves how thrilled she is for me. Charlie is one of those girls that can always put aside the shit in her own life and become completely immersed in the life of her best friend.

I smile a reserved smile at her. Even though Charlie is the

closest and most important friend I've ever had, I still find it difficult to gush to her about the things that make me happy. Mostly because I'm usually sure that the happiness is temporary or a fluke, and I don't want to hear the pity that results from the inevitable fallout.

"You been boinking?"

I bark out a laugh, spitting water out of my mouth in the process.

"*NO!*" I shout with more forcefulness than is probably necessary, thankful that there isn't anyone sitting in front of me. "No, we haven't been... *boinking.*" I chuckle under my breath. "We just decided last night to try and navigate everything."

"But there's been kissing right?" Her face is far too hopeful for me to withhold the information about my handful of kisses with Mack.

When I blush and nod, she squeals and starts bouncing in her chair, again.

"You have to tell me. Everything. I want all the details. I want to know what he smells like and where his hands were and how many times you thought about doing it and..."

"I'm not telling you all of that!"

"Oh come on, RJ! My sex life is like a desert right now. A barren wasteland. I don't even see any mirages on the horizon. You have to give me this sip of water to tide me over until I find the well of sexual healing."

I laugh again, tucking myself further into my seat and training my eyes on the field. The game hasn't even started yet, the players still passing the ball around a bit before the whistle blows.

"Well," I clear my throat. "You remember how you went to O'Reilly's last weekend and I was going to come with and never showed?" She nods. "It's because Mack came by." Her mouth drops open. "And we had our first kiss. And it was... I can't even explain to you how absolutely divine it was. It was out-of-this-world, heaven, pure bliss."

Her smile is so big it practically dominates her whole face.

"Why didn't you tell me before? This totally makes more sense now!" I narrow my eyes in confusion. Her smile drops just a bit when she clarifies. "When you found out he was your coach, you were so broken-hearted and upset. I was still assuming you hadn't gotten any lip-love. But if you had the all-consuming kiss *first*, and *then* found out he was your coach, I can see how that would shake you up."

I nod.

"Well, that isn't even the whole story." As the game begins, I tell Charlie everything she's missed over the past five days. She's been so busy, we've been like ships passing in the night.

But she reacts exactly like I think she will with every up and down. She fumes when I tell her about spotting Mack with Ronnie in Hollywood, and she aww's when she hears about him showing up at the apartment. She gives me her dirty-girl smile when I tell her that we basically dry humped on the floor. She's right there with me as I talk about practice and his moody behavior, my dad at the game, my argument with Jeremy. And I round it out with our conversation and kiss at the high school last night.

"Damn, girl. Your life is like a telenovela. I'm sorry I've been so busy for the past week and haven't been there for you."

Her words are said calmly, but I know she's feeling regretful. Charlie prides herself on being an 'invested friend' - those are the words she uses to describe it. She doesn't just want to be on the sidelines of your life. She wants to be in the game.

Some of that stems from her inherent need to know everything. She's not a gossip by any means, but this girl does love her some drama. Mostly, it comes from the fact that her heart is huge and her compassion is endless.

Charlie's in her last year of the nursing program at Glendale. Her hours are weird, her schedule throwing her all over the place. I'm not joking when I say we've been ships passing in the night. Sometimes she's heading to sleep just as I'm waking up.

I wrap my arm around her shoulders and squeeze her tight to me.

"You know what you just said is dumb, so I'm not even going to dignify it with a response." I plant a loud wet kiss on her forehead, then release her. "Besides, I was able to figure it all out on my own."

Her head tilts a bit to the side as she looks at me.

"Did you, though?"

"What do you mean?"

"I just mean, like, you said you guys are going to 'figure it out'," she replies, using air quotes. "What does that even mean?"

I shrug.

"I'm trying not to think too hard about it. There are

obviously things in the way, and we will just have to take it a day at a time. Neither or us wants to risk a disaster if people find out, but we don't want to not see where this is going, either."

She nods, her eyes trained on the field, lost in thought. After a moment she continues. "I know I was the one to suggest the sweaty locker room sex."

"Thanks for that, by the way. He knows about that conversation and I was thoroughly red-faced and embarrassed."

She laughs.

"Well, it sounds hot. And now that he knows about that idea, maybe it will actually happen." She wiggles her eyebrows up and down. "But I just want to say this one thing, and then I will be nothing but supportive, okay?"

I nod, knowing her heart will always be in the right place. Her pause leads me to assume she's trying to figure out how to word something delicately.

"It's about what Jeremy said to you... about the whole 'institutionalization' thing." She stops again. "Is there a concern there for you? I mean, at all?"

Before I can say anything, she powers forward.

"Don't get me wrong. Every person is entitled to their bit of insanity. You've seen me at some pretty low points, and I would *never* judge someone just for experiencing theirs. I just want to make sure you think about it all, and decide what it is you need to know moving forward. I mean, there's a difference between having one episode of madness after a horrible experience, and being literally psychotic. Just make sure you don't get yourself wrapped up in something you aren't capable of handling. You've already got enough mental instability around you with your dad. You don't need to take on someone else's mess too."

My heart warms at her words, so carefully articulated. She's always willing to support me while still making sure I'm able to see something important.

"I appreciate the concern, Char, I really do. But I don't think Mack is *actually* insane. I think Jeremy was playing it up to get me to cut him out of my life, which I don't think is fair. Regardless, I'm sure it's something we will talk about eventually. But I don't want to be so crass as to walk up to him and just say, *hey, my brother said you're a fuckin' nut job and that you were in the looney bin. Let's chat about that over ice cream*. It's something he'll need to bring up in his own time."

She nods and reaches over to squeeze my hand. I'm content

in that moment, just the two of us watching Jeremy and his teammates running around on the field. My brother cares about me, my best friend wants me to be safe and happy, and I have an amazing guy who I can't stop thinking about.

And apparently, Charlie can't stop thinking about him either.

"So, seriously. When are you going to bang him in the locker room?"

Chapter Eleven

Letting out a sigh of boredom, I look across the library to where Thomas is standing in an aisle of books, arms crossed, his brow furrowed in concentration. Then I look longingly at the exit, as if daydreaming about packing up and rushing out the door will make this endless day finally end.

We've been here for nearly two hours already, and I don't think we've even gotten close to feeling like we have the right type of outline put together for our project. It's been difficult to lay everything out when we haven't even begun the prep work for our *individual* papers and presentations yet.

We have the majority of the semester to work on them because they're supposed to be extensive, comprehensive projects about one author and their impact on literature in a larger context. Realistically, if we want Professor Markson to accept our dual-proposal, we need to have a well processed outline that is in sync with the proposals we will have for our individual projects.

But we're struggling to make the outline without any real concrete decisions about what should be leading *up* to the outline.

I sigh again and flick my eyes to the book in front of me, where I've been mindlessly flipping pages when I should be scanning the text for passages to mark.

"Found it!" Thomas plops into the seat across from me, big grin on his face. "I knew it was there. It was just filed in the wrong spot."

I force a smile.

"Awesome. I was surprised when you said the digital copy wasn't in the school's database. You'd think every university would have access to the same one."

"I know, right?" He flips the old book open on the table, amidst the handful of other books we've pulled so far that address the literary relationship and friendship between Edith Wharton and Henry James.

We spend about thirty minutes sorting through books and articles, marking important passages with sticky notes and typing up our ideas for how our projects might intertwine.

"You know what I think is so great about these two?" Thomas says suddenly, startling me away from the page I'm looking at. "They're not some stereotypical mentor/mentee romance, you know?"

My brow furrows as I look at Thomas, trying to understand where he's going with this line of thought.

"Okay, so James is this amazing, well-known author who made it clear that he was a bachelor for life. This beautiful young thing becomes his mentee. They have this amazing friendship and impact each others' work significantly, right?"

I nod.

"It would have been so easy for something to happen there, you know? Similar interests, creative minds. I mean, I know she was married, but shit like that happens, and didn't she end up having an affair with some other guy? Everything we can find about these two indicates they were invested in each other, just not romantically. I like that their relationship is a passionate friendship and sharing of the minds without making it into something that takes away from their work. It seems more special that way. I feel like a romantic entanglement would have potentially taken away from what they accomplished together."

I smile slightly.

"I'd never thought of it like that. I guess you're right." I grab my pen and tap it lightly on the pad of paper in front of me. "I think it's easy to assume a shared interest or similar passions will eventually make friendships lead to a romantic relationship. But you need a lot more than that. Do you think that's a valuable piece to play into the outline?"

Thomas nods and twiddles his own pen between his fingers.

"Yeah. Yeah." He pauses, looking off to a spot just off the side of my head. "But I mean, shared interests are a good thing, too."

I squint my eyes at him slightly, unsure what he means. We'd just established that there was value in the fact that the Wharton/James relationship was strictly friendship, and he immediately starts back-tracking? Before I can ask, Thomas clears his throat slightly and leans forward, continuing to fiddle with his pen and looking at the table where the books are laid out.

"So, in their case, it was a good thing. Because it would have significantly compromised their friendship and possibly damaged the impact their relationship had on the works they both put forward." He clears his throat again. "But I think other friendships can translate into something more when those factors aren't at play."

My eyes widen slightly and I feel my face flush with heat. *Now* I understand what's happening.

"Thomas..." I start, but my phone beeps. Probably Mack. And then it beeps again.

And again.

And again.

When my phone beeps for the fifth time in a row, Thomas breaks the silence.

"You gonna check it?"

I grab my phone from my ugly maroon Jansport backpack that has clearly seen better days. Flipping it over, I unlock the screen and scroll quickly through.

Mack: Still studying?

Mack: Because I think we should go grab In-N-Out again

Mack: Or tacos sound amazing

Mack: I'm just really hungry

Mack: And I want to see you, which is the real reason I'm bugging you. Text me when you're done ;)

A smile stretches out on my face. My fingers hover over the screen as I consider responding. Should I scrap my plans to do laundry and be an adult and hang out with Mack instead?

"Something interesting?"

Thomas' voice snaps me back to the table.

In the library.

Where I'm supposed to be studying.

"Sorry." I wipe the smile from my face, put my phone on silent and back into the front pocket of my bag. "It's nothing." Looking back at Thomas, I try to give him my full attention.

"What I was going to say, earlier... I just... RJ, do you want to go out sometime?"

His voice is so clear and earnest. Not like he's begging me to go on a date, but it's clear he really wants us to do something.

"On a date, I mean. I've liked you for a while and just... it took a while for me to... well..." His voice breaks off when he clears his throat again. A nervous tick. "What do you think?"

If this was something Thomas had asked me two weeks ago, I probably would have said yes. But I know saying yes today isn't in the cards. Not with whatever this new thing is with Mack. I can't even study without thinking about him.

"Thomas, I just..." I pause trying to find the right words.

"If you're about to say no, don't say it yet," he says, cutting me off before I tell him I'm figuring things out with someone else. "Just take a while and think about it. I know we argue a lot in class and I've probably really surprised you. But, I think you're great. Amazing, actually. And beautiful. And I don't want you to give me a knee-jerk reaction and say no, which is what I think you're about to do. Just... think about it. Take some time, and come back to me later."

I give him a slow nod, not responding. I should just tell him I'm seeing someone. But honestly I shouldn't share that with anyone, so I'll do him the service of 'thinking about it' before letting him down.

An awkward silence ensues as we turn back to our books and notes. I only allow a few minutes to go by before I let Thomas know that I need to get home to work on some other projects and get my life in working order before the new week begins. He looks surprised, but waves me off with a pleasant smile.

When I climb into my car, I quickly turn it on and give the A/C a chance to cool the warm musty interior. Leaning my head against the seat, I close my eyes.

Did Thomas really ask me on a date? It's been at least six

months since I've been asked by anyone. A year since I've said yes.

Even though it sent a small zing of pleasure through me to know someone was interested, that zing doesn't hold a candle to the steady hum of awareness I feel when thinking about Mack. In such a short period of time, I've come to find his presence intoxicating, cathartic, enraging, arousing... everything.

I glance at my phone, debating whether or not to call him. Eventually my fingers swipe open my screen and find his number.

"Hey," he says, answering after the first ring.

"Hi," is my only response, but even I can hear the overwhelming smile in my tone.

"How was studying?"

"Oh, you know. Boring and mind-numbing. After two hours I'm starting to reconsider this whole partnership thing with Thomas."

"How come?"

I shrug, and then realize he can't see me.

"I don't know. I just feel like it's adding all of this work that I don't want to do," I finally reply.

"Well, you shouldn't not do it just because it's hard," he advises. "If anything, you should push forward because it's hard. Because it means you're about to do something great."

I hum at his statement, appreciating it in sentiment, but not in my present situation.

"He also asked me out on a date."

Mack is silent on the other end of the line.

"I'm not sure that us working together is a good idea, even if we *can* create something super cool and get top marks on the project. I just..."

Mack clears his throat lightly as I let the end of that sentence trail off. When I don't add anything else he finally says something.

"So what did you say to him?"

"Huh?"

"When he asked you on the date. What did you say?"

"I didn't say anything. He cut me off and told me he wanted me to think about it."

"And are you going to?"

"What?"

"Are you going to think about it? About going on a date with him?"

"What? Why? Do you *want* me to go on a date with him?"

"Of course not."

"Mack, I was obviously going to tell him no, which is why he told me to think about it." My response is slightly clipped, and even though I regret it slightly, I'm also frustrated at Mack's implication.

He sighs.

"I just worry, is all."

"About what?"

"You're 21 and you're in college and you should be enjoying yourself if guys ask you out. And I'm older than you and you have to keep anything between us a secret. I don't want you to miss out on fun in college."

I laugh. I feel bad laughing when his tone is so concerned and thoughtful, but he still clearly has a lot to learn about me.

"Mack, where are you right now?"

"I'm sitting in my car in the parking lot outside of Target."

"Can you meet me somewhere?"

"Anywhere," he responds, lightning fast, like he has nowhere else in the world he wants to be other than next to me, wherever I am.

Fifteen minutes later, I pull my car into a space in front of the Glendale Recreation Centre. When I walk towards the main building, I can see Mack in a secluded corner, leaning on the backrest of a bench seat on the other side of a fountain.

I should notice what perfect weather we are having, or the cute kids running around on the grass in the park across the street, or even the fact that the water in the fountain is a really strange color blue. But just like every time I'm near Mack, the only thing I can focus on is him.

When I'm within a few feet of where is stands, he looks up from his phone. His eyes flicker over my face and down my body and then back up to meet my eyes again. But in just those few seconds I've already eaten up the pavement between us and I'm slinging my arms around his neck and pulling him close to me.

"I just want to be clear about something," I whisper into his ear.

His hands brace on my back, his hold strong, his head tilted down and mouth resting on the space between my shoulder and neck.

"I don't miss out on things because I have to keep us a

secret." I lean back in his hold, just enough to look into his eyes. "I've gone on first dates with five guys since I started college. I was never really invested or interested, so I've never considered myself to be someone that's missing out. I had other things to focus on."

My hands move to his neck, my thumbs reaching and lightly touching that day-old scruff on his jawline that I love so much.

"But you, I care about. With you, I'd be missing out." I lean closer and lightly press my lips to his. "I'm invested." Kiss. "And interested." Kiss. Kiss. "And my focus is on you."

Mack's eyes search mine for just a second before his lips tick up just slightly, and he presses our mouths together again. They part on an exhale, and it feels like we are breathing assurance into each other's bodies.

My hands stay gripped on his neck and my fingers twine into the short pieces of hair I can reach. I hold his face to mine because I want this glorious kiss to go on and on. And on.

"I've never felt like this," I whisper, as his kisses begin moving along my jawline and down my neck. "Never. About anyone."

"Me either."

He rests his forehead against mine, but keeps his eyes open. He stares into my eyes as his hands drift, slowly but with confidence, down my sides, coasting over my hips, and then back to my ass.

He grips me tightly and then walks me backwards a few steps until I feel my back pressed against the scratchy stucco wall of the Recreation Centre building. His mouth returns to my neck, where he licks and sucks, causing me to moan and squirm.

I can feel him pressed up against me, hard and firm, and I drop my hand between us almost out of instinct.

"*Fuck*," he hisses out as my hand rubs against him through his jeans. He moans and rolls his hips, his head falling back just slightly, his teeth biting into his bottom lip. I love that I can do this to him, that I can make him swear and moan and pant for me. It's empowering and I almost get just as turned on as when he's focused on me.

But then he's stepping back and away from my body, and I'm instantly hit with the cool air around us in the shade of the building. Then, just as quickly, I'm flooded with heat as my blood flushes my neck and cheeks.

Mack adjusts his jeans and rubs a hand over his face as he

takes deep, long breaths.

"As amazing as that was, we should probably cool it on the physical stuff, right?" he asks.

I swallow - or, I try to swallow but I end up making an awkward gulping sound instead - and nod, still trying to catch my own breath.

"Sorry if I pushed too far," I say, my voice barely above a whisper.

Mack laughs, more to himself than at me.

"RJ, you could never... and I mean *never*... push us too far," he says, taking steps back towards me and wrapping me in his arms. "I just want to make sure you realize I'm in this because of who you are and how I feel when I'm around you. Not just because I want in your pants."

"But it's still a *little* bit about getting in my pants, right?" I ask with a cheeky grin.

He laughs again and kisses the top of my head.

"You are too much." He steps back and takes my hand. "Lets get you home, miss."

I smile up at him and grip his hand tightly as he walks me back to my car.

*   *   *   *   *

The rest of my Sunday passes far too quickly, mostly due to the fact that Mack ended up coming over. We watched episodes of *The Walking Dead* that we've both already seen before and snacked on popcorn. But mostly we laid head-to-toe with each other and just talked about things.

Like Cherise and her boys and what little menaces they are. About Charlie and how close she and I are. About what Mack hopes to achieve in the future as a soccer coach, and what I want to achieve as a teacher. Essentially, we talk about almost everything.

Well... everything except for two topics.

Mack's accident and the things right before and right after it.

And my dad's alcoholism and the abuse Mack observed, as well as anything associated to that.

Those two items stay firmly on the *do not discuss* shelf.

When it finally hits around 11pm, we call it a night. Mack

gives me a sweet kiss on the cheek and on the lips before heading home.

And then I run frantically around my apartment trying to catch up on everything I didn't do.

On Monday, after another afternoon training filled with sneaking glances at each other, I'm sitting in front of the practice field waiting for Jeremy to pick me up when I get a text from Mack. My heart leaps when I see his name on my screen.

Mack: So date night with Jer?

Me: Yeah. Weekly thing, you know?

Mack: Family first. I get it. But don't forget that I want to take you on another date soon.

My cheeks flush and a smile breaks out on my face as I remember our conversation from the night before. He told me he'd have to figure out the logistics, but that it was important to him to take me out and show me he was also 'invested.' Swoon. But before I can craft a response, a new message pops up.

Mack: Love that smile.

I snap my head up and glance around. After a few seconds, I see him walking across the parking lot. He's freshly showered and wearing low slung track pants with a charcoal gray Glendale hoodie. Even from this sideways vantage point, I can see the smile on his face, a reserved grin that makes my heart race. And it only picks up when he turns his head slightly and we lock eyes.

A quick honk drags my eyes to Jeremy in the SUV idling at the curb. I lean down to grab my bag and trot quickly to Jeremy's car.

"Hey Jer!" I sing out, tossing my duffle into the back and clicking into the seat belt.

"Hey," he says, hesitantly.

When I glance up at him, I see him watching me with a curious expression, his brow furrowed. Then I watch as his eyes dart forward, out the windshield. To Mack. When he looks back at me, I see something between curiosity and disbelief.

When he caught us outside my apartment last week, I was

pretty sure he understood that there was something between me and Mack that was deeper than an appropriate coach/athlete relationship. But maybe he assumed his forceful approach to that conversation would squash things.

He assumed wrong.

"We heading to The Shop or what?" I ask, my voice still light, refusing to give into whatever stupid conversation he wants to have.

He just nods, putting the car into drive.

The ride to my favorite burrito place, which is a convenient ten minute walk from my apartment, is pretty silent. Almost awkwardly silent. I pass the time by flicking through emails on my phone.

I don't like this feeling. Jeremy and I have almost no secrets. We don't get into real arguments. We don't even really get frustrated with each other very often. It's like we've always had this 'us against Frank Jameson' mentality that keeps us on the same page, always at each others' back, no matter what. Our fight last week was incredibly uncharacteristic. For both of us.

But I can feel it brewing. An argument I don't want to have. He's going to say something about Mack, and I don't want to talk to him about Mack.

Mack is my secret. I don't necessarily want him to be a secret, like some clandestine affair. But there's something about keeping our relationship close to my chest that makes me feel like I'm cradling something sacred and special.

Something mine.

So many things that have been important to me have been taken away. I don't want this to follow suit. This pseudo-relationship-thing Mack and I have is the most beautiful thing to happen to me in... well, in a long ass time, if I am being entirely honest.

And I don't want Jeremy to shit all over my beautiful.

We sit, we order, we snack on chips and make small talk about Jeremy's game that Charlie and I attended. I'm just taking a huge, very unfeminine bite of my burrito when my phone dings. It's sitting on the table, face-down. My eyes look at it, then up to Jeremy. His eyes narrow just a bit. There's a pause, a lull, before we both scramble forward to grab the phone.

And Jeremy snatches it up right before my hand can get to it.

He takes one glance at the screen and mumbles an angry, "Shit" before slamming the phone down on the table in front of me, face-up. I don't look down at it. Jeremy's gaze is locked on mine, and he. Is. Pissed.

"Look at it, Rachel."

My eyes drop reluctantly down, and I see the words displayed on the lock screen.

Mack: Wish you were here.

When I look back up at Jeremy, he is rubbing his hand across his stubbled jaw.

"You said nothing was going on. Go ahead and tell me this means nothing, because that is so fucking far from what it looks like, I don't know how you could even try to pretend."

I say nothing, my eyes staring at the now black screen on my phone. *Wish you were here.* I can't help the small smile that sits on my face. And I know Jeremy sees it.

He leans forward in his seat, hands clasped in front of him on the table.

"How much more clear can I be, Rachel? He's your coach. He's crazy. And he's in it for one thing. I can't believe you're being so stupid right now."

"I don't know what you want me to say."

"I want you to tell me you're not making a horrible, *horrible* mistake." He shakes his head, looking at me with frustration and disappointment.

Disappointment.

Something I never thought I would see on his face when he's looking at me.

"I don't feel like I'm making a mistake." My voice is just more than a whisper. It's been a long time since someone has made me feel this small with just one sentence and a stare. Even my dad hasn't done this in years.

He shakes his head again.

"You're wrong. You can't see it, because you're only thinking about the emotions you're feeling. But let me tell you what emotions you're going to be feeling when you and Mack are found out. Embarrassment for having an affair with your coach. Shame for being kicked off the team. Guilt for Mack losing his job. And crippling fear for your future, because you won't have one."

"Don't you think you're being a little dramatic?" I ask, trying to find a way to shift the tone of what is clearly becoming a chance for Jeremy to rip into me.

Inside, I'm kicking myself for even asking that question when just over a week ago, Charlie and I were having the same conversation. Only then, I had been the one pointing out all of the consequences of something happening between us.

"No. Not at all." His response is quick and bold. There's no room for argument. "You are making a mistake. And you *will* regret it."

It sounds like a threat. And that straightens my spine just a bit.

"I don't want to have this conversation," I say, scooting out of the booth. "Not with you. Not ever." I pull a twenty dollar bill from the wallet clip on the back of my cell phone, throwing it on the table.

"You have no idea what Mack and I have. We may crash and burn, but he means something to me. I'm not going to just give up and not try because I'm scared of what might happen to me or who might be disappointed in my decisions. You know who has to live with the choices I make? Me. I do. Not you. So I am only going to say this one time, Jeremy."

I lean forward and stare him right in the eyes.

"This is none of your business, and I don't want to hear a word about it from you again. Stay the fuck out of it."

I stand back up and walk away. Out the front door without letting him respond. My anger burns off quickly as I hit the pavement and walk down the street in the direction of my apartment.

I hate to say it, but the walk home isn't as satisfying as I wish it could have been.

*　　*　　*　　*　　*

My stomach rolls, the nausea building quickly, as I look down at the phone in my hand.

I can't believe I just did that.

I'm sitting on the bench next to the practice field, my duffle at my feet, fully dressed for practice, nearly an hour early. But I'm not here to get in some extra practice with my teammates,

153

or to jog the field and stretch to warm up. I'm sitting here because I literally feel like I have nowhere else to go.

"Amy, I don't know what to do."

It was the tone of his voice that stopped me dead in my tracks when I dropped by his office just a few minutes ago. I was walking down the hallway with a happy heart and a smile on my face. If anyone had seen me, they would just assume Coach McIntosh was having a meeting with one of his players to talk about strategy or injury or a million other things. His door was cracked open just slightly, and I had just reached up to knock when I heard him.

"Amy, I don't know what to do."

He sounded devastated. Overwhelmed. Confused. How I was able to pull all of those emotions out of one sentence, I'm not sure. But it was all there. I knew I was encroaching on something private, something personal. Never one to seek out gossip, I had spun on my toes and was just about to walk away from his door and give him privacy when he spoke again. If he had just waited a few more seconds, I wouldn't have made a horrible decision.

"Even if my job is on the line?"

I froze. Incapable of moving forward. My eyes wide, I kept them focused down the hallway, away from Mack's door, and yet every nerve in my body was pulling me backwards to hear more. I took one step back. And then another. And another. Until I was standing directly in front of his office, leaning towards the crack in the doorway, straining to hear him speak again. I wondered if I had heard him correctly, and silently prayed that I hadn't.

"Yeah, last night at my house. I was shocked, but what can I do?"

And then there was silence when all I wanted was to read the thoughts in his mind and know what was happening. Even having heard that much, I still should have left. Why didn't I just leave? Instead, I inched my head closer, trying to see in through the opening between the door and the jamb. Mack's office came into view, and my heart broke when I saw him. He was at his desk, one hand to his ear holding his cell phone, the other bracing his head in place. His fingers were twisted into the hair at the crown of his head, his eyes shut tight as he listened.

"But I don't..." Pause. *"I don't want to just call it off. I can figure it out."*

I swallowed so audibly, I was shocked he couldn't hear it

from where he sat just ten feet away. It clicked in an instant. His job was on the line because of me. Something had happened. Something was making him worry about us continuing whatever we were doing.

But he was confused about what to do? *He should just end it! We shouldn't be doing this!* My head was screaming at me to step into his office and tell him we should call it off, take a break, avoid each other, anything. He would understand if I explained it. But then he exhaled with a whoosh, and said three words that made me realize he would never understand.

"She's worth it."

I gasped. That's how shocked I was. I literally gasped like some housewife in a 50's movie. I then took several large, purposeful steps away from the door, turned and bolted down the hallway. When I finally reached the practice field, I felt like I had sprinted the entire way without taking a breath.

"She's worth it."

He said those words. He'd implied he would take on whatever shit storm would rain down on him if word got out about our involvement. But that shit storm would rain onto me as well. In that moment, I should have had normal, altruistic emotions about wanting to protect Mack and his job and reputation.

But my selfish mind was firmly planted in the fact that the life *I* had worked so hard for would be upended if we kept moving forward. *My* scholarship. *My* degree. *My* career. *My* future.

And I wasn't ready to throw in the towel on everything I had accomplished.

Which brings me to now, sitting on the bench at the practice field, staring at the screen reflecting my call to Thomas. It took less than a minute.

Less than a minute to call him and tell him I had decided to say yes to the date.

Less than a minute to schedule something for Friday night.

Less than a minute to know I had made a horrible decision.

But the horrible decision is still the right one. Or at least, that's what I will need to remind myself. Over and over.

And over.

Chapter Twelve

I love my job as a Stocking Clerk at Candy's Crafts, a boutique shop on the main drag in Glendale. Sure, the name of the shop is horrible and the work I do isn't particularly important, but Candy is one of the nicest people I know.

Plus she lets me work whenever I have the time instead of scheduling shifts, so as long as I can put in around fifteen hours over a two-week period, she could care less if I was working in the middle of the night, which is perfect for my hectic schedule.

"How's the season going?"

The question takes me by surprise, mostly because I thought I was the only one here. The storefront closes at 5pm, so I assumed I would be working alone when I entered through the back door at 7pm.

"Hey, CC."

I try to infuse some brightness into my voice as I take an inventory of the scrapbook stickers we have sorted in the back, but my happiness sounds strained.

Mechanical almost.

"Things are good. Just busy. The usual."

She plops down at her desk, which sits in the corner of the warehouse-style back room, and begins shuffling through paperwork, her wild blond curls bouncing all over the place as she shakes her head slightly.

"That wasn't very convincing," she replies, glancing at me over the rim of her glasses. "Try again."

I mentally groan. CC has been a sort of mother-figure for me over the past few years. I've been working for her since the middle of freshman year when I realized that my scholarships covered school and housing, but not other important things like food, books, money to buy tampons, etc. She took a really quick interest in my life.

She comes to some of my soccer matches and we try to get coffee every few weeks. She's in her mid-thirties and single, and lies through her teeth every time she says she isn't interested in settling down or having kids. I know she wants them, and her interest in me has become a way for her to express some of her innate nurturing personality.

A big part of that personality is being able to read people like the top letter of an eye exam chart. I should have known she would be able to sniff out my faux-cheeriness.

I huff out a breath.

"I just have a lot on my mind. Nothing for you to worry your pretty little head about." I grab a box cutter and turn back to the boxes in front of me, prepping them to be unpacked and sorted.

CC laughs behind me.

"It's been quite some time since you've snipped back at me. Whatever it is, I hope you figure it out soon."

We both work in silence for a while. I know she's waiting for me to spill, but what am I supposed to say?

Oh I'm just having an emotional affair with my coach and he might get fired so I've accepted a date with a player on the men's team that likes me even though I don't like him. On top of that, I'm pretty sure my psychology grade is beyond saving, which could mean I lose my scholarship, and my brother and I are in a fight for the first time in years. Same old stuff. No big deal.

"Don't hurt yourself," she says softly from behind me.

I jerk back from the cardboard boxes and see that I've gone a little Jack-the-Ripper on them. Sliding the box cutter blade back into the plastic, I place it on the workbench next to me and take a seat.

CC takes a seat next to me without saying anything. After a few minutes I turn and catch her eye.

"Have you ever intentionally hurt someone to do the right thing?"

She raises her eyebrows.

"You're gonna have to be more specific than that, honey."

"Well, there's this guy..."

"Isn't there always?"

We share a small laugh, and my chest feels lighter. Talking to CC almost always does that. I take a breath and launch right in.

"Well, this guy... we technically can't date, because he works for the college. But we've been... flirting, I guess, with the boundaries of what we can do. And now his job is in jeopardy and I can't let him get fired over me when he has worked so hard to get his life to a good place. But honestly, I also don't want to have to deal with the consequences in my own life if we're caught. So I accepted a date with another guy. And I feel terrible about it. Like, really, horribly awful."

CC leans back against the wall and crosses her arms over her chest.

"That's quite the predicament you're in." I nod. "Did you ever think about just *talking* to the guy and explaining that you have to take a break until you *can* date? More often than not, communicating is the best way to work through a problem."

"But I heard him say he would give up his job for me!" My voice comes out high-pitched and incredulous.

"Why is that so shocking to you?"

I pause.

"What?"

"Why is it shocking to you that he would give up a job that is going to get in the way of you being together?"

I prop my leg up on the bench so it's resting between us, turning to look straight at her.

"It's not that it's *shocking*. It's that we are in completely different places if he is willing to leave his job when I don't even really know how I feel. We still barely know each other. It's been like, ten days since we met. Isn't that really fast?"

"It is fast, but sometimes you meet someone and feel a connection immediately. And it's okay to be in different places. That's usually how relationships progress. One person feels ready to take a step forward, and they reach out their hand to the other person in the relationship. You only move forward as a couple if the other person takes the hand and steps forward too."

"But I don't want him to ruin his life for me."

"But you're assuming that him *quitting his job* would be ruining his life. What if, in his mind, not being with *you* would ruin his life? And the job is just a job?"

158

I shake my head. That's not what's happening. But before I can verbalize that to CC, she begins again, her words soft and loving.

"You have to get it out of your head that you're worthless, RJ. You're *anything* but, and it sounds like this guy knows that."

I sit frozen with my mouth slightly open, unsure of how to respond.

Worthless?

It's been a long time since I've used that word to describe myself, but is that what I'm subconsciously assuming now? That I'm worthless?

I can feel that single statement, that single word, weaving around me like ivy and suddenly I feel like I have to get out of here. I'm not talking about this.

I stand abruptly, startling CC as my clipboard and paperwork falls to the floor.

"I have to go. I forgot I have some stuff to do."

I race to my bag that's thrown on one of the shelves. I'm nanoseconds away from opening the door and getting out of this situation when CC's hand closes over mine. I can't help but look up at her face, even though I'm showing her the handful of tears that are pooling in my eyes.

Her expression is warm, but tinged with just a small amount of concern.

"I'm sorry for pushing, but you need to know that you are loved, RJ. Not just a nice person people can get along with. Not just someone that might be lovable *one day*. But loved, right now, by many, many people. And it sounds like this young man can also see all of the wonderful things that make you, you. I would hate to see you push someone away because you don't feel worthy. You are *not* worthless, no matter what that shit of a father made you feel."

I exhale quickly at her words, my shoulders dropping slightly as the beginning of an anxiety attack grips at my chest. It feels like all of the air has been compressed out of my lungs and a buzzing fills my ears.

I've never talked to CC about my dad. Ever. And yet, somehow, she's gleaned from our interactions that my relationship with him is toxic.

My mind is racing with a thousand thoughts, but only one crystalizes.

I can't do this right now.

"I can't do this right now," I whisper.

She just nods and I turn the handle and walk out the door.

*   *   *   *   *

On Wednesday, I trudge through a rough morning conditioning, eat an early lunch with some teammates, and stare out the window through my entire Foundations of Learning and Teaching course.

By the time the afternoon scrimmage rolls around, I've decided I should just talk to Mack about what I overheard in his office. I've actively avoided thinking about CC's parting words to me, but I do agree that communicating with Mack is the best way for us to figure things out.

If I don't allow him to be a part of figuring out the solution to our problem, I'm eliminating his ability to be an active participant in the future of our relationship.

"Do you have time to chat after practice?" My voice is hushed as I stand next to Mack on the edge of the practice field. "It's important."

He's silent for a beat too long and I glance over. His brows are furrowed.

"Sure. I'll always make time for you, RJ."

My smile is uneasy, but I nod and quickly turn to jog out to center field to begin the scrimmage.

I don't like that my words put that expression on his face. He looked worried. I mean, I guess he has a reason to be worried. His job is potentially on the line, and the girl he's apparently willing to risk it for is about to have a super deep conversation about why he shouldn't do that. And why we should put our relationship on hold until I graduate in May. Seven months isn't that long. Right?

Right.

An hour later, our scrimmage is over and I'm certain I played like shit. I was distracted and stuck in my thoughts. Gina had a few choice words for me, but other than that, no one said anything. Hopefully I still get to play tomorrow.

But that isn't the priority.

I catch Mack's eyes and he tilts his head just slightly, indicating we should walk over... well, somewhere. The parking lot, his office. Just somewhere that doesn't include a bunch of my teammates.

"Hey RJ!" I hear from behind me.

My body freezes.

I can hear Thomas jogging lightly towards me, but my eyes stay locked on Mack, who is just a few feet from me, bending over to stuff a final ball into his mesh net bag.

"I made reservations for Friday at that new tapas place on the drag."

Mack's eyes snap up to mine.

"I was thinking I could pick you up at 6:30ish? That should give us enough time to get there, park, walk around a little, you know? Proper date stuff."

Mack's eyes are wild and confused and they flick between me and Thomas. But then he looks away, grabs his bag and practically storms towards the parking lot.

"RJ?" I turn to look at Thomas. His eyes look behind me at Mack's retreating form, then back to me. "Everything okay?"

I nod several times, surely looking like a bobble head. I'm only able to form an eloquent, "uh huh. Gotta go," and I'm grabbing my duffle and power walking in Mack's wake.

When I finally get to the parking lot, I see Mack chuck his bag angrily into the bed of his truck. I just stand there, watching him. Every nerve in my body says I should go to him, right this moment, and tell him the truth. Tell him about overhearing his call and how I reacted, so he knows why I did it but also that I regret it.

But I don't.

I don't go to him. I just watch him.

I watch as he runs his hands through his hair and grips the back of his head, his face turned downward.

I watch as he clenches and unclenches his fists, and gets into his truck.

And when our eyes lock through his windshield, and he shakes his head in what looks like anger or frustration, I do nothing but watch as he drives away.

*   *   *   *   *

"You said WHAT?!"

Charlie's voice is shrill. I haven't heard her sound like this in a long time.

"You heard me," I huff out as I towel dry my hair while I sit cross-legged in yoga pants and a baggy shirt on my bedroom floor. "Don't make me repeat it."

Charlie walks out of my room. I hear her banging around in her own room for a few minutes before she's back, with her arm extended and her finger pointing at me.

"No. I want to hear you say it again. If you are actually going to make this *colossal* mistake, you need to stick by it, mister!"

I sigh and throw my towel on the ground. She's in a mood. And the only way to get her to go away so I can finish getting ready for this stupid date is to tell her about the game yesterday. Again.

"I told him I didn't want to wait until May."

My stomach curls at the memory, and I can't maintain eye contact with Charlie.

It was one of the most difficult moments I'd ever faced. Mack, with his sweet heart and kind soul, his warm eyes and easy confidence, had come to me after we'd finished the home game against Cal Poly. He'd come to me looking tired and beaten down. Wounded.

"I don't understand what happened," he said in a hushed voice in the hallway outside of the locker rooms. "I thought we were figuring it out." He swallowed. "I thought..." but he didn't finish his sentence, as several of the girls came out of the locker room.

"See you at practice on Saturday!" Piper said, her voice the epitome of cheer as she basked in the glow of her three goals.

I gave her a small, forced smile and a wave, then looked back at Mack.

"I thought we were both in this, together. What changed between Sunday and yesterday?"

It took me a moment to muster up the courage to say what I wanted, and when the words fell from my lips I felt physically ill.

"I decided I don't want to sneak around, Mack."

"So you immediately accept a date with Thomas? Where is this coming from?"

I shrugged, because I didn't know what else to do.

"You know this thing between us is something special, and

162

you're just going to throw it away?"

I shrugged again, feeling incredibly immature, but also incapable of verbalizing anything that would advance the conversation.

"You didn't even want to talk to me about it? We could have figured something out. We could have waited until you graduated, or... or I could have..."

"It's not worth it to me."

I cut him off before he could say he would quit his job. But the words that popped out of my mouth were much more cruel than I had intended. His mouth parted in surprise and his brows furrowed.

"It's not worth it to me to put my life on hold until May. I don't want to have to wait."

He stared at me for a few seconds before I turned and walked as confidently as I could muster out of the practice facility to the parking lot. And then when I reached my car and closed myself inside, I cried. I cried all the way home, I cried in the shower, and I cried in bed.

I should have just told him.

I should have told him that I heard the conversation, and gone with the original plan to wait.

But after seeing Mack storm away after practice and seeing how dejected he looked at the game, I knew that the only way for us to move forward would be separately. And to do that we would need to put a pin in everything.

The longing glances would stop. The stolen kisses when no one was looking would stop. But only if I hurt him. I just wasn't prepared for what the words would feel like once they left my mouth. It was vile, and I could barely stand the sight of myself.

"I can't believe you said that shit to him." Charlie's voice snaps me out of a memory that's making me physically ill. "You should have just been fucking honest!"

She's shouting. Like, actually shouting.

"You don't live my life, Charlie," I say in exasperation. "You don't get to tell me what choices I should and shouldn't be making."

"You know what? Fine! But when you realize the mistake you've made, and you actually sit and reflect on what a miserable *bitch* you were, how hurtful you were to a man who has been nothing but open and kind and vulnerable with you, *don't* come talk to me about it. Because my response is going to be a nasty little *I told you so.*" And with that, she storms out of my room and slams her bedroom door.

I huff out another sigh. I feel like that's all I've been doing all day. Sighing about my life, when in reality, I've made these decisions myself, so I shouldn't be disappointed.

God, but the look in Mack's eyes. Actually saying the words *It's not worth it to me*? I don't think I've ever said something in such an intentionally hurtful way to someone who didn't deserve it.

But I can't let Mack quit his job or get fired over me. Especially when I don't think I would take the same risk for him. He took that step forward and reached back for me, and I literally spit in his hand and walked in the other direction.

I let out a groan and lean back against the foot of my bed. So this is what it feels like to be a bitch? I don't know how Gina does it every day. It's exhausting.

Chapter Thirteen

When Friday night rolls around, I'm nearly sick with anxiety. I fought with myself for hours today, talking myself in and out of calling Thomas and canceling. Ultimately, I chose to go with the flow. Going on a normal date like a normal college student is... well, it's normal. It's what I should be doing, instead of sneaking around and hiding with my coach, making out on the floor of my apartment and in dark parking lots.

Charlie has been stomping around the apartment all evening, making her distaste for the entire situation known. Her glares have not gone unnoticed, either.

"I'm leaving!" she shouts to me from the entry.

When I come down the stairs, ready for my own date, she's standing at the door sorting through her clutch. She's dressed to kill in a classy red cap-sleeved silk dress with a sweetheart neckline. Her hair is up in an incredibly complicated twist. I think it's called a chignon, but the only interesting hairstyle I know is the french braid, so I can't be sure.

She looks elegant and understated in her beauty, which isn't her normal look. She's much more of a 'check out my awesome rack' kind of girl, rather than someone who pays homage to Audrey Hepburn in the fashion department.

"Charlie," I breathe. "You look amazing!"

Her eyes flip up to me and for a brief moment, I think she's going to say something about how she's dressed. She looks vulnerable. Breathtakingly beautiful, but nervous. Not the Charlie I know.

But then her eyes narrow and she scans me up and down. She rolls her eyes and snorts.

"You couldn't manage anything other than jeans for Mack, and then you dress like *that* for this Thomas guy, who you don't even care about?" She shakes her head and struts towards the door.

I stand frozen halfway down the stairs in my black dress. The one dress I own that makes me feel beautiful. And Charlie has just made it clear that the dress is doing nothing to hide my shameful behavior.

"Have fun on your *date*," she mocks. "Try not to rip this guy's heart out too, would you?"

The slam of the door startles me even though I knew it was coming. I stay on the stairs for a few minutes, unsure what to do with myself. I just stand there, frozen, Charlie's words seeping through me.

It's a knock on the door that forces me out of my trance, and when I open it, my heart breaks at Thomas standing on my porch with a small bouquet in his hands.

"RJ, wow," he says with a sweet smile. "You look... wow, you look beautiful."

I must stand there for too long without saying anything, because his smile fades a little bit. "You okay?"

I nod too hard and open the door, indicating that Thomas should come inside. The minute he places a foot across the threshold of my apartment, I put a hand onto his chest to stop him.

He takes a step back, looking incredibly confused.

"I'm guessing you're not okay?"

When I finally find my voice, I'm surprised about what comes out of it.

"I'm sorry, Thomas, but I can't go on a date with you tonight."

He shifts slightly on his feet, and my heart clenches as the unsure look on his face.

"Did you..." he clears his throat, "... did you want to reschedule?"

There is a very tiny smile on his face and just the right amount of hope in his voice for me to know I'm making the right decision, no matter how my stomach turns over at my choice. I need to call it off now before I risk hurting him further. The last thing I need on my conscience is another wounded heart.

I shake my head slightly.

"No." My words are a whisper, but I know he hears them when that small smile slips away completely. "I'm so sorry, Thomas. You are handsome and smart and charming, and if I wasn't totally hung up on someone else, I would feel so lucky to be going on a date with you tonight."

"But you *are* hung up on someone else." I nod and he lets out a breath. "I knew I should have asked sooner. I just couldn't get up the nerve."

He shakes his head a little bit and looks down at his shoes. His shiny shoes, beneath his slacks, which has a collared shirt tucked into it. He's even wearing a tie, which he reaches up to adjust slightly.

"There's not any chance in the future, is there."

He doesn't say it as a question, so I know he already knows the answer. When I shake my head no in confirmation, he nods.

"Thanks for at least being honest," he says, taking a step back. "And you really do look beautiful, RJ. I'm sure if the guy you're hung up on doesn't figure his shit out quickly, there are loads of guys who would love to be on your arm."

If only he knew it was my own fault that I was alone. But I don't tell him that. Instead I allow him to hand me the bouquet and kiss me lightly on the cheek. Then I wave slightly and close the door on Thomas' retreating form. I walk slowly into the living room and sit down on the couch, staring at a blank television screen.

I feel out of control. My emotions. My fears. My decisions. It's like I never know what I'm going to do or say until right when I do or say it. I've never been that person. I'm 'thoughtful and intentional' according to Charlie. I'm 'a future thinker' according to Jeremy.

But tonight, I feel like none of those things. I feel lacking in any kind of plan or direction. I keep hurting the people around me.

And I can't stand it.

*　　*　　*　　*　　*

The slamming of the door jolts me where I've fallen asleep on the couch, and my eyes fly open. I stretch a little bit until I hear a mumbling whisper in the entryway.

"...such bullshit. Like I don't know what's happening. Of all the..."

Charlie's mumbled ranting stops with a halt when she sees me sitting on the couch. She raises an eyebrow and glances at her phone.

"It's 8:30. Was the date that bad?"

My face crumples and I look back down at my hands, willing myself to maintain control of my emotions.

"I didn't go."

Only a few seconds pass before Charlie is plopped down on the couch next to me, wrapping her arms around me and pulling me into a tight embrace.

"Did you call him and cancel?"

I shook my head.

"I told him there was someone else when he showed up at the door."

Even though I can't see her face, I can feel Charlie's wince.

"Ouch."

"I know. Not one of my finer moments. I haven't been having a lot of fine moments recently."

Charlie pulls back to look at me and I'm happy to see that her previous bitter death glare is replaced by her normal expression full of care and warmth.

"But you did the right thing, even if it hurt you both." She rubs her hands up and down on my upper-arms, attempting to soothe me. "It wouldn't have been fair of you to go on a date with Thomas when you're clearly in love with Mack."

I scoff.

"I am *not* in love with him, Charlie. I've known him for two weeks. I just..." I sigh. "He's just important, that's all."

"So important that you had to stomp on his heart?"

I let out a breath.

"He'll be fine. I'm sure he's already bowing down to the Ronnie Kade altar."

Charlie giggles.

"You know that's not true."

"Do I?" I sit back and curl my legs under a pillow. "I told you what Jeremy said. About how Mack used to, and I quote 'bang everything in sight.' It would be only natural for him to go back to that. I mean, he's gorgeous."

"Fuck Jeremy."

My eyebrows feel like they're about to fly off my face in surprise. I've never heard Charlie say something like that about my brother.

"Jeremy is using guilt about his own actions to manipulate the situation in a misguided attempt to protect you. And from Mack, who is basically someone who *used* to do what Jeremy is *currently* doing."

Her face is the picture of frustration, and I feel like I'm getting some insight into some of her irritations with Jeremy in the past.

"Are you going to let another man dictate your life choices? Your dad did it for years, and now you're letting your brother force you into a situation where you're either not together, or Mack loses his job and you are a pariah. This isn't *The Scarlet Letter*, RJ. You have other options without having to brand yourself with some shameful monogram."

"I'm not sure *The Scarlet Letter* really applies here, but…"

"Come on, I tried to make a literature reference. I should get mad points for that."

I let out a half laugh.

"Maybe." I pause. "Maybe I should try to talk to Jeremy again. Get him to see it from my perspective."

Charlie shakes her head.

"I don't think that's what you should do. I mean, it's basically his fault that Mack's worried about losing his job anyway, right? So you talking to him isn't going to make that problem go away."

My brow furrows.

"What are you talking about?"

Charlie's face blanches, her eyes going wide.

"Charlie, what do you mean it's Jeremy's fault that Mack is worried about his job?"

"Uhmmm…" Her eyes are burning holes into her hands, her feet, the wall. She is looking anywhere but at me. "I may have overheard something," she finally says in a mumble.

I sit forward, the pillow in my lap falling forward.

"What?"

"Well," she twists her fingers in her lap, "I may have overheard Jeremy on a phone call with Mack. I didn't hear everything, and I don't know the whole story, but it sounded like Jeremy was following up to make sure you guys weren't together. Like they had talked before… or something."

169

My mind is reeling. All of the blood in my body has flown to my cheeks and my neck, and I know I am bright red with anger as I sort through the information Charlie has just given to me. I can literally feel myself going from zero to sixty in almost no time at all.

Suddenly, I'm off the couch and slipping into my shoes, rushing around the living room in a frenzy.

"What are you doing?" Charlie asks, the nerves in her body clear in the shake of her voice.

"What do you *think* I'm doing, Charlie? I'm going to fucking murder my brother."

*   *   *   *   *

It takes me almost no time at all to find out that Jeremy and some of 'the Galaxy hotties' are grabbing drinks at Smoggy Tavern, thanks in large part to the fangirl pages that blast updates on their whereabouts. MLS stars don't get a lot of attention, but the ladies who focus on them sure are dedicated.

It takes me twenty minutes to make it from Glendale to Downtown LA, a miraculous occurrence on a Friday night when the Lakers are playing. I park in the public parking lot a few blocks down and swallow the frustration at paying the high cost that accompanies convenient parking in Los Angeles.

By the time I get through the doors of Smoggy Tavern, I'm sure my eyes are blazing in rage, as the doorman doesn't even bother carding me. I let my eyes scan the dimly lit bar. When I don't see Jeremy I plow through the crowd to get to The Alley, the outdoor seating area that Smoggy Tavern uses to accommodate smokers and crowds on busier nights.

As soon as I get outside, I see him sitting with a girl on his lap, laughing at some other guy at his table. They're wearing suits and look very clean cut and incredibly charming. Good thing I know better.

I storm quickly over to his table and see the shock on his face when I get close enough to catch his eyes.

"Rach? What are you..."

But before he can get a word out, I've slapped him across the face.

Hard.

The girl on his lap gets up quickly.

"I didn't know he had a girlfriend," she says quickly.

"Don't worry. I'm his sister. You can still make a play for his dick once I've left."

The words I'm spitting out of my mouth are laced with every ounce of the frustration that has boiled along the edges of my skin as I drove here. Jeremy's head jerks back in surprise at what I've said, the red mark on his face becoming more apparent as the girl quickly slips away.

"What the hell are you doing?"

"What the hell am *I* doing? How about, what the hell are *you* doing?" He just continues to stare at me. "Did you threaten Mack's *job*?"

My words come out incredulous, and I'm almost hopeful that he will deny them. I'd rather be wrong and feel like an asshole for slapping my brother.

But Jeremy's brow furrows in frustration, and I instantly know I'm not wrong.

"So that prick decided to tell you instead of doing the right thing and ending it?"

I lean in towards Jeremy, my entire body vibrating with unchecked emotions.

"No, you son-of-a-bitch. *Charlie* told me."

His eyes widen, just slightly. My voice is low to keep any neighboring tables from overhearing, but loud enough for Jeremy to understand how truly upset I am.

"Can you imagine what it was like to learn that my *brother* threatened a man with his livelihood in an attempt to manipulate a situation in a way that serves himself? Do you have any idea what it feels like to be me? To know that the one person I trusted to have my back, no matter what, has stolen away the small piece of happiness that I've tried to carve out for myself?"

Jeremy rolls his eyes, effectively throwing gasoline on my fire.

"I think you're being a little over-the-top here, Rach. *Small piece of happiness?* Come on. That's so dramatic. The guy's a douche."

"You have no fucking clue what you're talking about," I reply. "And I am letting you know right now, Jeremy. I will *never* forgive you for this. Manipulation, cruel words, apparently reveling in my distress." I shake my head at him. "Sounds like a page right out of the Frank Jameson playbook."

Jeremy's face loses a little bit of color at those words, and for a moment I think he's come to his senses. But then I see the resolve in his eyes. He stands quickly, grabbing my arm and pulling me towards the door back inside Smoggy Tavern.

"If my words and actions don't have any impact on you, maybe something a little more visual will do the trick."

I can barely hear him over the loud voices and laughter as he drags me further into the throngs of people surrounding the bar. When he stops suddenly, I almost plow right into his back.

"What are you doing, Jeremy?" I shout.

He steps out of my way and when I look at him, he points to my right.

When I turn to look, I allow my eyes a minute to adjust to the dim lighting that impacted my vision the first time I walked in. When I can finally see, I wish I couldn't. Because what I see decimates me.

Behind a roped off VIP section is a separate dance floor. It's fairly full, but not overflowing. Right in the middle is Mack. And wrapped around him like a vine is Ronnie Kade. Their movements are so sexual that I literally can't believe what's happening just a few feet away and in the eyes of the general public.

Their mouths are locked together in what looks to be a deep, passionate kiss that never ends. Ronnie's leg is wrapped around Mack's hip, which he is gripping roughly with one hand. They're grinding into each other in time with the music, his other hand squeezing her ass over her very, *very* short green strapless dress.

I'm rooted like a tree to the spot, staring at them. It's awkward and uncomfortable, but it's almost like I need to sear this visual into my brain.

When Ronnie lowers her leg and breaks their kiss, she turns in Mack's arms and begins rubbing her ass against the front of him. One large hand grips her hip, the other splays on her stomach. I can see Mack close his eyes and lean his head back, biting his lip in ecstasy as they continue what is obviously a rousing bout of foreplay on the dance floor.

It's a face almost identical to the one he made when we were together in front of the Recreation Centre. And seeing him just a few days later with Ronnie... well, I've never felt more like a cheap slut then while watching them together.

"I wanted you to see what he's really like," Jeremy's voice

cuts through the fog I was in. "You wouldn't listen to me, but this is the guy he's *always* been. You deserve better, Rach."

I turn sharply away from Mack and Ronnie and stare at Jeremy. Tears fill my eyes as we just look at each other. Finally, I simply turn away from him and walk out of Smoggy Tavern, back to my car in the overpriced lot, and drive away.

The visual of Mack and Ronnie stays with me even once I'm back in my bed, and I'm wishing I could rewind the past few weeks and start over.

*   *   *   *   *

To say I don't want to be at practice today is an understatement. My feet are sluggish, my hands are slow, and I feel like bursting into tears every time I catch sight of Mack on the sidelines as we complete rapid three-on-three drills.

What should bolster my flagging energy is Mack's appearance. He looks a little bit nauseous and a lot exhausted, and has been defaulting to Coach Johnson's lead all morning.

But in reality, I can't feel good that Mack looks so bad. Because his appearance and lack of focus is simply a reminder that he spent the night with Ronnie. I spend the entire practice fighting off images of the two of them twisted up in a sweaty mess in what are likely 1000 thread count sheets on Ronnie's round, rotating bed surrounded by mirrors.

Okay, so I doubt any of that's true, but it helps just a little to pretend she's a bad porn star instead of what she really is.

Gorgeous. Perfect.

The literal antithesis to my average and awkward self.

As the morning progresses, my upset mood sways back and forth between sadness and anger. At one point, I attempt apathy and disinterest, but fail. And unfortunately, for both me and for Mack, as practice wraps up, it stays firmly planted in anger that unleashes itself when I find myself in the doorway of Mack's office.

"Rough night, *coach*?" The words are from my lips before I can stop them.

Mack's head snaps up from his desk where he is taking notes, his eyes locking on me then straying behind me to the empty doorway, presumably to confirm that I'm alone.

"You could say that," he replies warily. Then his face changes just slightly, revealing just the hint of bitterness. "How was your date?" he spits out.

"My evening was absolutely fantastic," I respond with a fake smile. "It was pretty enlightening, actually."

Mack's eyes dart away at my words, then lock back in on me.

"I feel like you're trying to be a smart-ass but I don't know why." So matter-of-fact. "*You're* the one who set up a date with someone else, RJ."

Still standing in the open doorway, I step inside and close the door behind me.

"I cancelled my date."

Mack's mouth opens just a fraction in surprise. The anger that has been holding my heart in a vice finally loosens as sadness floods my body.

"I heard the phone call," I whisper. "With Amy. About you possibly losing your job."

Mack is silent as he watches me, shock still evident on his face.

I shake my head slightly.

"Accepting the date with Thomas was a knee-jerk reaction and a mistake. I was going to talk to you about it, about the fact I overheard, at practice that day when Thomas mentioned our plans. When I saw how hurt you were, it just seemed like an easier way to manage it. It would be easier to let you be mad at me than to risk losing your job. But when Thomas showed up at my house on Friday I couldn't do it. I knew it wasn't right. Knew that I was betraying something special."

I stand and walk to the small window, looking out at the sky without really seeing anything other than a blur.

"And then Charlie told me she thought it was Jeremy who threatened your job. Something about overhearing a phone call between the two of you. I don't even know the whole story, just that it was his fault. So I went out to find him last night."

I turn around and face Mack where he still sits at his desk.

"At Smoggy Tavern."

Mack's face goes slack and he looks down at his desk, his eyes moving rapidly across the papers scattered in front of him.

"And I confronted Jeremy. And then Jeremy dragged me inside and there you were, with Ronnie. On the dance floor."

A tear slips down my cheek and I quickly bat it away.

174

"And the thing is, I shouldn't be this upset because you aren't mine. So maybe us falling apart solves the problem, Mack."

I shrug, trying to play everything off.

"Maybe us 'figuring things out' just meant figuring out that we aren't a fit. It's not just bad timing. What you want in a girl... I can't be that and I don't want to be."

Mack's brow furrows.

"What I want in a girl? RJ, I..."

"I don't need you to clarify anything for me, okay?" I'm quick to respond, cutting him off mid-sentence. "We've been here before, remember? After the *first* time I saw you two together. I feel like we keep coming back to this place where we misunderstand or miscommunicate and then we both assume the worst. And I never thought I would be this jealous person. But knowing that the two of you have an obviously very... *very,* sexual history and that it was so easy for you to pick it up again... I just don't see how that leaves us in a space where we can move forward when that kind of life is the norm for you."

"But it's *not* the norm for me, RJ."

I shake my head.

"Don't lie to me, Mack. Not now. We have been brutally honest with each other. It has been the one beautiful constant in this non-relationship, so don't start lying now."

Mack is silent for a moment, his hands playing with his black wristband. The look on his face is different than what I've seen before. He looks stopped up, like he wants to say something but can't verbalize the words or can't force himself to say them.

When he stands abruptly and walks over to me, I'm startled. Before I even know what is happening, his hands are on my face, pulling me into a kiss. It's delicate and sweet, and it would be so easy to just fall into everything that is him and get swept up in it. But I pull away before it can go any further.

"RJ," Mack whispers, keeping his hands on my face, his eyes latched onto mine. "That *was* the norm for me. A long time ago. But it isn't who I am now and it isn't who I *want* to be."

I shake my head again, dislodging his hands and taking a step back.

"How many girls have you slept with since you've been in LA, Mack?"

"What does that have to do with anything?"

"Just tell me."

175

He pauses for a beat, and my stomach plummets when for a brief moment, I worry that he doesn't actually know. Maybe the number is too high. Maybe he doesn't remember because it is all a blur mixed in with alcohol and parties. A life I can't get wrapped up in.

"None."

My head jerks slightly in surprise.

"What?"

"None. Is that surprising to you?"

I just stand there, confused.

"But Jeremy said..."

"So, the *real* root of the problem," Mack says on a frustrated exhalation. "Jeremy."

He takes his hands and twists them into his hair, then down across his face in frustration and disappointment.

"Apparently I've been getting rave reviews."

His tone is slightly bitter, his eyes glassing into a frosty glare.

"What did my dear friend tell you about me?"

I swallow hard, unsure how to answer the question. Do I tell him what I've read online? What I've heard from the girls? What Jeremy has told me?

"Come on, RJ," he says, as he walks backwards and leans against his desk, crossing his arms. "You owe me a chance to hear what's been said."

I swallow hard, again, my throat dry.

"He said you slept around a lot after the accident," I finally get out. "And one time you had a threesome with strippers at the strip club in a public space."

I see the wince on his face, his embarrassment clear.

"And that you were institutionalized for a mental disorder or something, which is why you left the team in Chicago."

His head falls forward and he grabs the bridge of his nose.

"Anything else?" His words are small, his face morphed into a mixture of discomfort and frustration.

"He said you've only been in LA a few weeks and have already slept with a bunch of women."

Mack releases his nose and grips his hands against the desk he is leaning on, his eyes looking back up to mine.

"And your honest reactions to those things?"

I let out an uncomfortable laugh, shifting on my feet. When I realize I have bitten my thumbnail down too far, I quickly pull it from my mouth and grip both hands behind me.

"Honestly?" He nods. "Your past doesn't bother me, Mack. It's your present and future that matter, and I just don't see how I could ever fit into it."

He looks surprised at my response, what with how he tilts his head to the side and begins to assess me as if I am a puzzle he can't solve.

But before he can say anything to me, there's a knock on his door. I turn quickly and open it, feeling slightly flustered at being interrupted at what feels like a critical moment for both of us.

"What are *you* doing answering the door?" Gina's words are dripping with irritation.

"Gina, we were just finishing a meeting," Mack's firm response comes from behind me.

Slipping a sweet expression onto her face, she peers around me at Mack, who remains seated on the edge of his desk.

"Sorry, Coach. I'm a little early for our...," she trails off, her eyes flying to mine. "... *meeting*."

I look at Mack and have to do my best to not roll my eyes.

"I'm assuming we're done here?" I say, the nervous energy under my skin beginning to build.

Mack looks at me for a beat, his gaze hard and focused.

"We're finished for now, Ms. Jameson. But we're definitely not done."

I don't even have a moment to digest his double-meaning before Gina pipes in from beside me.

"Piss off the coach, RJ?" she whispers. "That polished look you used to have just keeps wearing down further and further."

This time I don't try to hide the roll of my eyes.

"Have a good meeting, Gina," I say clearly. "I hope you're not here to talk to Coach about starting a new juice cleanse." Her face blanches just slightly, her mouth going slack. "I hear those have been rough on you in the past."

"Fucking bitch," Gina mutters as I walk past her and down the hall.

Twenty minutes later, I'm opening my front door when a text comes through.

Mack: I meant what I said. We're not done

Me: That's very alpha-male of you and not really my style

Mack: I deserve a chance to tell you about my life from *my* perspective

I play with my phone for a few minutes, unsure of how to respond. Yes, logically he does deserve a chance to tell me about his life.

I guess.

I wouldn't want someone to go about their days assuming things about me without letting me separate fact from fiction. But what can he say that will change things?

We aren't a good fit. We're too different. We've lived very different lives with very different codes of conduct. What hope do we actually have of 'figuring things out' at this point?

Apparently, a part of me thinks there is the tiniest sliver of hope, because my response is direct and short, but eager.

Me: I'm free tonight

Chapter Fourteen

Mack and I are currently staring at each other, not saying anything.

I arrived at his house about twenty minutes ago and he has offered me something to drink three times, checked on the chicken baking in the oven twice, and has found at least a few reasons to get up and leave the room.

But now, here we sit. Just staring at each other in the small living room of the small back house he's renting from his sister.

I was surprised when I walked in, expecting it to look like the quintessential bachelor pad. White walls and dark furniture pointed at a black entertainment system with nothing personal on the walls or side tables - if there even were side tables. But I was pleasantly shocked at the warmth I felt in what was clearly a small home decorated by Amy.

The open kitchen and living room are decorated in soft colors with elegant finishes. Stainless steel appliances in the small kitchen, gorgeous granite countertops, flowers on the small wooden kitchen table. Throw pillows are on the couch, an area rug on the floor, photos of Mack and Anna at a park are on the walls, rustic wooden furniture mutes an expensive-looking TV and sound system. An open hallway in the corner leads to what I am assuming are Mack's bedroom and bathroom.

It doesn't feel like Mack just stays here. It feels like Mack *lives* here. And I like it.

But the warmth I felt at the design and style was quickly squashed by how awkward and uncomfortable our interactions have been since I've arrived. We've exchanged only a few words, and they've been so stilted and forced, so unlike any of our previous interactions. I feel like I have to say something before it gets even more awkward and uncomfortable.

"I like seeing you here," he says softly, startling me just a little bit after so much silence and staring.

"What?"

"You. In my space. I like you being here." I must look confused, because he presses on. "After our date, I thought about inviting you over here, for dinner. I was going to ask you to come over and have dinner with me, and see if I could get you to spend the night."

My breath catches just a little bit in surprise, but he either doesn't hear it or doesn't care.

"I'd already asked you to go to the Atwater game, but it was Monday morning when I sent that text, and the game wasn't until Friday night. That was too long. I've always been the guy who plays it cool or doesn't care enough to think that far ahead when it comes to the women I've... spent time with. But it was Monday and Friday was five days away and I wanted to invite you over so I could see you sooner. So I could kiss you again. So I could have you near me and wrap my arms around you, because having you against me felt so damn good."

My face and neck flush at his words, my body unable to resist reacting to some of the images that pop into my mind.

"But then you were in my office and you were my athlete and it quickly became clear that inviting you for dinner that night wasn't going to happen."

I just nod. I don't think he's said anything that warrants a response, just yet, so I settle further into the incredibly comfortable couch and curl my legs underneath me.

"But I was leveled, RJ. Literally crushed by the thought that it was over before it was ever given the chance to really begin. It made me feel out of control, and I can't... I don't know how to cope with being out of control of my life anymore. I've been there. I've felt that feeling of not knowing what's next and not knowing what decisions to make, or what's right and what's wrong. And I hate that feeling more than anything."

Well, it seems like we have one huge thing in common.

He stands up from the love seat he's been perched on and walks over to the couch where I'm sitting. He takes the seat next to me, close enough that I can feel the warmth from his body radiating towards me

I want to curl up into it and absorb everything he is.

When his hand reaches out for mine, I let him take it, threading our fingers together. I say 'let', as if I don't want him to hold my hand, but that would be a bold-faced lie. I love feeling that physical connection to him, even if it's just palm to palm.

"The reason I hate that feeling is because the last time I felt that way, I...", and then he stops.

When I look up from our entwined hands at his face, I see that he is struggling to speak. I'm not sure whether he doesn't know what to say, how to say it, or is afraid of the story he wants to tell, but I squeeze his hand once in reassurance.

I'm here, I tell him without words.

I'm not going anywhere.

He lets out a breath and untangles his fingers from mine. Before I can protest, he takes my hand and places it in his, then begins to stroke the back of it with his other hand. Soothing circles, something he did once on my wrist, although there was an innate sensuality in it last time. This time, though, it seems like he's trying to soothe himself with the slow movements.

"When I dropped out of college to join the Fire, I thought I had it made. I was barely twenty years old and I'd signed a decent contract. I suddenly had money when we didn't really have it growing up. The Fire had a reputation for being kind of a party team and I just went with it. I'd like to say that wasn't who I was, but that's a lie. I liked everything that came along with being a part of that group. I felt invincible."

His body turns towards me, but his eyes remain locked on his hands encasing mine. The crease in his brow is prominent, and I want to take my hand and touch it, knead it away with his worries and fears. Because I know he is about to talk to me about the accident, and Cherise, and everything that came after.

He's afraid to tell me.

And I don't want him to be.

"On the night of the accident... I'd found out earlier that day that Amy had been getting abused by her boyfriend. He would just... he beat the shit out of her, and he was a friend of mine. He was my *friend*. And I didn't know anything was happening!"

His voice raises pitch just slightly, his eyes finally finding mine.

"How did I not know?" he asks. But before I can respond he

dives in again.

"And when they were having a rough time, my *friend* told me all these horrible things about her and I believed him. I blamed Amy for it, and told her to figure out her shit, and she stuck it out longer, trying to change herself to be better when he was the one who was fucked up. My mom called and told me they'd broken up and I started spouting off until she told me what had really been going on. I felt like I couldn't breathe. How could I have treated her so poorly and not realized what was happening?"

He stands quickly, his words flying out. It's like a dam has been opened and he has to purge everything.

"I got completely obliterated and then got in that car. I don't even remember the accident, that's how gone I was. I remember getting in the car and then waking up in the hospital. I couldn't move. I was so fucking scared and when my mom told me about Cherise, I was just sick. It was like my body was set to this continuous state of nausea. The accident fucked up her spine and she'd never walk again. I got to walk away and she would never. Walk. Again."

He just shakes his head, his hands resting on his hips. Still so angry at himself, even though I know Cherise isn't. The love that woman has for Mack is unconditional. But he doesn't feel that way about himself. At least not right now, as he relives his past.

"It took months of physical therapy to get my leg back to rights. The Fire had the best trainers in there helping me get better."

"Wait." I interrupt. "They had trainers helping you? I thought you were released after the accident."

He finally stops his pacing at my interruption and takes a seat next to me again, but he doesn't take back my hand.

"When I was finally better, I started up with the guys again. Darren had been charged with reckless endangerment and got off with a million community service hours and a revoked license, and everyone just kind of played it off, like it didn't matter. And that started to eat at me. I knew it mattered. I knew Cherise's life had been changed forever and it was *our* fault. So… I tried to forget. I tried to lose myself in the things that made it feel better."

I shift slightly in my seat, lifting my legs and wrapping my arms around my knees. It's a defensive move. I know that. I'm pretty sure Mack knows it, too. But I can't help it, and Mack leans back against the couch, away from me, respecting that choice.

"When Jeremy said I was banging everything in sight...," he pauses, staring at the coffee table. "Well, he was saying that from the perspective of someone who didn't even really know half of what I was doing."

My stomach drops, and the blood in my body feels like it has all rushed to the space around my neck and ears. Can he be serious? Is this really...

"I had unsafe, risky sex with who knows how many women for like, six months because getting lost in someone else made me feel like my own shit didn't exist. Jeremy's story about the strip club... I'm sure it's true and there are probably a few other stories just like it. But to be entirely honest, I couldn't even ballpark for you how many women there were or talk to you about some of the crazier things. Because mixed in with that was enough liquor to black out a good portion of that stuff, and at the end, there was some drug stuff too. Nothing serious, but pain pills and anxiety meds that weren't mine."

I know all about anxiety meds and what they can do to the body. For a split second I get wrapped up in that one piece of information. As if I can ignore everything else he has said and just focus on that one statement that links us.

But he keeps talking. His breath sounds different.

Labored.

He's struggling.

"One night I was at home alone. I was alone for the first time in a long time and it just felt like... like too much. I felt like I was going out of my mind and was desperate for some semblance of normality. I was losing control of everything. I'd been confronted at the Fire for my behavior and slow recovery because I wasn't putting in the work. Amy and my parents were barely speaking to me because I was such an asshole. I didn't have any real friends or people who cared about me in my life. I had treated Amy like shit when she was getting abused and then nearly killed someone in a car accident. I just felt fucking *lost* and *worthless*. And I just wanted it all to *stop*."

In the same moment that I realize what he's telling me, I see him pull off the black band around his wrist. There, against his tan skin, is a mark a few shades darker, running about two inches on the length of his arm. My eyes widen slightly, unable to actually believe that the confident, amazing man in front of me ever felt as lost as I did. That we lived parallel existences even if our experiences were different.

"I was lucky," he says in a humorless laugh. "That's what the doctors said when I woke up strapped to a hospital bed. One of my coaches had come by my house on a whim to chat about me seeing a therapist, and apparently I'd left my front door cracked open. He came in and found me on the kitchen floor. And I happened to live five minutes from a hospital. They said I cut with intent, and most people who slice their wrists up and down bleed out too fast and don't make it. So, like I said. Lucky."

He breathes out again, this time slowly. He's tired of this story. He wants to wrap it up and move on. This is what he was talking about outside of my apartment when he drove me home, when he told me it's more painful to talk about his past than it was to experience it.

"My parents came up to Chicago and drove me out to a rehab facility in New York. I was dealing with my shit like some celebrity. It felt incredibly self-indulgent, but I knew I needed it. My guilt about Amy and the accident and Cherise. It was choking me and I couldn't breathe. I talked with them about the drinking and the meds and the women. While I was there I talked to the Fire and asked them to break my contract. I still wanted to play, but the Fire wasn't a good fit for the new lifestyle I wanted. And then when I was done at Oakhurst, I moved back in with my parents in Indiana and just kind of... existed."

He leans back against the sofa and crosses one leg over the other in that very masculine way. Ankle resting on knee, legs spread wide.

"I was at home for about six months when I finally got the courage to visit Cherise. And she was just," he blows out a breath. "She was amazing. And kind, and warm, and forgiving. And I spent about a year and a half overly involved in her kids' lives, driving up to Chicago all the time. She ended up moving to LA to be close to her mom, and I started to feel lost again. I was working at a fucking gym and I just felt like I wasn't doing anything with my life when Cherise was stuck in that damn chair. When Jeremy talked to me about the coaching job, it all lined up perfectly. I could move to LA and still help Cherise. Amy and her husband were already here and my parents always talk about retiring in Santa Barbara because they want to be involved grandparents. I thought there might be a chance I could finally turn all my shit around and get back to doing something I love in a way that wasn't destructive."

I don't realize how close we are to each other until I feel his hand reach out and tangle in mine again. He looks at our hands for a moment, then tugs it up and kisses my palm.

"I know my life was a mess at one point," he whispers, "but the man Jeremy is painting me to be is a man who was so incredibly lost that he couldn't even see the path at his feet, let alone a way out. I'm imperfect, and I'm a work-in-progress. But I'm not that lost guy anymore."

We are silent for long seconds, just staring at each other. As cliche as it sounds, it really does feel like we are falling into each others' eyes with how deeply we are wrapped into each other in this moment.

I lean forward and rest my head against his chest, my ear pressed against him so I can hear his steady heartbeat. His hands rest on my shoulder and twist into my hair, playing with the strands. I allow myself to stay like this and take just a moment to internalize what he has shared with me. And it's in that exact moment that I realize I've started falling for him, despite my aggressive attempts not to.

I lean back and look into his eyes, just inches from mine.

"So, why are you sharing all of this with me?" I finally ask.

I know my words sound immature and ignorant of a bigger picture, but I don't know how else to ask. I'm not sure what he wants from me. What outcome he sees on the other side of this mountain of a conversation.

"Cut right to the chase, don't you?" he asks with a small smile, still clutching to my hand.

When I don't respond and just continue to look at him, he finally speaks again.

"I guess I just wanted you to hear it all from my side. You can choose whatever you want, RJ. But I at least want you to make an informed decision based on facts if you're going to walk away from whatever we have. I don't want it based on Jeremy's misinformation and bullshit."

I just nod slightly. That makes sense. He's managed to answer most of the questions I would have asked had I felt the courage to do so. But I still have this unsettled feeling in my belly, as if I have a belt wrapped around me that is supposed to fit when I'm standing, but is too tight when I sit.

"So, to sum up crudely and in complete dismissal of nuance: you partied too hard, were feeling regret, got in an accident, had trouble recouping, partied harder, and then hurt yourself and had to go to rehab to work through your problems. Since then you've cared for the family you impacted, kept yourself employed, even if you were unhappy, and were able to eventually find a job that you thought would be a good first step."

"In the simplest terms, yes."

"I know I'm going to regret this question but, where does Ronnie and the bar the other night fit into all of this?" I feel his hand tense in mine. "I mean, you said you are this different person, and I think a lot of what you've talked about shows that. But Mack, the guy I saw at Smoggy Tavern looked like the guy you were just describing. He was medicating with liquor and women. I know there are plenty of people who do that and I'm not judging that behavior solely on its own. But it's something you're trying to not do, right?"

Mack's hand continues to hold mine, but his eyes are focused on the coffee table.

"I don't want to be dismissive of what you've been through. At all," I say quickly, interpreting his silence as shock at my reaction. "You lived on a roller coaster for several years and fought really hard to come back from that. I know... I know something about that. My life hasn't been all roses either. But I told you earlier that my real concerns about there ever being an 'us' have nothing to do with your past. It's all about who you are now, and who you want to be. And I just... I wonder whether who I am fits into the life you live now, even with how far you've come and how much you've grown as a person. I've had to fight tooth and nail for the life I've been able to scrape together for myself, and I'm not sure I am willing to throw in a plot twist."

Mack's eyes finally reattach to mine.

"A plot twist?"

I nod.

"You know, a character or event that changes everything. Sometimes it's just safer maintaining the status quo until you feel more secure."

Mack lights up just slightly at that statement.

"And I'm the plot twist that changes everything?"

A small smile escapes me.

"We need to work on your confidence, pretty boy."

"They're your words, not mine, RJ." His eyes bore into mine. "If you're even referring to me in those words in your mind, you have to realize that we have something here. Something special. And at the risk of sounding desperate, which is absolutely not my style, I am terrified you're going to let my one step backwards get in the way of the possibility of us moving forward."

I stand suddenly, feeling overwhelmed and unsure of what I want. His words remind me of CC's theory about relationships. How one person is brave enough to move forward and then reaches back and tries to encourage the other to follow. I wonder what she would say about times when someone takes a step back.

But right now, I have this beautiful, smart, warm man in front of me practically begging me to throw all of my eggs into his basket. He's wanting me to ignore what I saw last night with Ronnie, ignore the risks we face, and just run to him with open arms.

And I'm not sure I can do it

"Why are you running from this?"

I look over at Mack from where I stand at the window, feeling thrown off kilter by his statement.

"What do you mean?"

Mack shakes his head slightly.

"I mean that I can see you battling with yourself over there. I've seen you at war with your mind since the moment we found out I was your coach. Maybe even before that. I feel like you are trying to scramble away from us, like we are some combustible thing..."

"But we are!" I shout, interrupting him and startling myself slightly in the process.

I lower my volume, not wanting to be a crazy chick who screams when she's frustrated.

"We *are* combustible, Mack, don't you see? We have the capability to hurt people, and hurt ourselves, and change the course of what we want out of life. Does that not bother you?"

I curl my hands into balls, my breathing becoming labored.

"How can you not see the worst case scenario here? I could be kicked out of school, lose my scholarship, have nowhere to go when I have no way to take care of myself. I'd have to go back to... I'd have to go find some dead end job and live on food stamps."

My eyes start to well up, and I can feel the actual fear of these things coursing through my veins, lighting up my skin with a blaze of goosebumps. My heart pumps fast and fierce, my body feeling like it's heating from my chest outward.

"And you! You could be fired and never coach again when you're just starting to find your way out of the darkness. And that's just individually. What about together?"

I slam my eyes shut as I fight the tears that are trying to escape.

"I can't be strong for you, Mack. I'm too busy trying to be strong for *me*, and to get past my *own* shit and what happened to me. I can't be what you want, or the type of woman you normally look for, or what makes you happy. What happens if I give all of who I am to you and find out later I'm just a throwaway too!?"

The silence that follows my verbal outpouring is deafening. And as my mind rewinds and replays what I said, I feel the color drain from my face.

"What happened to you?" His voice is barely louder than a whisper, and I know the look on his face will be one I don't want to see, so I don't look.

I just stand there and say nothing.

"You said... you had to be strong for yourself. Because of what happened to you."

He says his words slowly, like he's turning them over in his head, trying to figure out any possible meaning behind what I said.

"What happened to you?"

Suddenly, my world shifts and I have to lean forward and brace my hands on the windowsill to steady myself. My breathing stutters and stops and starts as I gasp for breath because I feel like every item in this room is piled on top of me, holding me to the floor as my lungs claw for air.

Strong arms come around me, picking me up and carrying me somewhere. But I fight at the embrace, as I try to inhale something. Anything.

"... for me, Rachel, just breathe for me."

A hand slowly rubs my back as I curl onto my side and struggle, struggle, struggle to take any beloved oxygen into my body.

"Come on. It's just you and me. Just take a breath for me, sweetheart"

And suddenly I inhale deeply, the blurring on the edges of my eyes receding. I inhale again in a large gasp, my body scrambling for every last bit of air it can take in.

"That's it, Rachel. You're going to be fine."

Inhale. Exhale.

My mind feels fuzzy after my anxiety attack, and my body has broken out into a light sweat that is now chilling my skin. My eyes well with tears as I realize I've had my first full blown attack in years, and I hate that I allowed myself to get to a point where I wasn't able to calm myself down.

But I notice something different. Something that doesn't normally happen when I come down from an attack. I find myself wrapped in a warm cocoon, against a hard body, with the scent and feel of safety hitting each of my senses.

I burrow deeper into the warmth, reveling in the security I feel in Mack's arms. After a few minutes has passed and I feel like my heart has finally slowed and my breathing has returned to normal, I move my head slightly until I'm looking directly into Mack's eyes. We are snuggled together on our sides, our faces inches from each other, as Mack rubs my back in slow, steady circles.

"You would never be that to me, RJ," Mack whispers, his gaze combing my features. "You could never, in a million years, be throwaway."

He leans forward slightly, and presses his lips to my forehead, then my temple, and my entire body finally releases into a puddle wrapped in his arms as I let go of the final piece of tension and anxiety left over from my attack.

We lay wrapped in each other for who knows how long.

It's safe. It's warm.

My heart rate picks up and calms at the same time. And his hand never slows on my back. Not even when his phone rings.

And rings.

And rings.

Not even when there's a knock on the door.

But ignoring it doesn't do either of us any good when the door just opens and I hear her.

"Mack, what are you doing?"

His hand stills, and when my eyes dart to his face, I see him staring above my head at the front door.

"I thought we had *plans* for tonight."

And the way she said plans, I have a very clear picture of

what she means.

I know Mack feels me tense in his arms, and I can simultaneously feel him struggle with whether or not to hold me tighter or let me go.

"Don't worry, Ronnie, I was just leaving." I say, pulling myself out of Mack's arms, righting myself and standing too quickly.

Mack reaches out to brace me, but I lean on the edge of the couch instead, shying away from his hands.

"RJ, you shouldn't go anywhere right now. You need more time to calm down. You could get in an accident." His tone is desperate, and I can only imagine what he's thinking.

I shake my head, pushing away from the couch as I find my balance.

"I'll sit in my car for a few minutes and if I don't feel better I'll call Jeremy."

I walk briskly to the door, grabbing my purse from the table next to it.

"RJ, we still need to talk about..."

"About *what*, Mack?" I respond, not looking at him as I dig through my purse for my keys.

All of the calm and serenity I felt in his arms just a moment ago has faded, replaced by my own insecurity.

"About the fact I just embarrassed myself by having a full blown panic attack for the first time in two years? About the fact that you and I have no business being anywhere near each other because we keeping saying and doing stupid shit?"

I pause as I see Ronnie shuffling back and forth in the doorway out of the corner of my eye. I look to Mack, my eyes probably watery, my body exhausted, my mind a mess.

"Or about how you *double booked* for tonight?"

His eyes widen slightly as I turn and storm past Ronnie, barreling through the yard between his house and Amy's.

I think I hear him call my name once, but then I hear the door to his house slam closed and I keep moving towards the street, my steps never faltering.

*   *   *   *   *

I'm not surprised when I'm snuggled into pajamas, staring

blankly at the TV, and I hear a knock at the door. When a minute goes by and a knock comes again without the slightest move from me, Charlie glances at me for a second before pausing the movie and walking to the door. I hear it open, I hear murmuring for a few minutes, and then I hear the door close just as quietly as it was opened.

But I *am* surprised when Charlie returns and takes a seat next to me, pressing play and continuing on as if nothing happened.

I look at her for a full minute before she finally looks back at me.

"What?" she asks.

"Who was at the door?"

She rolls her eyes.

"You know who it was. Don't play games."

My brow furrows in frustration.

"What are you talking about?"

Charlie re-pauses the movie and turns to face me, her legs crossing in front of her on the couch.

"You weren't going to answer it because you want him to sit out there and suffer because you think he did something wrong."

"You don't even know what happened! You don't know if he *did* do something wrong!"

"Exactly!"

She doesn't shout the word at me, but it comes out like a whip, cracking into the space between us.

"If something horrible had happened, you would have told me. But you walked in here and plopped down next to me to watch this stupid sports documentary, and you *hate* documentaries by the way, like nothing was wrong. So I think whatever is going on now is *your* fault, not his."

I feel the blood rush to my face in anger, but I can't seem to form a sentence in response. Is she right? Am I the one that messed up?

Charlie must see something shift in my face because her expression softens. She adjusts herself so she is sitting right next to me, her arm wrapped around my shoulders.

"No one is perfect, Rach. Being in a relationship is hard work. Sometimes you're the one to forgive, and sometimes you're the one being forgiven. But no matter what, both people have to want the same outcome for it to really work."

She leans away from me so she can see straight into my

eyes.

"That man has done nothing but fight for you. I won't pretend to know all the details. I won't try to make you believe that he hasn't done anything wrong, because I don't honestly know. But from the moment I saw you two together it was clear what he wanted. It's important that you figure out what you want, too."

We sit there for a minute staring at each other without speaking when I finally figure out what to say.

"And if I don't know what I want?"

She gives me a soft smile.

"That's the beauty of being an adult, RJ. Sometimes you have to make the hard decisions based on just the information you have. Take that organized brain of yours and scan through the information you have about Mack, about you, about the life you lead, and the future you want. And then decide. Is he what you want?"

I sink into the couch and think on her words for a few minutes as she goes back to her movie.

I run through the list of cons. The things standing in our way. My concerns. But when I get to the end of that list, all I can think about is the way that I felt in Mack's arms just an hour ago as he calmed me and talked me through my anxiety attack. That feeling of safety, like nothing I've ever known before.

But even though I have all those warm feelings towards him, and I knew earlier that I was beginning to fall for him, is it fair for me to try and be in a relationship? After I've been so hot and cold with Mack from day one?

"And you may want to pop out and let him know once you figure it out because I may have told him to chill outside and wait for you," Charlie suddenly blurts out.

My face snaps to her calculating and very pleased smile. After a very small internal cuss-fest, I slowly stand from the couch and make my way to the door, taking a deep breath and releasing it before reaching for the handle and stepping out to the front patio.

Mack sits on the stoop with his elbows on his knees, his chin resting in his steepled fingers.

I clear my throat once. Twice.

"Sorry you were out here so long," I finally manage. "Charlie didn't say you were still here until just a minute ago."

He doesn't say anything, so I step forward and sit next to

him, wrapping my arms around my flannel covered legs.

Just as I'm about to ask why he's here, I look up at his face and I'm startled by the look of sadness that has overwhelmed his features.

"This isn't going to work."

The words are out of his mouth for a good thirty seconds before I'm able to respond. And it takes every ounce of strength in my body to ask him this simple question in a way that is calm and collected.

"What do you mean?"

He exhales and drops his hands, grabbing my left with his right and twisting our fingers together.

"Us. We aren't going to work, are we."

It isn't a question. It's a statement. And I am shocked at the level of devastation that travels from the ears that received the words, to my brain that digests them, to my heart that breaks at their meaning.

"I can't try to be in a relationship with someone who doesn't see the same things that I do."

"What do..."

"Why did you storm out of my house earlier when Ronnie showed up?"

I shrug slightly.

"I was upset. I reacted. She was clearly there for your *plans*."

My reply is laced with sarcasm and tinged with bitterness.

"*My* plans," he says, more to himself than to me. "You really think that little of me? You think I would invite you over to talk about my past and the pain I experienced, with the plan of fucking Ronnie after you left?"

The disbelief in his tone hurts my heart, but it's the acceptance I hear that kills me. He can't believe that I would think so poorly of him, but at the same time he's already accepted the idea that I do. My mind is racing, trying to come up with a way to tell him what I really think. But the words I play in my head don't sound right, because in all honesty, I'm not entirely sure what I think.

Do I think he would intentionally hurt me? No. Definitely not. But do I think he is capable of 'double booking,' as I so eloquently put it earlier? Maybe. And that's a hard thing to realize. Because it says more about me than it says about him.

"I have a hard time trusting people," I finally say, my words

193

barely a whisper. "Sometimes it's just easier to believe the worst than to give someone the benefit of the doubt."

"Why?"

I shrug again, hating how immature it makes me look.

"I'm used to the people in my life letting me down. If I don't rely on anyone, that won't happen. If I believe they'll let me down from the start, the sting isn't so bad when it inevitably happens."

"I swear that you are both the most and least self-aware person I've ever met. Sometimes you say things that make it so clear that you know who you are and what you want, that you've made life choices based on intentional decisions and well thought out plans. And then there are other times where you seem so clueless and so clearly ignorant about why you do things."

I scoff and pull my hand from his.

"Excuse me?"

"You ever think that you might shut people out because of your dad?"

And that gets my back up. I stand quickly.

"I am *not* talking about this."

"Why not, Rachel?" he says, rising to block me before I can storm into the house. "Why won't you talk to me about this? You have a fucked up dad who ruined the way you see men? No one would blame you for that! It's actually a very common problem and you can probably find heaps of information online about it. But you can't just continue to shut people out when things aren't perfect. You have to talk about it."

I try to push past him to get the door and he side steps, blocking me again, placing his hands on my arms and holding me still.

"You have to talk about your panic attacks. You have to talk about whatever happened to you when you were in high school that you keep locked up tight. And you have to talk about why you're so quick to believe the worst in a man who is falling in love with you!"

I freeze.

He leans towards me slightly, catching my eyes that are stuck wide open at his admission.

"I don't know how many times I can tell you that I am crazy about you for you to believe me. I don't know what I can do to prove to you that *you* are what I want, and that what we have is worth risking everything for." He drops his hands. "But I can't be the only person who is willing to take risks, RJ. I want to be with someone who is willing to take a risk on me, too."

When I look up at him, I see that same sadness in his eyes that was there when he first arrived ten minutes ago.

He straightens, though. Resolve wipes the sadness from his face.

"And I don't think you're there yet. Whatever it is you need to work through, I get that. We all have our baggage. But if we aren't at the same place, we can't move forward together, RJ."

His words are again so similar to CC's from just a few days ago, and my heart tumbles over itself. He leans forward and kisses my forehead, his hands resting softly on my neck. I close my eyes at the tears that are brimming to the surface, as his breath whispers over my skin.

And I don't open them again until he's gone.

Chapter Fifteen

I wander through the next few days in an absolute haze. Laundry, grocery shopping, homework. I go to practice on Monday and Tuesday, and I spend the majority of time away from Mack, working in the gym with the other keepers. I attend classes, work on my projects, play a game against Santa Barbara.

And I clean.

Charlie's on her semester break due to the strange nursing program schedule, which makes things even worse. She watches me wander around the apartment in the evenings dusting this and scrubbing that.

She knew something was wrong over the weekend when I came inside after talking to Mack, my eyes glassy, and curled up next to her on the couch. I didn't say anything to her as she stroked her hands through my hair and continued to watch her movie. She didn't ask me any questions, which I greatly appreciated. Sometimes a girl just needs to be alone with her thoughts, but not alone.

Compound my behavior that night with the fact I've been roaming the house like a cross between a zombie and a maid, and I know her concern is growing.

I hate cleaning.

"Okay, that's enough," I hear her say from behind me.

I look back at her from my position on my knees in front of the oven. I'm drenched in sweat, my hands covered in some weird oven cleaning foam, and my back aches. So as much as I don't want to have whatever conversation is finally coming my way, my body readily accepts the mini-break it receives.

"I don't want to talk about it, Char," I say, wiping my forehead against the sleeve of my shirt.

"But you're cleaning. *Cleaning.* Like a crazy person." She shakes her head. "I don't know whether to shake you or thank you, but I can't let you just keep going. It has been almost four days."

I let out a light huff of laughter, but I don't respond. I just remain with my knees on the floor, resting on my heels, the silence stretching on between us.

"What happened?"

I sigh.

"He called things off."

She says nothing. When I look up at her, her face is contorted in confusion.

"Wait. I'm lost. What?"

I close the oven door and turn it on, allowing the heat to do the rest of the work. Standing and walking to the sink, I replay the conversation at my door last night.

"He told me he was willing to take a risk on me, but I wasn't willing to take a risk on him. And since I'm not ready, we aren't going to work."

I scrub my hands clean, drying them on the towel folded neatly next to the sink, then refolding it and putting it back into place.

"And the thing that kills me, is that he's right." I look over at Charlie. "I'm not willing to take the risk."

"You're just saying that because you're scared of feeling something..."

"I know what I'm feeling Char," I interrupt. "I'm sad, true. I'm crazy about him, yes. But I also know that he and I are a huge, huge mistake. We are too different, and we have too much against us. I could be kicked off the team and lose my scholarship and..."

"Would you cut the shit about the team and the scholarship!?"

My head jerks back at her sudden increase in volume, the exasperation evident on her face.

"You are one hundred percent using those as excuses, and it's bullshit."

"Excuse me?"

"You heard me." She takes a step towards me, her expression full of frustration. "You have this amazing guy who wants to be with you *so* badly. Yes, you could lose your scholarship and get kicked off the team. But you don't think that a man willing to risk his job for you would be willing to help you come up with a solution? Maybe he'd be willing to wait a few months? Have you even opened up the possibility of keeping your hands off each other until May? Didn't you two clear the air after you pretended to want to go on a date with Thomas?"

I shake my head. "It's not that simple."

"Why? "

"It just isn't."

"Why!?"

I continue to shake my head, hoping she'll drop it. But she just stands there watching me, waiting for me to reveal something to her.

"You don't know what it's like," I whisper. "I can't go home if I fail. I can never go back there."

"I know, sweetheart." Her tone, so placating, sets me off.

"No you don't!" I shout. "You have NO idea what I went through."

"Well I would if you would ever tell me!" She looks at me across the kitchen, her arms folded. "I've known you for over three years. We are *best* friends. I have told you the most ridiculous, embarrassing and crazy things that have happened to me. I've told you all of the stupid shit I've done. But there is some big secret that you keep hidden away, some secret from your past that you don't want anyone to know."

"Why is it wrong to keep some secrets?" I ask.

"It isn't wrong to keep things to yourself. But I feel like there's something going on in your mind and heart that is unresolved, and talking about it can help. I watch you live every day without really living. You are friendly and at the same time you are so closed off with people. But I have *never* seen you glow like you did when you met Mack."

I scoff.

"It's true!" She shouts again. "Even after you found out he was your coach, it was like your soul was lighter. You were practically flitting around the apartment."

"I don't flit anywhere," I respond.

She gives me a small smile, and I can feel the tension begin to dissolve.

"Oh, you flitted. All over this bitch, you were flitting and floating."

I smile.

"You know I love you, right?" she asks. I nod once. "I would never, ever try to make you tell me about your past if you didn't want to tell me. I get it. But have you ever talked to anyone? I mean, professionally?"

I nod again.

"I saw a therapist after..."

"Good. Do you feel like you should go back? Like, maybe there are still some things to work through?"

I sigh.

"Maybe. I just... I would have to talk to Jeremy about it, and ask for his help. I used up all of the free sessions Glendale provides to students, which is why I stopped going."

I cross my arms and lean onto the kitchen island.

"I just know he will want to know why I want to see a therapist, and I don't know if I'm ready to tell him."

She reaches across and places her hand on my arm.

"I know you're protective of your secrets, RJ, and there's nothing wrong with that. But you might feel a lot better if you finally let someone help you carry them."

*   *   *   *   *

I've never had a practice as brutal as today's. And it had nothing and everything to do with Mack.

Rain was pouring down hard and thick, the field covered in mud. And it seemed like none of us had our heads on straight. We weren't working as a team, and to be honest, I felt completely useless during my drills. I kept slipping. I kept throwing my body in the wrong direction.

I kept watching Mack.

And he didn't look at me once.

I should have been happy. He was trying to make it easy, either on himself or on me. But it was still miserable to go from avoiding eye contact because I didn't want everyone to know I kissed my coach, to desperately seeking eye contact as some sort of validation that he was feeling as torn apart as I felt.

But like I said, he didn't look at me once.

"Well that was the worst practice ever," Piper mumbles as we change in the locker room.

I give her a small smile.

"Yeah, we've seen better days."

"Plans for the weekend?" she asks as she begins to unbraid her long hair.

"Jeremy and I are gonna see a movie or something," I respond as I chuck my cleats and practice gear into my duffle.

I called him yesterday and asked if he was free tonight. Normally he's traveling or has plans on a Friday night, but he just so happened to be free. Serendipitous.

"Sounds like fun. I wish I had an older sibling who wanted to take me out all the time," she grumbles with a smile.

I laugh, say bye to the girls, then sprint from the locker rooms to the awning in front of the stadium to wait for Jeremy. And as I sit on the benches out front and wait, I replay in my mind what I'm going to say.

I've thought about it for two solid days, whether or not to talk to him about what happened in high school. I got shit sleep last night and woke up cranky after allowing my brain and emotions to wind up and up and up. And when I finally dragged my ass out of bed, I thought about it during my conditioning this morning, during class this afternoon, and when I got back home and began working on my Psych paper.

Now that I'm waiting for him to pick me up, I know that I'm making the right choice, no matter what happens. If I've decided I need his help, it isn't fair to ask for it without being completely honest.

Two short honks have me grabbing my bag off the ground and ducking my head low as I sprint through the rain to where he sits in his SUV.

"I'm glad you called about getting together," he says as he shifts the car into drive.

"Me too. It's important we make sure to spend enough time together."

He stays silent for a moment, but then makes a right out of the lot.

"I didn't know if you were still mad about Friday."

I roll my eyes and twirl my phone in my hand.

"Just because you were a dick doesn't mean I'm going to stop talking to you."

"I'll address the 'you were a dick' comment later. We hitting

Mama Sita's?"

I nod.

"Yeah."

Mama Sita's is a popular Southern California burrito chain with a spot about two miles from my house.

"Do you mind if we drive through and head back to the apartment though? There's something important I want to talk to you about."

When I get nothing but silence, I turn to look at Jeremy and catch his eyes locked on mine, his face showing an almost grave concern.

"Why can't you just tell me now?"

"Because I want us to be at home. It's important."

"Yeah, I got that. Just tell me now."

"Jeremy, stop. I'll tell you in a bit."

"Are you pregnant?"

"What!?"

"Are you?"

I can't believe he would even... ugh!

I can feel the blood rushing to my face, demonstrating in a more than obvious way how angry his question makes me. My fists clench and I glare right back at him.

"When did you become this person who always jumps to conclusions about me? Can't I have just normal sister-brother stuff to talk about? Does it always have to be that I've fucked up in some way?"

Jeremy sighs.

"Sorry. I'm just on edge today."

I cross my arms and continue to throw daggers at him with my eyes.

"Well I don't give a shit. I don't know *what* has happened to our mojo in the past few weeks, but I feel like I barely know you anymore. You hardly speak to me, and when you do, you're either angry or making huge assumptions."

"Rachel, I said..."

"And even more frustrating is that it feels like you don't know *me* anymore, either. When did I become this person that you think so poorly of? Why can't you believe in me? It's like everything that comes out of your mouth is tailor-made to make me feel like shit."

Jeremy sighs again, but we don't speak, apart from ordering, until we pull into my apartment's parking lot.

As he sets his food on the counter, I can see him moving his mouth, talking to himself. It makes my mouth tick up in a half smile. Jeremy's always done that. It makes him look a little bit crazy, but none of the good ones are sane anyways.

"I'm sorry my faith in you isn't what it used to be," he finally says, pulling out my burrito and setting it on the counter in front of me.

"I just don't understand why," I reply. "We've always been so close. What happened?"

Jeremy turns and opens the fridge, pulling out a bottle of Coke. When he turns back around, his face is like granite.

"I just have some personal stuff going on. I'll tell you one day, but not today."

He plops the bottle onto the counter and grabs two glasses.

"Today, we talk about you. What's going on?"

My stomach drops and I feel like I'm starting to lose my breath. My skin goes instantly clammy and warm at the same time. I know the signs of an anxiety attack looming in the distance, and luckily this isn't it.

I take a deep breath, resolving myself to what's about to happen as I try and blurt things out in chunks so I can get it all out.

This is going to be hard. And it's made even harder by the fact that Jeremy is still looking at me with that same face, the one that says he's really worried. And I know this is going to be just as hard for him as it is for me.

"Well…" I clear my throat, trying to remember what I wanted to say but drawing a blank. "Sorry, this is hard. Uhm…"

"You're making me nervous, Rach. Whatever it is, just rip off the bandaid."

"Okay." I shake out my arms, trying to loosen the tension that has taken over my body. "I'm wondering if I can borrow some money so I can go back to therapy."

Jeremy's head jerks back.

"Therapy? Why?"

"I just… have some things I need to work through."

"And you can't talk to me about it? I can give you some advice."

I shake my head.

"I appreciate that, I do. But this isn't about getting advice. This is something I need to do. For me."

He pauses, surveying me, like he's trying to figure it out

without me saying anything.

"Wait. You said *back* to therapy."

I nod.

"Yeah."

"When did you go before?"

"Freshman year until the middle of sophomore year, but I ran out of free sessions so I stopped going because I can't afford it."

God, getting out that entire sentence was like trying to sing a note when you're out of breath, so you just push on and your voice begins to sound thinner.

Jeremy slowly unwraps his burrito, his eyes focused on the task.

"And you can't talk to me about it? I mean, I'll give you the money, no problem. I'm always here to help you. But if you're going through something I want to be able to help, you know?"

I pick at my own burrito, struggling to get the words out.

"It just has to do with... dad."

"What about dad?"

"Just some stuff from senior year."

Jeremy stops chewing on the bite he just inhaled, swallowing loudly.

"Did something happen?" At my silence, he prods again. "Rachel, if something happened..."

We stand in silence, staring at each other.

"Please tell me."

His voice is a whisper, and I know I have to tell him. I can't protect him from this truth anymore.

I let out a rush of breath.

"After you left... he... got worse."

"What did he do?"

"God. He... he called me names. Which I know sounds like no big deal, but hearing him call me a whore and worthless and a fucking dyke on a daily basis was... I don't know. And it wasn't just that. He started hitting me."

"Rachel..."

"He slapped and choked and punched and kicked. Over and over. For three years."

Jeremy leans over and braces himself on the counter, his face white.

"It got so bad that I..." I stop, my stomach twisting at the idea of revealing my darkness to Jeremy. "I tried to kill myself."

"Oh my god," he whispers, before he awkwardly folds in on himself and sits on the floor, his back to the cabinets.

I fly around the island and wrap my arms around him. At first he's almost limp in my arms, but then he clings to me, so tight, so close, like he can banish away anything harmful or hurtful if he holds me tight enough.

"Rachel I'm so sorry."

We stay like that, holding each other, for ages. Jeremy whispering apologies, both of us emotional and upset.

"I'll give you anything you need. You need therapy, I'll cover it. You need to go to the gym to beat the shit out of a bag, I'll take you."

I let out a half laugh through my tears.

"Thanks, Jer."

He pulls back and looks at me.

"How did I not know? I could have..."

But I shake my head, almost violently.

"You didn't know because I didn't tell you. I hid it. It's not your fault."

Jeremy wraps his arms around me again, holding me close as we sit on the kitchen floor. After a few minutes of silence, just as I'm about to get up, he speaks again.

"I should have known something was wrong."

"No, Jer..."

"I should have known!" he almost shouts. "I could see you were more withdrawn every time I came home. I could see you were thinner, and unhappy. You always looked a little more pale. And that one time I saw bruising and you said it was..." he can barely choke out the words, "... it was from practice. It was that asshole beating you! I knew something was wrong but I was so wrapped up in my own shit I didn't even notice!"

"I promise you," I whisper, "I promise you that this is not your fault. I did everything I could to keep you from knowing."

"Why?"

I shrug.

"I didn't want to burden you. You were finally free and I didn't want to add to..."

"Seriously?"

I just sit and stare at the floor, unsure how to answer when I know he won't want to hear it.

"You are never a burden, Rachel. Never. Not ever." I can feel the sting of tears again at his words. "You are the best thing in my life, Rach."

"But I didn't want to risk you being on his side."

The words are out of my mouth before I can stop them and I slap my hand over my mouth like a cartoon. I can't believe I just said that out loud, and when I look up at Jeremy, his face is enraged, mortified, astounded.

"You think..." he braces his head with his hands, "... you think I could ever... *ever*... believe you deserved anything like that?"

I'm shaking my head as he's speaking, already trying to reassure him.

"Not now I don't. But I was 15 when it started getting really bad. I was alone and had no one to talk to. I just had dad telling me how worthless I was. Blaming me for everything. Telling me you hated me and thought it was such a waste of time to see me when you came home."

I blink back tears, trying to explain to the person who has always been there for me what the thought of losing him did to me.

"I was worried you'd agree with him, and then I'd be *completely* alone, because I wouldn't even have the thought of you."

Jeremy's head drops back against the cabinet behind him and he stares at the ceiling, collecting his thoughts.

"I know that's not true now," I continue. "I had a really great therapist at the College Counseling Center. She helped me work through a lot, see how he abused and manipulated me to satisfy something inside of him that has nothing to do with me. But now, I have other things to work on."

"Like what?"

I let out a small, humorless chuckle.

"Like actually believing I'm worth something. Knowing it's true because I've had a conversation with a therapist, and believing it's true deep in my very bones? Those are two separate things." I clear my throat. "And I have a hard time opening up to people... to guys... and I want to be able to."

When we connect eyes again, I know he sees it.

He can see that while, yes, most of this is going to be for me, some of it is for Mack.

"He's in love with me," I whisper, finally letting the tears stream down my face. "He's in love with me and I don't know if I'm even capable of loving someone back. And I don't know how to fix it on my own."

He wants to say something about Mack. Lessen his value to me, assure me I don't need him. But he stops himself.

Instead, he does exactly what a big brother should.

"Whatever you need, Rach. I'm here."

*   *   *   *   *

I can't fall asleep when I try to that night, so I open the laptop my brother gifted me for my high school graduation and look up Mack's Facebook page.

I haven't looked at it since the day I found out he was my coach, and when I go to it I see not much has changed. No status updates. No photos. Nothing.

But when I click on the box on the bottom right, I see a little green dot next to his name that lets me know he's online.

I waver for a moment after opening up the tiny chat box, wondering what I'm doing. But ultimately I can't help myself.

Me: Are you there?

The marker pops up letting me know he's seen the message, and for a brief second the little bubbles glow on the screen to indicate he's responding.

But then they disappear.

And the little green dot disappears too.

I sit blankly staring at the screen. He closed his computer or his app to ignore me. My heart drops.

But for some reason I don't let that deter me, and I end up sending one message after another in rapid succession.

Me: I'm sorry.

Me: I'm sorry for thinking the worst of you time after time when you've done nothing to actually deserve it.

Me: You said you're falling in love with me and I don't even know if I can love someone back. But I'm not sure how to fix it.

Me: And I don't know whether you think I'm worth the time it would take. To wait for me to figure out what's broken in my mind and my heart.

Me: But you should know that I'm going to try and figure it out. I'm gonna try to work through a few things.

Me: And in the end, no matter what happens between us... even though I hope it's something good... thank you for showing me that not everyone lets you down. And that sometimes you can meet someone who's worth the risk.

I sit silently and re-read the things I've written. The words sound stiff and formal, but they're honest and real. I can only hope I've conveyed how I really feel in a way that resonates with him.

I close my laptop, switch off my light, and crawl under the covers.

And this time I fall straight to sleep.

*   *   *   *   *

When I wake up the next morning, I stumble through my routine. I eat my banana, drink my orange juice, and throw my hair up into a messy bun.

I race back up the stairs to grab my phone off the nightstand, and stop short when I see what's on the screen.

Mack: You're worth the wait.

And my face breaks into a smile I can't contain for the rest of the day.

Chapter Sixteen

The next few days pass without much incident.

I go to work and chat with CC about insignificant things, even though I know she wants to push and talk about the day I stormed out of work.

I get together with Piper to work on our Psychology papers and we head to the tutoring center together to get some help.

I email back and forth with Thomas as we push forward on our joint project.

He doesn't mention our failed date and neither do I.

I visit the College Counseling Center and book in an appointment with Regina, the same woman I met with before. She's actually in the waiting room chatting with the receptionist when I get there and greets me by name, letting me know she's happy to see I'm back and looking forward to meeting again.

I go to practice and conditioning.

I see Mack.

We don't speak. But unlike Friday, our eyes linger. I feel like hope and fear and confusion radiate from both of us.

It's encouraging to feel like I'm not alone in this.

*　　*　　*　　*　　*

"Rachel, can I see you for a minute?"

I hop up from where I'm stretching on the grass and jog

over to where Coach Johnson is standing on the sidelines.

"What's up Coach J?" I ask, trying not to pay attention to how close I am to Mack, who stands just a few feet away looking at his clipboard.

Coach Johnson sticks out his clipboard and places a whistle down on top of it.

"It's time to start this practice coordination Coach McIntosh has been talking about nonstop for the past few weeks. He says you're eager, so I'm assuming you're ready to go?"

My mouth hangs open. I'd completely forgotten that Mack talked to me about this. About coaching my fellow teammates.

"I, uhh… I don't…" I feel like a bumbling idiot, unable to form thoughts.

No, I want to say. *No, I'm* not *ready to go*.

"McIntosh, I thought you said you'd discussed this?" Coach J says, looking over at Mack, who I realize is no longer looking at his own clipboard and is instead looking at us.

"Give us a sec?" Mack waves me over to him, and then leads me a few feet away. "I thought we'd talked about this, RJ. I wanted to give you a chance to coach so you could get some experience under your belt."

My voice comes out whiny and panicked. So mature.

"We talked about it but I didn't know when it was gonna start! I don't feel ready at all!"

"Take a deep breath and look at me," he says.

When I look into Mack's eyes, I see a confidence I don't feel. I see a trust that I don't think I deserve. And I see someone who believes in me implicitly, even if I'm struggling to always believe in myself.

"Have you been watching tape when you're supposed to and do you feel prepared to play Long Beach on Friday?"

"Yes."

"And you've been listening to Coach J and myself sharing our strategy for the game, reviewing Long Beach's strengths and weaknesses?"

"Yes."

"What did I say two weeks ago that I wanted the offensive players to work really hard on, because there are several teams coming up who have issues with the same thing?"

"You said you wanted them to work on set pieces because Santa Barbara, Long Beach and a few of the teams at the upcoming tournaments are weak at defending their goal from corner kicks and penalty kicks. Piper said the girls were having some issues, though, and that the practices aren't going so well."

Mack chuckles slightly.

"You're ready to go, RJ. Just don't forget what you said to me right now, and you'll do fine."

He gives me a slight push on the shoulder, sending me back over to Coach J. I'll be honest, I don't feel a whole lot more confident now than I did when Mack pulled me aside. But at least I have a tiny idea of what I can do to coach the offense today.

Set pieces.

Things start off slow and definitely awkward. The team has already had a change in coaching structure and style with Mack coming in mid-season, so there's some obvious resistance to my leadership at first, especially from Gina. Which doesn't surprise me. I feel like my instructions are stilted, even when I'm directing them in a simple warm up drill to practice handling balls that have been kicked high.

Piper, Erin, Kristal and some of the girls I've played with for several years are quick to be supportive, though, and by the time I tap Piper to do corner kicks instead of Gina, who huffs as she stands observing with her water bottle, I feel a lot more confident in what I'm doing. It helps when I realize I've provided a piece of feedback to one of the girls and Coach J says, "Good eyes on that, Rachel."

Maybe I'm not completely useless at this.

When Mack takes over from me about ninety minutes into our two hour practice, I feel an energy coursing through me that I don't normally get when I play. Just the short period of time I spent 'coaching' made it feel like I was looking at the field and the players in a completely new way. Like they were chess pieces and if I had the right strategy they'd be fine.

"Great job, RJ!" Piper says as we change after practice.

"God, I was so fucking nervous," I reply, taking a seat on the floor and leaning back against the lockers. "Was it really okay? Be honest."

"It was a bullshit practice," Gina spits from my left, "and Piper only liked it because you threw your minion a bone by letting her practice set pieces with the starters."

"Why are you such a bitch all the time, Gina? It's important for everyone to practice in case someone gets injured. That's literally the *reason* teams have more than just starters," Kristal snarks back.

"Fuck off, Kristal. Saying that your roll on this team matters over and over again doesn't mean you're gonna get to play any time soon. Your goalkeeping is as nasty as your face."

"Uncalled for, Gina," I say standing up. "Your toxic attitude is a waste of space on this team. You should focus more on teamwork and caring about the other women you play with. It might help with *your* resting bitch face."

The rest of the girls make 'ooooooooh' noises, but I quickly snip at them to focus on changing and getting home, and leave the locker room still in my workout gear.

I need to talk to Coach J about Gina. Having a hateful, bitter player on the team that says nasty things to teammates, completely unprovoked, does nothing for team morale.

A change needs to be made, and after watching their practice today, I have just the suggestion to make that can hopefully move us in a more positive direction.

*   *   *   *   *

About a week later I find myself jogging on the treadmill at the athletic center reflecting on my most recent meeting with Regina.

I've gone to twice-weekly therapy appointments since I talked to Jeremy about returning. It's going really well, and I love that I get to meet with Regina again. She never holds anything back. In our third session, she was quick to point out that I wasn't being entirely honest about my reasons for going back to counseling.

When I finally admitted that I had fallen for a guy and was struggling to figure things out, she gave me that slow nod therapists give you, internalizing the information, and then moved on to discuss Jeremy and my dad. But I knew it wouldn't be that easy. We revisited the conversation about Mack in the fourth session, which was this morning.

"We've talked a lot about your relationship with your dad and brother over the past few sessions, but today I want to talk

about you and this young man you've been seeing. Mack. You've said repeatedly that you don't know how to make it work. What does that mean?" she asked me.

I knew I couldn't tell her that he was my coach. I could be honest with her about everything except for that.

"Well... I guess I just keep waiting for him to do or say something that my dad would. And I know that's not fair to him, but it's how I'm wired. Jeremy's the only man in my life that I trust implicitly. His motivations are clear. With Mack, I'm just not so sure."

"What about his motivations is a concern to you?"

I had to pause at that and really thing before I gave her an example.

"He has a really good heart, and he's so handsome and kind," I started, thinking about how Mack had refocused his life and tried to do right by Cherise. "But he has a really... dark past. Drugs and sex and drinking to really unsafe levels... anything to numb himself from some of the stuff he went through."

"I'm assuming you know this because he's talked to you about it?"

I nodded.

"Yeah, he sat me down and basically shared his whole history. He hurt someone in a car accident and tried to drown his pain and guilt. He... he got help though." I stammered the last part, unsure if I should share the part about Mack attempting to take his life. That seemed so personal, something I shouldn't share without permission.

Regina made a soft humming noise and looked back at her notes, jotting something down.

"And how was his family through that period?"

I shrugged.

"I'm pretty sure they were supportive. His parents got him into rehab and back on his feet. When he moved to California he moved in with his sister and they seem to have a great relationship. He's gotten a really good thing going in his life, now."

"Does that bother you?"

I squinted my eyes in confusion.

"What? Why would that bother me?"

"Well, without going into too much detail about it, you basically told me Mack went through a very dark period in his life, but he came out the other side almost entirely unscathed, with the help and support from his family. He has a job, a steady future, good relationships. And you didn't have any of that."

My head jerked back in shock.

"Excuse me?"

"You also had a dark period, where things were so bad you tried to kill yourself. And when you came out the other side you were alone. Jeremy didn't know, and your relationship with your father was a big part of the reason you made the choice you did. You didn't have the same support system, and you went off to college and tried to be independent and do everything on your own. You've placed all your value in getting a degree and a job so you can have the freedom you believe will solve all of your problems."

I blinked.

I blinked again.

"No that's not... I'm not jealous of..."

But I couldn't finish the sentence. My mind was too busy scrambling, trying to rebuild the carefully crafted world I had built in my head. Regina was silent as I sorted through the shattered pieces that lay littered on the ground.

"But I can't actually believe that I don't trust Mack because I resent him for having a caring family," I finally said.

"I don't think that's what has happened, Rachel. I think it's that for the first time, you are seeing a demonstrated example of how things could be if you'd had support and care after your suicide attempt. And I think it highlights for you some of the insecurities and imbalances you feel based on current happenings in your life."

When I didn't have anything to add, Regina continued.

"Rachel, you have very specific ideas about what will make you happy. And there is nothing wrong with setting goals for yourself and working hard to achieve them. But you also have to teach yourself how to adjust when things don't go according to plan, and how to build and maintain important relationships in spite of any setbacks. That's life. And it seems like that's what is happening to you now. Your relationship with Jeremy is a bit unstable. You're worried about completing your coursework to the specifications needed to retain your academic scholarship. You are entering a relationship with a man, and because you don't recognize your own worth - your words, not mine - you question his motives. In your mind, everything of value in your life is sitting on the edge of a cliff and a slight breeze could send *it tumbling down."*

I nodded.

"That's exactly how I feel," I whisper.

"But Rachel, nothing in the world is that finite. Think hard about these questions for me okay? Jeremy. Things feel raw and strange right now. But what do you think is going to be the outcome of it?"

After a moment, I responded the only way I knew how.

"We'll get through it. We are all each other has."

Regina nodded, sitting forward and looking at me closely.

"And if things were to continue to feel awkward and stilted, what would you do?"

A tear slipped from my eye.

"I'd force us to have a hard conversation so we could fix it."

"Exactly," she said with a smile. "You wouldn't just allow the circumstances around you to happen to you. You would do something about it. And your coursework. What are you doing about it right now?"

"I've been studying with a friend and working on a project in a pair instead of alone. And I've been going to the tutoring center to have someone read over the paper I'm working on."

"And lets say you end up getting a lower grade than you need for your scholarship. Think of worst-case-scenario stuff. How would you handle that?"

I turned my head to look out the window.

"I guess I'd... I don't know. I'd speak to my scholarship advisor to see if I could take a different class or a winter term elective to make it up."

"And if that didn't work?"

"Well... maybe I could find a different scholarship, or continue part-time on just the athletic scholarship until I could figure out what to do next."

I could see Regina beaming at me out of the corner of my eye.

"All wonderful ideas. And those are just things you came up with off the top of your head without help from people who will want to help you stay enrolled, people who know the ins and outs of that kind of stuff."

I nodded, feeling a small brick of worry fall away from my shoulders.

"And Mack."

My head snapped back in her direction.

"What about him?"

She smiled softly.

"You're nervous about your relationship because of the relationship you had with your dad. You said you're waiting for him to do or say something that hurts you significantly, or that shows you can't put the same implicit trust in him that you place in Jeremy."

"Well... I don't know about that." But I relented when she gave me a knowing look. "Okay fine, yes. I guess that's a realistic description of how my mind is working. Fine."

"Has he done anything so far that would make you think he doesn't deserve your trust."

I pulled my legs up and crossed them on the couch, thinking through everything as quickly as I could. The knee-jerk reaction would be to bring up Ronnie and the night at Smoggy Tavern. But we talked about that, and if I was completely honest, even though it devastated me at the time, I didn't think he would ever do something like that if he was in a relationship.

There was the fact he was worried about losing his job and didn't talk to me about it. But would I have done the same thing? I mean, I kind of did, but in a backwards way. He was willing to potentially lose his job to save us. I was willing to lose us to save him. Both of our reactions were about sacrifice and putting each other first.

And maybe he got a bit overzealous when it came to his reaction about Thomas. But it was practically a mirror image of my reactions about Ronnie. His was just more fueled by testosterone.

So if I was honest about it - really, really honest - I knew how to answer Regina.

"No. He hasn't done anything to make me think he doesn't deserve it."

"Good. And if, in the future, he breaks your trust, or he hurts you, what will you do?"

I laugh.

"I don't know. I mean, it will depend on how he does it. Mack would never actually hurt me, like, physically. But if he broke my trust or hurt me emotionally, I guess... well we would need to talk about it before I made a decision about what to do."

"Yes. And that's a great answer, want to know why? Because it demonstrates that you value communication and working to solve problems."

"But I haven't been doing that. I've been jumping to conclusions and making assumptions. I've been hurting him when I was so worried about him hurting me."

"And that's based on the fact you were worried about trusting his intentions. Now that you've realized you don't necessarily have anything to worry about, might that change how you respond next time?"

I shrugged, feeling horrible. All this time, I was thinking he was the problem. But in reality it was me.

"I hope so. I want to be better for him. I mean, that's why I'm here."

Regina removed her glasses and sat forward, pinning me with a stare that was a cross between motherly concern and that look a teacher gives you when they think you can do better.

"Rachel, be careful with a statement like that. You're placing too much value on you in relation to him. But the whole reason you're here to begin with is because you struggle to place value in you just on your own."

"So you're saying I have to be better for me. Regardless of how the relationship turns out."

She nodded and gave me a sweet smile again.

"That's right. Because if you learn to develop your sense of self-worth, but it's entwined with his presence in your life, and things don't work out, that value will disappear and you'll be back at square one again."

"Hope for the best, expect the worst."

She shook her head.

"No. Not at all. Hope for the best, accept the rest. You can only control yourself and your actions and reactions. You can't control someone else, and living a life braced for all worst-case-scenarios isn't healthy either. That's why I said earlier that it's important to learn to adjust when things go off course from what you've hoped for. So, like I said, hope for the best, and accept the rest."

God, she made so much sense. What I loved so much about Regina is that her conversations with me were just that - conversations. She didn't just ask me how I was feeling and then ask for clarification. She didn't make mmmhhhmmm noises like you see on movies. She gave me advice and suggestions on how to solve my problems.

She closed her notebook.

"Lets review quickly okay?"

I nodded and she held up one finger.

"First of all, it's important that you remind yourself what your true motivations are for returning to therapy. It's not about Mack, even if that is what initially prompted the visit. It's about focusing on finding value in yourself, and being able to trust those around you. Because if your value in yourself is strong, then the actions of those around you won't have a life-altering impact on you if they let you down. And that's because your intrinsic worth is not based in what others do that you can't control. Right?"

I nodded again.

"Right. And if I create value in myself based on a relationship, I'll have to start over again if the relationship fails."

She touched her nose then pointed at me.

"Exactly."

She held up a second finger.

"Second, you are feeling a little off-kilter with certain important areas of your life. Jeremy. Academics. Mack. But you yourself listed how you will approach each of these very important facets if things don't go according to plan. This week I want you to spend time thinking about those, because forward thinking is really important when setting yourself up to be strong in the face of difficult situations. Begin preparations now so you aren't blindsided later. For example, visiting your advisor now to discuss options for what will happen if you continue to struggle academically could help you feel more in control of what will happen next. But also remember, you want to be prepared for difficult situations, but not always assuming that something bad is going to happen."

"Okay, and talking to Jeremy and Mack now can begin the process of repairing some of the issues."

"Bingo."

I smiled, feeling a lot more in control of things and a little more sure-footed than I felt when I arrived.

The slamming of the gym door snaps me out of my memory of the morning and the fantastic conversation I had with Regina. I look over to my right and see Gina storming across the room towards me, anger rolling off of her in waves.

"You fucking *bitch*," she seethes as she gets closer.

I quickly stop my treadmill and hop off. Looks like she was

bumped from starter today. I stand without a defensive posture, trying to remember the prep conversation I had with Coach J about how to handle the inevitable fallout.

"What can I do for you Gina?" I ask, keeping any malice from my tone.

"Don't act like you don't know what just happened," she spits. "I got bumped from starter and your little minion is taking my place!"

"I'm aware that decision had been made," I respond. "Did you have any questions or concerns about it that Coach J was unable to answer?"

She growls at me, her hands clenching into fists.

"This is all your fucking fault, you stupid fucking cow," she screams, causing other athlete's heads to turn our way.

"Gina, I made the recommendation that Piper should be moved to starter for multiple reasons, which I am sure Coach J reviewed with you. Mack said they wanted to give you another two games to demonstrate that you were the better player and that you were capable of working effectively with the team. You failed on both, which is why Piper has replaced you."

Gina's face is bright red and her body practically vibrating with rage.

"You are going to pay for this," she hisses, before storming away from me and out the door.

I breathe in deeply and exhale, trying to remain calm. That girl has a way of getting under my skin like no one else can.

But I have to admit to myself, as a slow smile creeps onto my face, seeing her skin turn that particular shade of red was incredibly satisfying.

Chapter Seventeen

At the crack of dawn the following morning, a Friday at the beginning of November, our team packs up into a bus and shuttles down to San Diego again, this time for the Southern California Small College Tournament, affectionately called the SC2.

Being a smaller school means athletic teams struggle to get funding for travel, so it's a big deal that the Athletic Department is supporting this trip down to San Diego. The women's team has made it to this very important tournament for the first time ever, though, so they were kind of obligated to pretend they cared.

The games we play this weekend will determine if we get to play in the College Cup in December. The men's team has made it before, so it's pretty much a given that they will attend this year. Our chances are still a bit more uncertain, and the pressure we all feel to perform this weekend is high.

The joint bus ride with the men's team and requirement to play in multiple games over several days also means we need to stay overnight in San Diego, so the athletic department also splurges on hotel rooms for us. Shitty hotel rooms, with cigarette burns in the horribly stiff bed spread. But still, it's a trip out of town for a bunch of healthy, energetic college students to meet and interact with other healthy, energetic college students.

It's disgustingly exciting and I've heard it's like a mini-Olympic village. Lots of sex and drinking and debauchery once each team is done playing. To say all of it makes me terribly uncomfortable would be an understatement.

"Think we should get out that black light before we crawl under any covers?"

I snort out a laugh and throw a shin guard at Piper.

"God, no. I'll sleep in filthy, ignorant bliss over finding out the sheets are diseased."

Piper giggles too.

"Blurg. So gross."

And yet she still crawls onto her double bed and splays her body out, face down into that same bed spread.

"Don't get too comfy, missy. Coach said we needed to go on a 4 mile run during our free time since our first game isn't until tomorrow morning. Some of the girls are meeting downstairs in about an hour."

When all I hear is a groan muffled by the bed, I lean over and smack Piper's butt.

She yelps.

"Alright! I'll be ready in an hour. Leave me be until then, por favor."

And she plops back down on the mattress.

While Piper rests face down on the diseased bed spread, I plunk in my headphones and crank up my tunes. Unpacking is unnecessary for just a two-night stay, but it's something to do with my hands that doesn't require a lot of brain power. My hope is to focus on this meaningless task instead of the other million things I want or need to think about.

After about 10 minutes, there are no items left to unpack and I glance around the room, trying to find something to keep me busy. I roll my eyes and smile when I realize I can hear Piper snoring softly, her face still buried in the bed spread

When I walk to the window and pull back the curtain to look out, I bark out a small laugh when I see we're facing a brick wall. Classic. But when I press my forehead against the glass, I can see a sliver of life beyond and the ocean in the background.

Such a perfect metaphor for my life.

When I finally get brave enough to look out the window and into my future, I can't actually see anything. But if I press a little harder, I can see hints of things to come, and I can try to prepare for them.

As my mind flips over and over the conversation I had with Regina yesterday, I realize that if I'm going to begin looking forward, I need to focus on building foundations for the important relationships in my life.

And I know exactly where to start.

*   *   *   *   *

"I'm just gonna get a few more laps around the block to cool down," I say to Piper as we finish up our required run two hours later. "I'll catch up with you in a bit, okay?"

Piper strikes a pose, her hands on her hips.

"Girl, come on! Don't push yourself too hard the day before a game."

I giggle at her wrinkled nose.

"I promise, cool down laps. You know I'm intense about cool downs."

Piper huffs but gives me a small smile and waves as she heads into the hotel.

I start into a slow jog around the block, and when I'm a decent ways away from the hotel I pull my phone from the band on my arm. My heart pounds loudly in my chest as I scroll to Mack's number and press the green button.

I spent the entire jog with the girls thinking about what I will say to him. Do I have the ability to really express how I feel? Am I brave enough to be honest? Will he be open enough to meeting me half way?

"Hey."

His voice is a low rumble through the phone, and it sounds like he's trying to be quiet.

"Hey, it's RJ."

He chuckles, understated and warm.

"Yes, I know who it is. What can I do for you?"

I lean up against the back of a bench on the side of the road. "Can we talk?"

And I'm met with silence.

"I mean in person. I just have a few things..." I let my voice trail off, feeling a little unsure now that it seems like I will have to convince him to see me.

"Sure, just... give me 10 minutes and I can head out. Where do you want to meet?"

I exhale a relieved breath and look around quickly for points of interest or ways I can tell Mack where I am.

"There's a park about 3 blocks away from the hotel on G Street. Wanna meet there?"

"Yeah, I'll look it up and head out in a few."

We hang up and I walk across the street to the park, finding shelter from the sun under a huge oak tree. Or maybe it's maple. I can't really tell the difference, but it is an absolutely massive tree. The roots are growing up out of the ground in thick ropes. The trunk is thick, the foliage full and green.

One of the things I love about living in Southern California is that it's perpetually spring and summer, with tiny little hints of rain and cold. But the leaves always stay full and beautiful. Nothing ever dies.

Unless there's a fire. But that's a different thing, right?

About 15 minutes later, I see Mack round the corner and start towards my spot sitting on one of the tree roots. I rub my sweaty palms against my black running shorts as I repeat things over again in my head, reminding myself of what I want to say.

I know you said you'd wait and be patient. Can you do that for another six months? Because I am in love with you and will do anything not to lose you.

Short and sweet. Simple and straightforward.

Hopefully Mack thinks so too.

When he finally sits down next to me, I take a moment to breathe him in. That familiar warmth, that slight touch of sweat and soap. It elicits memories of joking around after a practice, of him kissing me against my front door, of his home the night he explained his past to me.

God, I'm so hopeful and so terrified at the same time.

"Hey," he says, his tone slightly guarded, his eyes trained on whatever is in front of him, and not on me.

But my eyes are glued to him. To his jaw and his stubble and that slight curl at the nape of his neck where his hair grows unruly.

When I continue to stare and fail to respond, he finally turns to look me in the eyes.

"You wanted to talk?"

I clear my throat and give an embarrassed smile.

"Yeah... yes. Thanks for coming."

I rub my hands on my shorts again.

Stupid nerves.

"I... I know you said you'd wait... and, be patient," I start, my eyes fixed on my hands that grip just slightly to the hem of my

222

shorts. "Can you do that for another six months?"

I chance a glance at him and see him staring at me with a slight frown, his eyebrows furrowed in the middle. Not exactly the response I was hoping for. But instead of letting the silence linger, my traitorous honest tongue takes over.

"Because I'm in love with you and I don't want to lose you just because I've got all this bullshit going on in my head."

I brace my elbows on my knees and drop my head in my hands.

"And I'm working on it. I promise. I'm meeting with my therapist again and she's amazing and she helped me see in just a few sessions that I'm living my life braced for men to treat me like shit and for everything I've planned to fall apart. But I don't want to live that way."

I look over at him again, hoping he can see the plea in my eyes, and that the absolutely ridiculous stream-of-conscious thoughts tumbling out of my mouth are making sense.

"I want so much to be with you and explore whatever this is in real life, and not just in secret. To see if you really are the man I think you are. A kind, good man who makes me laugh and smile more than anyone. But I also want to make sure I'm staying focused on my future and a life I worked really hard for, a life I had to fight for. And if Regina can help me work through a handful of things in just a few weeks, imagine how much more normal and not broken I can be if we date after I graduate. The season's almost over and I won't be back next year and I'm not trying to go pro so I won't be at spring trainings. So we could just, I don't know, email and text and talk occasionally or something. Which I know might not be enough for you right now, and I'll totally respect that if that's the case, but I'd rather have you in my life in some way, even just in small doses, than not have you at all. Because in like, six weeks, you have become this life force that keeps the blood pumping in my veins and I can't imagine what it would be like to not have you. I mean, not that I *have* you, have you. Like, I'm not your boss or girlfriend or anything, but you're so important and I can't imagine..."

And my words get cut off when Mack stands abruptly, walking away from me.

My heart plummets and my eyes prickle at the corners.

I knew I was rambling but I didn't think that he would just get up and...

But then he turns around and looks at me, and whatever

reaction my heart just had is now in reverse.

Because the look he is giving me…

It's not angry, or upset, or disappointed.

No.

It is full of hope, and longing. And love.

He's standing 10 feet away, hands braced at his hips.

I stand slowly and rub my hands on my shorts again.

"You are…" he stops and shakes his head, letting out a humorless chuckle. "RJ, you are *not* broken."

I squint my eyes in confusion. Out of everything I said to him about loving him and waiting until I graduate to date, he focused on that?

"If you end up taking only one thing away from knowing me, I want it to be that. You are *not* broken. In *any* way. You've been banged up a bit by things I might not really understand, and you've been worn weary by burdens that you've carried for years on your own with no one to help you lighten that load. But RJ, shit." He shakes his head again, taking a few steps towards me. "You are anything but broken. You're beautiful and resilient and…"

He stops and rubs his hands up and down his face.

"And I'm in love with you," he finishes, his eyes connecting with mine again. "So in love with you that I have been barely seeing straight for the past few weeks wondering if that was the end."

I stand suddenly and practically rush him, my body colliding with his in a hug so tight and warm, I wonder how I will ever let go. His arms wrap around my middle and mine are squeezing tight around his neck and shoulders, our cheeks pressed together.

"I don't want that to be the end," he whispers into my ear, kissing me softly just beneath it. "Six months is nothing when considering the potential of forever without you."

Chapter Eighteen

I groan internally when I see the caller ID display on my phone. *Frank.* I've never programmed him in as *Dad* - it's just Frank.

"Don't answer it," Mack whispers from his spot next to me on the bus. When I look at him in question, he continues, "It's either something you don't want to hear, or it's something that will make you upset. You don't need that today."

My first instinct is to brush him off, tell him it isn't a big deal. But then I remember what I promised to myself. That I would open up those protected parts of myself to Mack, and trust him with those pieces of vulnerability that I think make me weak.

I nod slightly, clicking the *ignore* button.

"You're right. I don't need his particular brand of crazy today."

Mack gives my knee two taps, then turns back to focus on the paperwork in front of him.

Sitting next to each other on the short bus ride from the hotel to the arena is weird. Normally I sit with Piper, and she sent me a *why are you sitting with coach?* text when I stopped at the front of the bus and slid in past him to get to the empty seat by the window.

I didn't respond, figuring the excuse I had crafted this morning didn't even make sense, and that the time on the bus would provide me with extra time to come up with something.

But of course, my mind is blank.

He didn't act surprised when I sat next to him. It's not even just that he wasn't surprised. He barely responded. He didn't move out of the way or rearrange his stuff. He didn't even look at me at first. The only reason I know he was aware I was sitting next to him was the ghost of a smile that sat on his face when I turned to look at him after a few minutes.

Telling me to ignore Frank's call was literally the first thing he said to me.

But he has been sitting for the entire 10 minute bus ride with his knee pressed to mine, and I cannot for the life of me calm the butterflies that are soaring around in my stomach and around my heart.

From touching knees.

So pathetic.

When the bus comes to a halt, I glance outside and see the stadium.

Shitshitshit.

"What's wrong?" Mack asks.

"Did I say that out loud?"

He laughs.

"Yeah, now what's wrong?"

"I don't have a reason why I sat next to you," I whisper to him.

Mack shrugs.

"Don't worry," he says, his volume a bit higher. "I used to get nerves before tournaments too. Glad to hear they passed so quickly." He pats my shoulder and turns to walk out of the bus.

I shuffle after him, feeling slightly relieved that I don't have to come up with a fake excuse, while simultaneously pissed that he made me sound like a nervous Nellie in front of the rest of the team.

"So glad to hear I'm not the only one who feels like they're gonna upchuck before a game," Piper says as she bounces down the steps. "I thought I was the only freak on the team." She gives me a cheesy grin before scooting past me to grab her duffle from underneath the bus.

I grab my duffle as well, following the team through the parking lot and towards the stadium tunnels. I am dressed and ready to go by the time I glance at my phone again. Two missed calls and a text from Jeremy.

Jeremy: He's coming to the game. I'm on my way.

My stomach drops. Why would he come to another game? There is legitimately no reason for him to come. I can feel my blood pumping faster as it throbs through my body, anger and frustration rippling across the surface of my skin.

Me: Don't come. I'll be fine.

I almost send it.

I type it completely, and then stare at it as my teammates mill around me, laughing and joking and excited about the game.

I stare at a text I want to send to my brother, in an attempt to save him the frustration while everyone around me enjoys themselves.

But then I delete it.

It's not my job to protect Jeremy. By doing that, I've created a barrier between us that is now one of the causes of a rift that I can't stand. If he wants to come and be supportive, so I can be like every other normal person on this team, I should let him.

But I also have to tell my coach that there is a potential distraction.

I hop up from the bench next to the lockers and go to the hallway just outside the locker room, where Mack and Coach J are talking quietly. They stop immediately when I approach.

"What's up, Rachel?" Coach J asks.

It throws me for just a moment, since my focus had been on sharing with Mack. But Coach J's question reminds me that I'm here to tell my coaches, plural, about a distraction. I'm not here to cry to my future boyfriend about my asshole dad.

"The game against USD a few weeks ago, there was a heckler in the crowd that caused some problems."

I provide the information as a statement, not a question, because I know they remember. Everyone remembers Rachel Jameson's dad calling her a dyke loud and clear.

"He's coming today, and his presence will cause problems for me. You need to put Erin in as starter. I'd like permission to not go on the field."

When all I hear is silence, I glance up at both of them, my eyes previously trained on the ground.

Coach J's eyes are furrowed in confusion, while Mack just watches me with a neutral expression.

"I've already informed Coach J that your father will be at the

227

game," Mack says, "and we both agreed that it would be best to keep you on the field."

Now my head cocks to the side with my own confusion.

"That makes no sense. Last time I could barely pay attention when he was here. I almost lost us the game. This game is way more important."

"I'll let you two get on the same page," Coach J says, and walks back into the locker room.

I stare after him for a moment before turning my attention back to Mack.

"I'm so lost. Was he mad?"

Mack shakes his head slightly.

"I'd already told Coach J that your dad was coming, and that you were still going to play. He was probably just wondering why you were telling us for what seemed like a second time to him, and why you would say you should sit out when I *just* told him you were good to play anyway."

"But I'm *not* good to play, Mack. I'm gonna choke again, and I... wait. How did you know he was coming?"

"Jeremy called me."

My head jerks back.

"What?"

"Yeah. He was worried and said he couldn't get a hold of you. He wanted to make sure someone was keeping an eye on things to make sure you were okay."

I let out a sudden burst of uncontrollable laughter, and Mack breaks into a grin.

"Well, I guess he's at least accepted the idea that you might care about me."

"I worry *everyone* can tell how much I care about you," he replies.

My face blushes bright red.

"I'm serious, RJ. I feel like it's stamped on my forehead sometimes. I feel like my eyes are always glued to you, even when I'm supposed to be watching another player on the field or listening to someone speak to me."

I shake my head with a small smile.

"I love that," I whisper.

Mack clears his throat.

"Well, we should get back inside. My decision is final, just so you know. You're playing. You'll be fine. The team will be behind you if there's any problems."

I stand with my arms crossed, and watch as he turns and enters the locker room.

I feel like I need to do something, but I'm not sure what. There's an anticipation coursing through my veins in place of the anger that was boiling to the surface earlier.

Then suddenly, it occurs to me.

I shoot into the locker room, just as Mack is calling everyone to attention.

"Can I say something quickly?" I ask, and see every eye in the room shoot to me. I hate being the focus of attention, but I have to push past it.

Mack waves a hand out in front of him.

"The floor is yours."

I clear my throat nervously, glancing around the room and catching Piper's eyes. I latch onto her beautiful spirit in an attempt to calm myself.

"I'm sure you all probably remember the USD game, when there was a man shouting really horrible things at the team from the stands."

A few nods. A lot of curious looks.

"Well, it's no coincidence that he singled me out that day. That guy is my dad."

A few gasps. A lot of open mouths.

"He's an alcoholic, and he was physically and verbally abusive to me when I was growing up. I know this might seem like a random thing to share with the team, but I promise, I have a reason."

A few wide eyes. A lot of pitying stares.

"He's going to be here today, in the stands. I spoke with Coach McIntosh about possibly starting Erin, since I have a hard time concentrating when he's around. I can normally shut out most things and focus - but not him. I just wanted to be honest with you, a group of women I care about deeply, that I will do everything I can to help you win this game, but that this one thing may impact my performance."

I catch Mack's eyes.

"Recently I realized that you can't work well with anyone unless you're open and vulnerable, and willing to take risks."

Mack gives me a small smile and I turn my head to let my eyes wander through the group.

"But in this case, the majority of risk rests on the team as a whole, not just on me. I don't think it would be fair for me to go into this game with a potential distraction without you knowing. I wanted to make sure you understand what today will be like for me, and I wanted to make sure I have your permission to play."

There's a super intense silence when I finish. I glance around again, catch Piper's eyes watching me with approval and a smirk. Erin and Kristal are sitting together watching me with beaming smiles. And when my eyes connect with Mack's again I see pride and respect and love radiating from him.

"Oh, come on. That's bullshit," Gina grits out.

And all of those eyes I hated having on me finally turn away and latch onto another target.

When my eyes laser in on Gina, I see her standing in front of an open locker, her hands on her hips, her face twisted in a scowl.

"She wrapped it up in a pretty bow, but what she just told you all is that she's going to be a deer in headlights today as the rest of the team busts ass trying to win this game. I think she should be asked to sit out today."

"Gina, stop being a fucking bitch." I turn to see Piper taking a step forward. "No one wants to hear your shit."

"Is it possible for you to shove your nose any farther up RJ's ass?" Gina spits out. "You're already a starter today. You don't need to push any farther. And you're a total idiot if you can't realize she's a liability. Besides, whether I'm a bitch or not is irrelevant when what I'm saying is true. She's going to lose this game for the team."

The silence in the room is so heavy I can feel the weight of it on my shoulders.

"A vote, then."

My eyes fly back to Mack's in surprise, and I'm sure I'm not the only one to respond this way.

"My original plan was to put RJ in because I believe in her ability to overcome her issues with her dad. It was her decision to share with you why her dad's presence will potentially be a problem. She wanted to open up to you and ask for your permission to play, even though I had already told her what my decision was, because she values the collective team perspective."

He clears his throat, eyeing the room.

"And even though I *detest* the way it was phrased and think immature, catty behavior is uncalled for on this team," he says, glaring at Gina, who suddenly loses a shade of color, "it is a valid point that RJ's capability as a keeper may be impacted. I think RJ did the right thing in letting you all decide, as a team, whether she should be on that field. So, a vote. A team decision."

After a few moments where I see some uncomfortable glances my way, I know I have to say something.

"I won't be upset, whatever decision is made. It won't impact how I feel about any of you. I'll totally understand. And if it helps, I'll just step out," I point to the door and begin taking steps in that direction, "so everyone can say what they want."

I'm out the door quickly, pacing the hallways. But it's only a few minutes before Piper comes flying out the door with a shit-eating-grin on her face.

"Pull on your gloves, bitch! It's time to play!"

*   *   *   *   *

I can't stop smiling when I get off the field an hour and a half later. Not only did we win, but I was on. Fucking. *Point.* And the icing on the cake is that my dad didn't make a peep during the game, so I'm assuming Jeremy showed up at some point and either forced him to stay quiet or kept him from even attending the game.

I guess letting him protect me isn't so bad.

What is bad is when I get outside the locker room after showering, ready to head back to the hotel, and I find Jeremy and Mack together, talking quietly.

"What happened?" I ask, startling them both.

They exchange a look that means something only to them, before Mack turns towards me, his expression grim.

"Your dad's here," is his response.

My eyes flick from Mack where he stands to Jeremy, who is leaning sideways against the cinderblock wall, not fully looking at me. I'm trying to decipher the underlying tension swarming around them, but I'm unable to see what they're not saying.

"...And?"

Mack looks to Jeremy again.

When my eyes track back to my brother, I gasp. Now that he's pushed away from the wall and turned fully towards me, I can see his split lip and the cut on his eyebrow, as well as the bruises already forming under his eye.

"Jeremy, what the hell happened?" I ask, rushing towards him to inspect his face.

But he brushes me away, waving his hand in the air dismissively.

"It's nothing," he replies. "Dad's face looks worse."

"What!?" I shout. "Jeremy, will you just tell me what happened?"

Jeremy shakes his head, just slightly, mostly in disbelief.

"That stupid fuck thought he could show up tonight and not get the shit beat out of him is what happened," he barks out. "I don't know how he found out about this tournament, but I made sure he knew he wasn't ever welcome back at one of your games."

Jeremy makes an angry noise, then curses and touches the cut on his lip.

"I waited outside for him and when I saw him stumbling up to the entrance, I made it clear that he wouldn't be attending. The asshole sucker punched me. So I wrapped my arm around his neck and dragged him out to my car. He got in a few good hits but he's fucking wasted. I knocked him out and threw him in the backseat. He's gonna sleep it off until I drive his ass home."

We are all silent for a moment. I let Jeremy's words play over again in my head. He beat the shit out of our dad. Part of me wants to laugh and part of me is upset because I would never want Jeremy to risk getting in trouble or getting hurt.

When Jeremy found out that Carter cheated on me in high school, he drove home from college that very day and confronted Carter as he was leaving football practice. I was coming out of the women's locker rooms when I saw them through the chainlink fence, arguing in the parking lot.

Jeremy had taken Carter by the shirt and slammed him up against the expensive truck Mr. Lincoln bought just two weeks earlier as a present for Carter making team captain. I raced as fast as I could towards them, but by the time I got there, Carter was flat on his back and Jeremy was hitting him over and over in the face.

I had to throw myself in between them to get him to stop punching. Who knows whether he would have been able to stop.

He spent a night in jail because dad hadn't wanted to bail him out and his coach had to come to town to do it. He was charged with assault and had a bunch of community service.

I'd bought him a thank you card.

I'm jolted back to the present when suddenly, Jeremy turns and punches the cinderblock wall of the tunnel.

I'm so stunned, I don't react.

I just watch as Jeremy hits the wall over and over again.

It isn't until Mack wraps his arms around Jeremy and pulls him backwards that I realize Jeremy's blood is now marking the wall where he split open his fist.

Tears track down my cheeks as I watch Mack quickly and quietly bring Jeremy to his knees on the floor of the tunnel where we stand. Mack remains with his arms locked around Jeremy's torso, inhibiting Jeremy's ability to move.

I rush to kneel down in front of them, my knees touching Jeremy's. And when I lean in close and try to catch his eyes that I realize he's crying too.

"Are you okay?" I whisper.

He's quiet for a moment, staring at the wall behind me, before finally shaking his head.

"I should have protected you from him," he whispers back.

I lean forward and rest my forehead on Jeremy's chest.

"No," I reply, although I know my words are slightly muffled. "We talked about this. It wasn't your fault."

I lean back and look him in the eye again.

"You are what kept me sane, Jer. Knowing you were out there and that you loved me and you didn't think the horrible things Frank said you did."

Mack's arms begin to release when he sees Jeremy isn't going to throw any more punches. Jeremy takes the opportunity to shift his body so he's leaning back against the wall. But he doesn't say anything. He just stares blankly at the ceiling, tears streaming from the sides of his eyes, down his cheekbones to his neck.

I scoot over and sit next to him, just how we sat a few weeks ago in my kitchen when I first told him what happened. I lean my head on his shoulder and wrap my arms around his muscular right bicep, trying to think of words that can comfort him.

"I promise you that I've never wanted to hurt myself again. I just had one moment of weakness where I couldn't see any flicker of hope. But my life is so different now, and you're a big part of that. Your support and encouragement and love. It helps make me feel strong."

He lets out a long exhale and then leans his head down, placing a kiss into my hair.

"We're a mess, kid."

I laugh a little, wiping away the last of my tears.

"But we're gonna be okay," I reply.

And when we both lift our heads and look at each other, I know we both believe it's true.

*   *   *   *   *

The three of us slowly make our way to the parking lot outside of the arena. I told Mack that before I get on the bus back to the hotel with the team, I wanted to see my dad. Jeremy said it was a bad idea, but relented when I told him I needed to say something to him that was important.

Mack has stayed mostly quiet in the moments since Jeremy's breakdown in the tunnel, but I can tell he's brimming with questions. As Jeremy walks ahead of us, I hang back just a few feet and let my fingers brush against Mack's palm.

"We'll talk," I say quietly. "Don't worry."

He looks relieved, and opens his mouth to say something when he's interrupted by an irate Jeremy.

"Where the fuck is my car?" Jeremy shouts.

My head whips to the left, then I let my eyes roam over the few dozen cars still parked and the families and spectators walking through the lot towards their own vehicles.

"Are you sure you parked it here?" I ask, walking away from him to scan further down the line. A black SUV isn't going to stick out like a sore thumb, not like my Trusty Rusty does.

"Yes, Rachel, I'm not a complete idiot," Jeremy calls out to me as he walks in the other direction.

I laugh as I turn away from him, cutting between a few cars to go to the next lane and continue the search.

"You sure about that?" I call back even louder, a teasing lilt to my voice.

When I emerge from between two vehicles and step out into the next lane, there are no cars driving anywhere near where I am walking. Which is why I'm startled when I hear a screech from behind me.

I turn my head just slightly but before I can see anything I feel a sharp pain on my right side.

I feel my feet lift off the ground and wind rushing around my body.

And then I don't feel anything.

Chapter Nineteen

The first thing I hear is a siren.

It's really far away, but getting louder by the second.

Then I hear voices.

Lots of them.

I hear someone shouting.

Then others talking around me in hushed conversations.

And then I hear whispers right by my ear, so close I'm surprised it wasn't the first thing I heard.

"You have to be okay," the whisper says. "Please, please be okay."

And then I feel soft lips on my forehead and fingers holding tight to mine.

I groan and instinctively try to curl up on my side.

"Oh, thank god," the whisper says on an exhale. "RJ. RJ it's Mack. Just stay still for me okay?"

I open my eyes then, and find his beautiful chocolate ones peering down at me.

"Hi," I say.

He smiles.

"Hi pretty girl," he responds, lifting my hand and kissing my knuckles, holding my hand to his chest while he reaches over and places his other hand on the top of my head.

I smile back, although weakly.

"I think I'm okay," I whisper. "I don't think anything's broken."

He nods, still smiling at me.

"I think you're right. But I want you to stay still until someone with a lot more knowledge can take a look and tell you for sure, okay?"

"Okay."

We stay staring at each other as the siren gets louder. Mack kneeling on the asphalt next to where I'm lying on my back, holding my hand, stroking his thumb along the back. When the responders finally pull into the lot, and their lights pass over his face, I can see that Mack's eyes are glistening, and there are a few tear tracks down his face.

I lift the hand he holds and place it against his face.

"I'm okay," I whisper.

He nods and turns his face in my hand, kissing my palm.

The next hour goes by fast and slow at the same time.

The police arrive first, and they arrest my dad for driving while intoxicated, along with a few other things. You know, because he hit a person, then crashed into a parked car, then got out of his car and tried to stumble down the road.

The paramedics arrive next and look me over. They clean up my few cuts and decide it's best for me to go to the hospital to get checked out, since I'm feeling a decent amount of pain in my right thigh and hip. But they tell me I don't have to be transported by the ambulance, which is great because: *expensive*.

Mack and Jeremy nearly get into a fight. Apparently, Jeremy told Mack he needed to go back to the bus and make sure the rest of the team was okay. Needless to say, Mack was not pleased. But eventually, he kissed my forehead while I sat in the back of the ambulance, and sauntered off through the parking lot.

Jeremy then never left my side, his presence soothing and irritating at the same time. But I don't let on about the irritation. He already feels shitty enough for leaving his keys in the car on accident.

"I don't want to go to the hospital, though," I say to Jeremy as he helps me into a cab. "I'm sure I'm totally fine."

He gives me a look that makes me laugh because he looks so much like an exasperated older brother. But then I clutch my side in pain from jolting my body with laughter.

"You just got hit by a car. I'm taking you to the fucking hospital."

I laugh again as he closes the door and goes around to climb in the other side.

"Why is everything about us so dysfunctional?" I ask him, only slightly seriously, once we are en route.

He shrugs.

"Who wants a boring life, Rach?"

"*Me*, Jeremy. *I* want a boring life."

He smiles and reaches over to squeeze my hand, then turns his head to stare out the window.

"You know this wasn't your fault either, right?"

He nods too quickly, and I know instinctively he's going to tuck this away with a dozen other things that he believes he's done to wrong me or other people he loves.

"Jeremy..."

"Let it go Rachel," he says, softly but firmly, cutting me off. He looks over and gives me a small, insincere smile and squeezes my hand again.

I turn and look out my own window, wishing desperately that my sweet brother could instinctively know that I don't blame him. I've seen the fire of self-hatred continuing to catch and grow inside of him over the past weeks.

And I don't think my words are enough to put that fire out.

*   *   *   *   *

When Jeremy and I pull up in front of the hotel four hours later, I barely have my door open before Mack is there, reaching to support me as I climb out of the back seat.

"I've been trying to get a hold of you both for hours," he says, his voice filled with emotions that I'm too tired to catalogue.

"My phone is still in the SUV," Jeremy offers up as he circles the back of the cab. "Rachel's broke in the accident."

Jeremy steps towards me, likely to help me to my room. But Mack steps forward and puts his arm around me, using his other hand to take mine and assist me.

"I've got her," Mack says, staring at Jeremy, who suddenly looks slightly unsure.

After way too long of a silence, Jeremy nods and steps back, his face looking slightly offended but resigned at the same time.

"I'll call you on your hotel phone in the morning around 9am, okay?"

"Sounds good," I reply. "Love you, Jer."

He gives me a small smile, then hops into the cab and heads off, likely to pick his car up from the arena parking lot. We weren't sure about the damage, but I don't think it was too bad.

"Let's get you inside," Mack says, leading me into the small lobby.

I walk slowly, wincing with the pain. I was incredibly lucky not to have fractured or broken something, but I still have to deal with strained ligaments in my hip and leg, bruising all over the right side of my body, general soreness and the asphalt scrapes on the side of my face and arms where I hit the ground when I crashed back to the ground.

Telling the doctor that I didn't want to take any pills is something I'm already starting to regret.

"Do you want me to walk you to your room or..." but before finishing, he trails off.

"... Or?" I ask.

He clears his throat and being so close to him I see his adams apple bob when he swallows.

"... Or do you want to stay in my room?"

His question is asked very quietly, almost like he's embarrassed to ask it or is afraid the empty space around us will hear him. When I stop walking forward, mostly in surprise, he's quick to explain.

"I just want to make sure you're okay, I swear. After watching you fly into the air and not being able to go with you to the hospital, I just..." he breathes deeply and lets out a harsh exhale, "I just want to hold you close to me tonight. To know you're really okay when you could easily have been seriously hurt."

My heart speeds up slightly and I feel blood rush to my neck at the thought of spending the night in Mack's room. But I know instinctively nothing is going to happen that's too much for me. And the thought of getting to snuggle up next to him and look into his eyes before falling asleep?

What girl could resist?

"I'll stay in your room," I say just as quietly.

Our eyes stay locked on each other for several beats before we finally begin making our way towards the elevators that will take us to Mack's room.

Mack's *hotel* room.

He swipes us into 806 and walks me over to sit on the edge of his bed.

His *king sized* bed.

"Do you want a water or something to snack on?" he asks.

I shake my head.

"Did you tell the girls what happened when you got to the bus?"

Mack exhales harshly.

"About that," he says, walking over and sitting next to me. "Gina came to see me tonight, bawling her eyes out, as soon as we got off the bus."

"What?" I ask, my face scrunching up in confusion.

"Trust me. I was confused too," he responds, rubbing his hands over his face. "It took a while for her to form sentences I could understand, but she said it was her fault. She called your dad and pretended to be someone from the school inviting parents for the tournament. Gave him all of the details for the games."

"Are you serious?" I ask in a whisper, shocked still by this information and unsure how to process it.

"I guess she had just hoped his being here would make you decide not to play," he continues. "She said she had no idea anything so horrible would happen and that she was really sorry."

I nod once and squeeze the bridge of my nose in frustration, trying to deal with this news along with the slowly increasing pain in my body.

"You okay?"

I nod again.

"I don't want to think about Gina. I'm just really sore and tired and want to go to sleep. Can I use your shower?"

"Sure," he responds, standing and walking over to the bathroom.

He flicks on the light and wanders in. I hear the water running and things moving around before he returns and takes both of my hands, helping me to stand.

"Take your time. Soothe your muscles. I'm sure they're sore from the game as well."

"Thanks Mack," I say, before slipping into the bathroom and shutting the door behind me.

I slowly peel off my clothes and leave them in a pile in the corner before crawling under the water and relishing the hot spray that instantly covers my body. Like every other time I take a shower, I place my hands flat on the wall and direct the water to hit my head, then trickle down my body.

I've often stood in this exact position and contemplated a next decision, practiced something I was going to say, or tried to reflect on an experience. Tonight is no different.

My dad hit me with a car. My brother is going through something deep. I'm probably going to have to sit out the rest of the soccer season. And I'm about to spend the night in Mack's room.

If I'm totally honest, even though everything else in that list is important, the only thing I can think about is sleeping in Mack's arms.

"RJ?" I hear from the other side of the curtain. "I brought you something to wear. I've set it on the sink, okay?"

"Thanks," I reply, and then I hear the door snick shut again.

After spending a bit longer letting the warmth soothe my aching body, I flip off the water and dry off. I grab the clothes Mack has left for me - a blue t-shirt and pair of gray sweats - and slowly pull them on, inhaling that delicious Mack scent that wraps around my body.

When I finally step out of the bathroom, I find Mack stretched out on the bed with his arms behind his head with the television on. But his eyes are locked on me.

I limp to the door and flip the light, leaving the room cast in just the blue hue from the screen. I walk back to the bed and crawl up from the bottom, all the while keeping my eyes glued to Mack's.

His arms wrap around me when I get close enough, tucking me into his chest and resting his chin on my head.

"What did the doctors say about your injuries?" he asks quietly, as his hands begin to make soothing circles on my back that make me snuggle even closer.

"Some strained ligaments is the most of it, apart from the bruising and small cuts and scrapes. But the ligs are probably going to be enough for me to have to sit out the rest of the season."

"I'm sorry, RJ," he whispers into my hair, kissing my head.

I pull my arms out from where they are tucked into his body and wrap them around his waste. I slip them under his shirt and press them into the solid muscles of his back, kneading the tension away that I can feel in his body.

"It's okay," I whisper back. "I'm going to be fine."

He pulls away just slightly so he can look down at my face, into my eyes.

"When I heard it, when I heard the car hit you and your body hitting the pavement, I thought you were dead. I know the car wasn't going that fast, so it makes me feel like an idiot to say out loud. But that was absolutely the most terrifying moment of my life. I ran towards you and it felt like my feet were melted into the ground - I couldn't get to you fast enough."

He lifts a hand and places it on my cheek, sliding his thumb along my cheekbone.

"And then I saw you crumpled on the ground and it felt like my soul died. In that instant when I thought I might have lost you, I felt everything that I am begin to dissolve and float away, like my body could no longer be bothered with holding me together. And when I realized you were going to be okay, I saw how clearly and truly and deeply I have fallen in love with you. You are my everything."

His face is so pained right now that I can't help but stretch up and press my lips to his to try to soothe away any hurt or fear that he felt earlier tonight. Our mouths part and his tongue flicks against mine, causing the butterflies low in my belly to take flight. All I can think about is him and breathing him in and touching his body and holding him close.

"I love you," I whisper, bringing my hands forward under his shirt and letting my palms coast over the dips and planes of the tight muscle of his abs and chest.

He lets out a light moan and twists his legs together with mine. I feel the hardness of him press against the softness of me and I can't help but undulate my hips against him in search of some form of relief from this fire inside that has erupted out of nowhere.

"God, RJ," he whispers in my ear as his hands slide along my hips and grip at my ass, giving him more leverage to push against me. "I want you so much." He rolls me to my back and I grip his shirt, tugging it off over his head.

The moment his shirt is off he begins to slowly push up mine, kissing up my stomach as he goes. And when my shirt stops just under my breasts, he takes his time kissing and nipping the skin on my ribs, his tongue slicking along the underside of my right breast before going to the left and repeating the motion.

His eyes lock on mine for a moment, giving me the opportunity to direct. I give a slight nod and the shirt gets pushed farther, baring my hard nipples to the cool air of the hotel room.

And I can't help but squirm, letting out a sharp cry of pleasure and need, when his warm mouth closes over the tip of one, licking and sucking.

"Look at you," he whispers. "So sensitive."

He moves to the other bud with his hand, flicking his thumb back and forth against the tip, over and over. And over.

And then suddenly he reaches between us and pulls my shirt down, re-covering my body. When I look at his face, I see his eyes are clenched tightly.

"This isn't what I wanted to happen tonight," he says in a voice laced with sexual tension. "I really did just want to hold you close."

"But I thought..."

"I am in love with you, RJ. We can have sex someday, absolutely, when you're ready. And it is going to be *fucking* amazing."

He rolls slightly so he's laying next to me instead of resting on top of me.

"But tonight isn't the night. Not when you were hit by a car today, and there are other soccer girls in the hotel, and I'm still your coach."

I nod and exhale a breath, suddenly frustrated with myself.

"I'm sorry," I whisper.

But he shakes his head.

"You have nothing to be sorry about. I *loved* that. Every second. But I shouldn't have done anything other than kiss you and hold you and let you fall asleep in my arms. Because holding you close to me is the only thing these arms have wanted since the moment I met you."

I give him a small smile and snuggle back into his arms, kissing his bare chest.

"We have the future in front of us, RJ. Just remember that. We don't need to rush anything today."

A few moments of silence pass before I muster up the courage to talk to him about sex. About the future and sex and us.

"I know we just did... *that*..." I say, my face flushing red, "... but I just want to be clear with you about me."

243

He nods, his eyes focused on my face.

"I chose to wait to have sex with someone when I knew it would mean something. I appreciated, so much, that you stopped things tonight, because you're totally right. My body fucking hurts right now," I say, and we both laugh.

"But I don't want you to spend tons of time racking your brain trying to make my first time some perfect candles and roses thing from a movie. I already know it's going to hurt and be kind of awkward. And if we spend too much time thinking about how to make it *perfect,* I think we might both be let down."

"Let me just stop you right there," he says with a smirk. "I can absolutely promise you that when I'm inside you, I am not going to be let down."

I laugh and slap my hand on his chest.

"You know what I mean!" I say with an exasperated smile.

He nods and kisses my lips.

"I know exactly what you mean," he whispers. "It will be special, and I will take care of you. But no flowers, candles or rotating beds."

"Oh my god," I giggle, unable to contain myself. "Indy. You're so ridiculous."

His eyes light up at the use of his nickname, and he tightens his hold around my body, pulling me up so my face rests right next to his.

"Cherise was right about you," I say to him, still giggling slightly as I rest nose to nose with him.

"What was she right about?" he asks.

"She said you're a keeper," I reply.

"No, I'm a sweeper. *You're* a keeper."

"Fine," I say, laughing again. "I'm a keeper. And you're a sweeper. You certainly swept me off my feet."

"Oh my god, it's too much cheesiness," he says, shoving his face into his pillow.

It's another fifteen minutes of ridiculous puns and silly expressions of love before we finally turn off the glow of the television and crawl under the covers together.

And when I rest my head on his chest and hear the steady beat of his heart - when I feel his strong arms wrapped tightly around me - I realize that Mack has taught me an invaluable lesson:

Any love worth keeping is worth waiting for.

Epilogue

"You can't be serious," I say, rolling my eyes. "You didn't even *go* to Indiana. Why are you rooting for their basketball team?"

"Have I not been clear before? I'm from the Hoosier state. I'm a Hoosier forever. Indiana basketball is the only basketball that exists," Mack replies from his place next to me on my couch.

We're completing our March Madness brackets. I have North Carolina taking it all, and Mack has his beloved Hoosiers even though they haven't won since 1987.

Sometimes I wonder if I'll ever understand him. But I'm sure having a blast figuring it out.

After the crash last November, a lot of shit in our lives changed. Some for the good, some for the bad. But we've taken it all in stride.

I wasn't able to play soccer for the rest of the season, but the Athletic Director decided I could keep my scholarship to finish out the year, contingent on my helping coach the team. I thought that decision was all Mack, but apparently Gina went directly to the Athletic Director's office to make sure he understood the whole situation with the accident. I wouldn't say she and I are friends or anything, but her whole 'I'm a cactus' routine has finally fallen away and she's not so prickly anymore. Our team didn't win the College Cup, but we did come in fourth, which is still amazing.

Mack and I kept our distance as best as we could after our

night in the hotel room. I didn't know how we were going to manage to last until May without really spending time together or talking. But Mack solved all of that when he stepped down as the coach after our last game in December. With Jeremy's help, and very intensely communicated support, Mack got a new position as the head coach at Occidental College. I guess MLS players have a lot more pull in the soccer world than I realized. On his last day, we went on a real date. He took me back to the Atwater Village Fun Center and I kicked his ass.

Speaking of sex (yes, I know I added that in there awkwardly, but be honest... you were curious), I finally understand what the big deal is. It was exactly like I thought it would be for me that first time. Awkward and a bit painful. But the good thing about handing my v-card to someone who loves me? We were able to talk and laugh through it a bit and adjust. It was still emotional and intimate and special. And then after the first time, we practiced. A *lot*. I like to think Mack's diligence as my coach in bed has been a reflection of my willingness to be taught.

CC was thrilled to hear that Mack and I decided to 'get our shit together,' as she likes to refer to the time directly following the accident. She is a huge fan of his and loves to compliment his looks and body, even though it makes his cheeks flush. I love watching that happen and laugh every time.

My dad went to jail for a little bit, and when he got out, Jeremy gave him two options: rehab or he would never see or hear from us again. Dad told Jeremy to fuck off with his worthless dyke of a sister. We've officially blocked his number with our phone company, and deleted his contact from our phones. It's been an adjustment, knowing that I'll never talk to him again, but I feel like I am mentally so much healthier now. Even Regina says she can see a huge difference, and I haven't had any more anxiety attacks.

Thomas and I didn't end up doing the joint presentation. Ultimately, our research was weak and it felt forced, so we gave each other a high five and went back to fighting in class. And with Piper's diligence, and some support from the tutoring centre, I was able to scrape by in my psychology class last semester. Barely. Needless to say, I won't ever be pursuing a career as a psychologist.

"You guys are both idiots," Jeremy says, returning from the kitchen with a box of cold pizza. "It's gonna be Villanova again.

For sure."

"I'm calling Michigan State," Charlie says.

The three of us look at her, a little surprised.

"How do you figure Michigan State?" I ask. "It's been a long time since they've been notable in March Madness."

"Their coach and the starters on the team have been together for three years. They recruited really strongly over the past few years as well. Two of their players were originally recruited to Indiana and North Carolina and then they transferred. I just think they're positioned for success."

I'm surprised nothing has flown into my mouth with how wide it's hanging open. Charlie, Miss 'Tell Me What Happens On The Basketball Field,' has just thrown us all for a loop.

"Wow," Jeremy says. "That was... a really great overview."

I nod, but after he looks away, I mouth what the fuck? when I catch Charlie's eyes. But she just shrugs and looks back at the TV.

There's something going on between her and Jeremy and she hasn't been very open with me about it. But in all honesty, we are still ships passing in the night now that she's in the last months of nursing school.

"I still think Indiana is gonna take it all," Mack says, sinking into the long portion of our L-shaped couch and hauling me on top of him.

"Indy can take it all right now, if he wants," I whisper into his ear.

He freezes underneath me, then he's pushing me off of him so he can stand up and he's dragging me towards the stairs.

"Where are you going?" Jeremy calls. "The game's about to start!"

"We're gonna go play our own game!" I shout back as we race up the stairs to my room.

"Don't be disgusting!" Jeremy shouts. "I don't want to know that!"

I just laugh and follow Mack down the hallway. He opens my bedroom door and hauls me inside.

"I love you, Indy" I whisper as I wrap my arms around his neck and pull him close.

It's true that I've been a lot happier over the past few months. But ultimately, that's because I've taken the time to learn to love myself and understand what it is someone like Mack sees in me.

So when he looks me in the eye and says "I love you too. So much." I can believe him.

And that means everything.

Acknowledgements

First, I want to thank YOU - thank you for purchasing my very first book. As a new author, it is incredibly nerve-wracking to put my work out there and essentially wait to be judged. But ultimately, thank you for giving me a shot. I hope you loved it, and that you'll consider posting a review so more people can find my work.

Lots of appreciation to my beautiful sister and wonderful mother, who have been my cheerleaders since day one. When I started writing and sent them the first few chapters, wondering what they would think, they immediately came back to me and told me to keep going. Without your push, I might not have continued.

Thank you to every friend and family member who sent me words of encouragement, liked my posts on Facebook, shared information with friends, and on and on and on. When an author is at the beginning, it is the endless support and care of the people in their life that help move things forward. I appreciate you!

And last but not least, a really large thank you to my husband, who allowed me to pester him with endless soccer-related questions, even though there wasn't that much *actual* soccer in this book. Yes, babe, I know. You're Argentine and know all the answers :)

About the Author

Jillian Liota is a Southern California native currently living in Kailua, Hawaii. She is married to her best friend, has a three-legged pup with endless energy, and acts as a servant to two very temperamental cats. When she isn't writing, she is travelling, reading a good book, or watching Harry Potter.

Always.

To connect with Jillian:

Sign up for her Newsletter
Rate her on Goodreads
Visit her on Facebook
Check out her Website
Send her an Email
Stalk her on Instagram
Add her on Amazon
Follow her on Pinterest
Tweet her on Twitter

More from Jillian

Did you love Charlie and Jeremy? They get their own happily ever after in the follow up novella, *Keep Away*. Make sure to grab the next book in the Keeper Series!

Looking for something with a little more steam? Check out the Hermosa Beach Series, set in a beach town filled with wealth, secrets and love that will shatter your heart.

And if you're in love with contemporary romance, the Like You Series follows single mom Annie and sexy biker Cole, as well as upbeat barista Carly and her surly neighbor Fin, as they navigate the trials of finding romance in the face of loss.

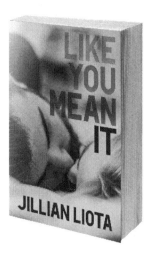 

All titles are available for purchase on Amazon, and can be read in Kindle Unlimited. Happy reading!

Made in the USA
Coppell, TX
20 December 2019